A
PATTERN FOR
MURDER

The Bait & Stitch Cozy Mystery Series

Book One

Ann Yost

Book and cover design by eBook Prep
www.ebookprep.com

May, 2018
ISBN: 978-1-947833-36-4

ePublishing Works!
www.epublishingworks.com

FOREWORD

N ow you can experience the smells and flavors of the Keweenaw Peninsula, just like Sheriff Clump! When you finish the story, page ahead to the recipe for Hatti's favorite oven-baked pancakes—known as Pannukakku within the Finnish community—which are not to be missed. Enjoy!

ePublishing Works

DEDICATION

To Helen Emmons,
the best listener, friend and mom,
with love.

CHAPTER 1

When folks call the Keweenaw Peninsula a dying country, they're not talking about homicide.

Don't get me wrong. This isn't Mayberry. We get our fair share of roadkill and hunting accidents. One time in the 90s an ice fisherman fell asleep with unfortunate results. But, mostly, people die of old age and, whenever possible, in the summer when the ground is soft enough to dig a new hole at the old Finnish Cemetery on Church Road.

I'm talking about crime, you know, 'out damned spot', murder, most foul, sleeps with the fishes. Homicide. We don't get much of that. And when I say, not much, I mean none. Zip. Zilch. Zero.

So when a body turned up on the sand beneath the Painted Rock Lighthouse the morning after the Midsummer's Eve *Juhannus* festival, everyone else was just as shocked as the victim. Maybe more.

It was only natural that I would become involved. I'm no Jessica Fletcher wannabe. But on the northernmost sliver of Michigan's Upper Peninsula, a witch's finger of land that crooks into Frigid Lake Superior, where the deer outnumber the people, we are all used to wearing multiple hats. And there's the fact of proximity. I found the body. Well, I and Larry, my stepdad's well-mannered basset hound and his acolyte, a hyperactive miniature poodle named Lydia. The three of us found the body. Eventually.

But let me start at the beginning.

My name is Hatti Lehtinen and I've spent most of my twenty-seven years on the Keweenaw Peninsula in the bosom of a close-knit (some would say suffocatingly close-knit) community composed of descendants of Finnish miners. I'm tall, a shade under five feet seven inches, with wheat-colored hair and blue eyes and when I'm with my sister, Sofi, who is several inches shorter and considerably more curvaceous, and my cousin, Elli, who is an elf, we look like a set of Finnish nesting dolls. At least we did until my marriage imploded and I chopped off my waist-length braid. Nowadays I look less like a Nordic doll and more like a chrysanthemum that's past its prime.

My marriage, which is either over or on hiatus depending upon your interpretation, occurred during my brief escape from the Keweenaw. I'd gone downstate to law school, a move my mother called "running away from home," and which was, in fact, the most out-of-the-box thing I'd ever done until, near the end of the first year, I met and married a tall, dark, intense lawyer named Jace Night Wind and relocated to Washington, D.C., a move my mother referred to as "out of the frying pan and into the fire." The "I-told-you-so's" started six months later when Jace, just returned from a business trip, strode into our Capitol Hill apartment and announced, unilaterally, that the fledgling union was over. I'd been in the middle of mixing up a batch of dough for *Joulutorttut,* which are prune tarts traditionally baked at Christmas time and when I departed, three days later, the dough was still in the mixing bowl. During the sixteen-hour drive home I felt like the Hebrews fleeing Egypt without the unleavened bread.

I moved back into the Queen Anne Victorian home on Calumet Street in Red Jacket with my folks. It has yellow siding, white gingerbread and there are still glow-in-the-dark stars on the ceiling of my childhood bedroom. For a while I felt disembodied. I'd wake up not knowing where I was. My life felt like a time capsule that had been dug up too soon.

It was mostly emotional fallout but partly culture shock. After the frenzied pace of D.C., it felt strange to wake up to nothing but the sound of snow falling in the winter and black flies buzzing in the summer.

The Keweenaw is a symphony of natural beauty despite the ravaging of its natural resources. One hundred years ago, our mines provided ninety-five percent of the world's natural copper and wood from our white pine forests was in great demand. Nowadays we depend upon the tourists curious enough about our lifestyle to drive nine hours from Detroit or Chicago.

Anyway, back to me. I lived in a cocoon of numbness that worked pretty well until I started to get random panic attacks and brain freezes. My sister frog-marched me into class with the owner of Heart and Hand, a studio that offered a combination of yoga, meditation and self-defense moves. Sofi figured that one of those disciplines would knock some sense into me and I guess it did because Pops (my beloved stepdad) installed me as summer manager of his shop, Carl's Bait.

It wasn't a huge leap of faith since, in all honesty, the position was mostly honorary. Pops's longtime assistant, Einar Eino, a gnome-like octogenarian who is an expert in tying fishing flies, predicting the weather and in speaking as few words as possible on any given day, handled all the earthworms and red wigglers. And the cash register. All I had to do was show up and chat with the customers.

It worked out fine until the afternoon Einar had to drive an order of casters (maggots still in the chrysalis stage) to a customer in Racine and I was the only one on hand to accept a shipment of crickets. When the insects were found dead the next morning and I had apologized for failing to read the note reminding me to feed them, Pops said I had a choice. I could go with him and my mother on their long-awaited vacation to Helsinki or I could accompany my great Aunt Ianthe and her best friend, Miss Irene Suutula on a two-week visit to the Painted Rock Lighthouse Retirement Home to provide assistance to the home's proprietor, Riitta Lemppi, who happens to be my second cousin.

It wasn't a hard choice. The second to last thing I wanted to do was spend two weeks with a bunch of old people but the very last thing I wanted to do was to observe my own first anniversary on somebody else's second honeymoon.

I went to the lighthouse.

The experience turned out much better than I'd expected. Riitta (pronounced Reeta) appreciated my efforts in the kitchen, with the cleaning and laundry and I actually enjoyed spending time with the old ladies, re-learning how to knit and play canasta. I loved hearing their stories, teasing them and being teased and I loved the walks on the shoreline of the largest fresh water lake in the world, the one that Longfellow called Gitche Gumee.

It was a pivotal time for the long de-commissioned lighthouse. It had been a private residence until its owner, Mrs. Johanna Marttinen died and now, a year after that event, it was scheduled to become an endowed retirement home for low-income seniors. The official transfer of ownership of the lighthouse to the Copper County Board of Commissioners was to be the focus of our Midsummer's Eve or *Juhannus* Festival and Arvo Maki, our leading citizen, chief cheerleader, head of the local Chamber of Commerce and the Boosters Club, the Historical Society and a member of the county's Lighthouse Commission and all-around Grand Pooh-Bah, was pulling out all the stops for a grand and glorious celebration. As we prepared a flower-strewn maypole, food carts with pasties and lemonade and soft-serve ice cream and even that symbol of summer, a faux wedding, no one could have predicted that the only thing anyone would remember about that weekend was the swan dive off the fifty-foot lighthouse tower.

But then, as Pops says, life doesn't come with a bell around its neck.

CHAPTER 2

The celebration of Midsummer's Eve goes back to pagan times. After the advent of Christianity, the Finns began to call it *Juhannus,* because it occurs on the approximate birthday six months before Christmas, of Jesus's cousin, John the Baptist.

Usually the weather is perfect in mid-June. The black flies that swarm and choke us in May, have disappeared and the lake water is starting to warm up. The sunrises are early and beautiful and the sunsets, late, and glorious. This year was no exception and with the retirement home's grand opening, the lakeshore was the perfect place for a blow-out festival.

Certainly Arvo thought so. At the last minute, fearing that he hadn't provided enough amusement for the hordes of tourists he expected, Arvo decided we needed to stage a wedding, since Midsummer is considered a propitious time to marry and, any wedding, even a fake one, would be entertaining. Naturally, he appointed the volunteer bride and groom, which was why, at a quarter to five in ninety-degree heat on the longest day of the year, I was sweating my brains out in my tiny bedroom up in the lighthouse tower while my sister tried and failed to zip up the size zero dress our grandmother (*Mummi*) had worn for her wedding back in the Ice Age.

Thinking about ice just made me hotter.

"I give up." The words sounded strange coming from Sofi. She is six years my senior and she owns and operates her own shop, Main Street Floral and Fudge. She is also the single parent of a teenager. Sofi is the embodiment of *sisu,* a uniquely Finnish quality of tenacity and endurance the practical meaning of which is "never quit."

"*Mummi* was a twig," she said, with a sigh.

"What am I, a trunk?"

"Let's say a branch. There's just not enough material here to cover your back, is the thing. You'll have to wear something else."

"Hold your horses," Riitta was breathless as she rounded the top steps of the iron staircase that leads from the second floor landing up through the tower. "I can solve this. Look." She handed Sofi what looked like a wheel from a child's tractor. "Duct tape!"

"Won't that hurt the dress," I asked.

"*Mummi* will never know," Sofi said, exchanging a look with Riitta. The latter produced a pair of scissors as my sister unrolled a length of tape. Together they attached the stuff and smoothed it down. "It works! I just hope nobody mistakes you for a UPS package and tries to open you with a *puukko*." A *puukko* is a small, curved belt knife carried by most outdoorsmen on the Keweenaw and by outdoorsmen I mean men.

The tape pulled at the fine hair on my skin and at the skin itself.

"Is it going to hurt when it comes off?"

"Yes," Sofi said. "A lot."

Strains of accordion music drifted through the open window in the tower. It was Mendelssohn's Wedding March.

"It's time," my sister said. "Got any last minute questions about the wedding night?"

My real wedding night, the one that had happened a year earlier, flashed through my head and I felt tears prick the back of my eyes.

"The tears are good," Sofi said. "It will make you seem like a more believable bride."

I stepped carefully down the narrow circular stairs to the second floor landing where all the regular bedrooms were located and then down the wide walnut staircase that led to the ground floor. The lighthouse, a sturdy structure with a sixty-foot square tower had been constructed in 1917 using the pale red sandstone striated with lighter streaks and spots that came from the nearby Jacobsville Quarry. The shoals of Lake Superior had been considered so dangerous that round-the-clock surveillance was required, so the house had been built to accommodate two lightkeepers and their families which meant there were two front doors, two kitchens, two parlors, two cellars and so on.

After the light was decommissioned in 1939 and the structure sold to a Chicago industrialist, August Marttinen, the kitchens were combined as well as other downstairs rooms, and the electrical wiring and plumbing were modernized. The Marttinen family used the lighthouse as a summer cottage until the early 1970s when August died. After that, the widow, Johanna, and her young son, Aleksander, lived in the structure year-round.

During her last illness, Johanna and Riitta, her home health nurse, had talked of Riitta's dream of opening a retirement home on the Keweenaw and Johanna had decided to will the lighthouse to the Copper County Board of Commissioners for that purpose along with five million dollars to subsidize it. There was, however, a caveat. Johanna, who hadn't seen her son in twenty years, stipulated that he would get both the lighthouse and the money if he returned to claim it within one year. He hadn't returned and the lighthouse now belonged to the county.

A white satin runner, sprinkled with rose petals, stretched from the foot of the front porch steps all the way across the lawn to a bamboo archway decorated with birch twigs and roses. Spectators in webbed lawn chairs, put down their knitting and got to their feet to honor the bride and, stupidly, I felt those tears again.

Under the archway, Arvo beamed, his wide-shouldered, sturdy physique impressive in the purple robe and white cassock he'd filched from the choir room at St. Heikki's Finnish Lutheran Church in Red Jacket. His face was ruddier than usual, no doubt due to the heat, so that his white teeth flashed and his blue eyes twinkled. My eyes shifted to my bridegroom, short, scrawny, amusing and feckless. Captain Jack Vinirypale's blue eyes twinkled, too, and his smile lost nothing from the fact that it was toothless.

My groom had dressed to the nines for the occasion. He wore a freshly laundered wife-beater tee shirt set off with a red bandana tied around his thin neck and a pair of ancient dungarees that clung precariously to his slim hips (he could have used the duct tape to keep them up). The piece de resistance was a red trucker's cap emblazoned with the word *Pulsit.* When I reached the altar he clutched my waist to balance himself as he lifted on tiptoe to speak into my ear.

"*Hei,* gal," he whispered, "can't wait for the weddin' night."

Arvo's pale eyebrows lifted and he blinked at me. His curls, once butter yellow had turned white and they gleamed in the sunshine. He opened the book in his hands and opened his mouth to speak. No words came out, as it dawned on him that he'd brought along a plain old hymnal instead of the Book of Worship that included the wedding service along with the rest of the sacraments. He flashed a panicked look at me and I mouthed the words, "dearly beloved."

The brief pause that ensued was co-opted by Mrs. Flossie Ollanketo, the oldest resident of the retirement home, who is stone deaf and an excellent lip reader. Mrs. O. never misses a chance to fill in a silence.

"My stars!" The exclamation seemed to explode in the peaceful afternoon. Mrs. O. can't hear her own voice and invariably shouts. "Doesn't Hatti look a picture in her *mummi*'s dress?"

The remark wasn't addressed to anyone in particular but Miss Thyra Poonjola, a tall, dour woman in her seventies, took up the gauntlet. She was perpetually bitter, a result some said of her sudden drop into poverty when her brother died after gambling away their savings. Miss Thyra did not like living on charity at the lighthouse. She glared at Mrs. Ollanketo and then at me.

"A picture? Henrikki (my real name) looks like a picture of a stuffed sausage. She is much too fat for that dress."

"Oh, no, no." My great Aunt Ianthe cannot bear any unkindness, especially if it is aimed at one of her family members. "Hatti is not fat. She has big bones, like my side of the family."

It was a valiant, if ridiculous, defense. Aunt Ianthe is my stepdad's aunt.

Miss Irene, long in the habit of punctuating every conversation with a not-too germane reference from the King James Bible, chose a verse from Ezekiel.

"Prophesy upon these bones and say unto them: O ye dry bones, hear the word of the Lord!"

No one knew what to say to that and Mrs. Ollanketo filled in that pause, too.

"Fat can be a good thing," she yelled, an impish grin on her wrinkled face. "Perhaps Hatti is already in the family way."

"A baby?" Aunt Ianthe was moved to utter a mild expletive of excitement. "*Voi kahuia!* What a splendid thing for the family, isn't it, Irene? And, of course, for Jack."

"For unto us a child is born," Miss Irene said. "Isaiah."

"Oh, for Pete's sake," Miss Thyra exploded. "You are all imbeciles. There isn't any baby! This isn't a real wedding!"

Mrs. Ollanketo grinned at her. "Who's Pete?"

"Is this thing over," Jack asked. He leered at me. "I'm ready to kiss the bride. And have a beer."

Arvo, aware that he'd lost control of the situation and determined to accomplish the real business of the day, raised his voice.

"I now pronounce you man and wife," he said, "and, this being the 365th day since the death of the late Johanna Marttinen, I pronounce the Painted Rock Lighthouse the official property of the Copper County Board of Commissioners. Henceforth, it will be used as a retirement home for the elderly of the Keweenaw who find themselves with a limited income and Riitta Lemppi is hereby appointed to a life term as director."

"Hear! Hear!"

Erik Sundback, attorney for the late Mrs. Marttinen, borrowed the phrase of approbation from a long-ago British Parliament. Sundback, who was of an age with Arvo and, in fact, looked remarkably like him, owned a condominium in Houghton on the banks of the Keweenaw Waterway near his law practice. He had spent countless hours during the past year up in Copper Country working, gratis, on the lighthouse commission. Both Arvo and Riitta, the other two members of the lighthouse commission, said they could not have handled all the paperwork without him. When I saw the way he looked at Riitta, I wondered how much was altruism and how much, attraction.

Perspiration beaded on my upper lip and I began to worry about dehydration for the older folks. The accordion player, Mrs. Marta Mikola, may have felt the same way. In any case, she struck up Bach's Brandenburg Concerto which she executed in polka time. Captain Jack responded by grasping my shoulders and lunging at me in an attempt to reach my mouth with his and I, caught unawares, staggered backward, nearly falling on Lydia. The abrupt movement was enough to loosen the adhesive on the back of the tape and as my bodice dropped unceremoniously to my waist I thought that Sofi was right about removing the tape.

It hurt like hell.

I barely had time to register my topless state (or my pain) when I felt the weight of a pair of hands and the security of a man's sports jacket on my shoulders. At the same time, I inhaled a scent of expensive aftershave and I turned to thank Sir Galahad, whoever he was. But as I gazed into a pair of unfamiliar eyes which were the exact color of the lake when the sun caresses it first thing in the morning (turquoise), I couldn't come up with any words. I stared at the lean, tanned face with its straight nose, firm, dimpled jaw, and expressive eyebrows that matched the perfectly styled hair. It was old gold, like a pirate's doubloon.

"Geez Louise," I whispered, finally. "It's Prince Charming."

He grinned at me, revealing a set of gleaming white teeth.

"Hardly. I'm Alex Martin, at your service."

"Alex?" I couldn't think with that much male beauty in front of me. His perfectly sculpted lips twisted.

"Otherwise known as, the Prodigal Son."

"This the brother was dead and is alive again," Miss Irene said, "and was lost and is found. The gospel according to Luke."

CHAPTER 3

"**D**on't romanticize this, Irene!"

Miss Thyra, who had drawn herself up to her full impressive height, barked at the smaller woman. She pointed a bony finger at the newcomer.

"This is not about a fatted calf. This man is Judas. He's here to betray us. He's here," she intoned, revealing that she was no stranger to drama, "to steal our home."

"I think you mean my home," Alex said, unperturbed. "I am the one who grew up here. It was my mother who died last year and left me the lighthouse and the residue of her fortune. This is my inheritance and I am here to claim it."

"It's too late," Arvo said, in a hoarse whisper. "Time has run out. You had a year and the year is up."

"I doubt whether the court will see it that way," Alex said, pleasantly. "After all, I was only informed about the provisions of the Will last week. And I have arrived here within hours of the deadline."

"Look," I said, finally finding my voice. "You don't understand the situation. My cousin has turned the lighthouse into a retirement home for folks who have nowhere else to live. They have come here in good faith and it's their home now. You can't throw them out."

He lifted a golden eyebrow.

"I suppose they could take up residence at the clubhouse. I have had an offer from a golf course developer."

Aunt Ianthe's response to his sarcasm revealed our communal state of mind. We all tend to think of what's good for the community.

"We don't need a golf course," she said, quite seriously. "There's a driving range at Eagle River and Pat's Par Three down at Chassell."

"For heaven's sake, Ianthe." Miss Thyra sounded bitter. "This has nothing to do with golf. It's about profit. This-this-interloper wants to make money by selling our home." She narrowed her light, colorless eyes at him. "He's willing to sell us down the river for filthy lucre that I would guess he does not even need."

Alex Martin nodded. "You are quite right. I don't need the money. And yet, the property belongs to me. Why should I hand it over to people I don't even know? I am neither a philanthropist nor a fool, as it happens. Perhaps you would like to make me an offer."

"Of course," Aunt Ianthe said, happily. "We can use Johanna's trust fund money to buy the lighthouse. It is a perfect solution!"

"Not really," Arvo said, dispiritedly. "The trust fund is part of his inheritance. That belongs to Mr. Martin, too." He looked at his co-commissioners, Erik Sundback and Riitta. Alex followed his gaze and then went very still.

"Riitta?"

There was a hoarseness in Alex's voice as he zeroed in on my cousin.

"Hello, Alex," she said, her face pale, her voice expressionless. "Welcome home."

"Let me echo that sentiment," Erik Sundback said. He introduced himself to the heir. "Your dear mother would have been so pleased to see you here. But, why not come inside for a drink? We can talk about this situation and figure out the best solution." After the honest comments of the others, Erik sounded like a used car salesman. I tried to remember that he wasn't personally affected by any of this.

"Yes, yes," Arvo said, "Erik is right. We will work something out. In the meantime, we should get the ladies out of the sun, eh? And get ready for tonight's festival."

Alex Martin couldn't seem to take his eyes off Riitta. He watched her haul Mrs. Ollanketo to her feet and help support the heavyset old lady as she tottered toward the house. At nearly forty, my cousin Riitta has retained her long, honey-colored hair and her slender figure. The only sign of age are a few laugh lines radiating from eyes the color of robin's eggs. She's a good person who seems to glow from within and Erik Sundback isn't the only man interested in her. For Tom Kukka, the doctor who takes care of the old folks at the lighthouse, Riitta is the North Star.

It seemed fairly obvious that Riitta and Alex had met before but it must have been more than twenty years earlier, since he had left the Keweenaw at that point and never been back. I was thinking about that as I clutched the Prodigal's jacket around me and started to walk toward the lighthouse, up the front porch steps, down the corridor and to the wide, walnut stairs that led to the second floor. It wasn't until I got to the landing that I realized I wasn't alone.

"I'm not stalking you, I promise," his pleasant voice was low in my ear. "I'm not even stalking my jacket. The light keeper's study up in the tower was always my favorite room and I'm planning to make it my headquarters while I'm here. Under the circumstances, I don't think it would be prudent to ask for a bed."

"My bedroom is that little closet up in the tower," I said, my heart trip-hammering in my chest.

He laughed. "Then we'll be neighbors. Don't hesitate to drop in for a cup of sugar."

Was he flirting with me? This sun god who had returned to the Keweenaw to blow up the hopes for a retirement home? I ignored a flutter of excitement in my stomach and frowned at him.

He gave me a slow, nearly irresistible grin. "What's a girl like you doing in a dying place like this?"

"The Keweenaw isn't dying," I snapped. "The people here are living their lives just like anybody else. The mines are closed and the jobs are gone but we have a close-knit community that is forging a new identity and we have irons in the fire in terms of tourism."

His grin widened. "I meant what are you doing at an old folks home. You have to admit, it's a dying place."

"Death," I said, tight-lipped, "is not a popular topic of discussion around here."

"Not discussing it doesn't make it less true. I like you, princess, but I'm damned if I can see any point in giving up millions of dollars so a handful of ancients can spend their last hours in my childhood home."

He didn't look quite as royal after that. I'm not going to lie. He still looked really, really good, but somehow, he was less attractive. A little less, anyway.

When we reached the second floor, a teenager wearing nothing but shorts and running shoes passed us on his way down.

"Hey, Hatti," he said. "Wardrobe malfunction?"

"Something like that." In spite of my irritation at Alex Martin I remembered my manners. "This is Alex Martin," I said. "His mother used to own the lighthouse. Alex, this is Danny Thorne, Riitta's son."

Alex held out his hand but, after a few seconds, he let it drop. The two stared at each other with matching looks of disbelief on their faces. The faces mirrored each other. Two sets of turquoise eyes flared under identical thatches of golden hair. Danny came to his senses first, mumbled, "excuse me" and clattered down the steps. Alex watched him go then looked at me. We were still staring at each other when Miss Irene joined us on the landing.

"Hatti, dear, I know it was a make-believe wedding," she said. "But is there going to be a baby?"

CHAPTER 4

I stood at the window in my bedroom and watched a stream of vehicles serpentine their way along the dusty, unpaved road that connected the interstate with the lighthouse. From fifty feet up they looked like toy cars as they threaded through the randomly planted white pines on the landward side of the house. One by one the vehicles disgorged human beings, coolers, beach umbrellas, chairs and blankets and I could hear the sounds of chatter and excitement as they moved through the early evening sun toward the lighthouse yard and the shoreline.

It was quite a turnout and I took my hat off to Arvo and his public relations czar, Betty Ann Pritula, the host of KPLW's morning show, *"The Finnish Line"* or, as Pops likes to call it, "The Finnish-me-off Line." Betty Ann considers herself a cross between Edward R. Murrow, Martha Stuart and the town crier. She is a craft maven and a household tips guru who provides lectures on how to make wreaths of out pussy willow branches, how to spice up tuna casserole by adding cilantro and how to get red crayon out of the coat of a white cat.

Betty Ann also keeps us informed of everything that's happening from the church picnics, Girl Scout meetings, major birthday celebrations, sales at the shops in town and most of all, Arvo's festivals. The thing is, she doesn't just tell us about the events. She coaxes, cajoles and guilt trips us into attending them. Needless to say, Arvo simply adores her.

I placed Alex's jacket on a hanger, removed what was left of my grandmother's dress, pulled on a red-striped tank top, red shorts and red flip-flops. The brush I ran through my hair made no real difference. The chrysanthemum leaves pretty much always did what they chose. I stepped out onto the landing and noticed the door to the lightkeeper's study, which is also called a watch room, was standing open and Alex was out on the gallery gazing at the lake.

At this distance he looked no older than Danny. He spotted me and came back inside.

"Thank you for the jacket," I said, handing it to him. "It was a lifesaver."

"Come in for a minute," he said, accepting the garment. "Have you been in here before?"

"Briefly. Captain Jack gave me a tour when I first arrived."

"Captain Jack?" He grinned. "Your new husband?"

"I'm not sure we're actually married. Arvo never even said the vows."

I looked around the room at the heavy, mahogany desk, the old-fashioned secretary in the corner, the wooden rocking chair, the rag rugs on the floor and the floor-to-ceiling windows that covered the curve of the room. Outside, some six or eight feet along the low-railed gallery, there was a stationary ladder composed of iron footholds that led to the lantern room. And, in the center of the ceiling was a circular opening with a rope ladder that could be released to allow someone to climb up to the lantern room or down from it.

"This was always my favorite place in the house," Alex said. "Up here in the tower, overlooking the sea, I was a sea captain or a pirate. I was king of my world, master of all I surveyed."

"Pretty heady stuff for a young boy."

"Pretty lonely stuff, too," he said. "I wasn't allowed to go to school. Mother brought in tutors."

"Why?"

"She had a kind of agoraphobia. Of course I didn't understand that at the time. I just felt the restrictions and resented them." He looked out the window again. "This seems like a good place to go over my mother's papers. She used to keep them up here in the desk. I imagine they're still here."

"What're you hoping to find?"

"Oh, nothing in particular. I like to be thorough." He was lying and I wondered why. He shrugged at my inquiring look. "That's how I've been so successful out in L.A. I do not let grass grow under my feet. Or, in this case, maybe I should say I don't let sand accumulate."

"So you're determined to take the lighthouse away from Riitta and the others?"

A cloud darkened his handsome face.

"I have only one long-standing, unalterable policy, Hatti. I don't let anyone take advantage of me."

"Alex," I said, because I just couldn't seem to help myself, "did you know Riitta before?"

He looked away from me and back through the window at the water. It was six o'clock and the sun was still well above the horizon. The rays hit the water at a slant, illuminating the ruffles of foam as the waves came into the shore. They reminded me of the precision of a well-trained marching band.

"She worked here as a maid, one summer after high school. You can imagine how she bewitched me, I, who had had no friends before that. My mother realized her mistake and finally gave me permission to leave which I did. I cared about Riitta but I cared more about freedom."

"And Danny?"

It was unconscionably rude but he seemed so open and so thunderstruck.

"I didn't know about Danny. She never told me."

"Do you think your mother knew?"

Alex nodded. "That's why she included the caveat in the will. She wanted me to come back to the Keweenaw. She wanted me to meet Danny."

It was a sobering thought and cast a new light on Alex's part in the lighthouse drama.

The evening was long and festive and culminated in a brilliant display of Northern Lights just after the sun finally set around ten thirty. The light display morphed into a ferocious storm, one of the kind that had killed tens of thousands of sailors and sunk some six thousand ships.

That night Lydia joined Larry and me in our little tower bedroom and, thanks to the crashing thunder and the brilliant lightning, the dogs were plastered against me on the bed.

It had been a tumultuous day and a crazy night and I was dog-tired, too tired, in fact, to think much about the fact that it was my first wedding anniversary and I was in a narrow bed sandwiched by a basset hound and a poodle. I breathed in with my left nostril and out with my right the way Chakra, my yoga instructor, had taught me and I could feel sleep approaching. I was almost there when I heard a familiar, angry voice.

"You ruined her life," Danny Thorne shouted. "You owe her, dammit!"

"Quiet down, son." Alex sounded half amused. "Do you want the Canadians on the other side of the lake to hear you?"

"Don't call me son." Danny's voice had dropped to a menacing growl. "What are you going to do? Are you going to give her the lighthouse?"

"First thing I'm going to do is apologize. I didn't know about you but that's no excuse. I should never have left your mother with no support. But as far as ruining her life, it seems to me she got the better end of the deal. She got you."

"Those are just words," Danny said. I pictured the way his brow furrowed when he was angry. "They don't mean anything. What I want to know is what you're going to do for her now."

"And what I'm going to do for you?"

Alex spoke in a pleasant, conversational tone but I shivered at the insult and expected Danny to mount an impassioned defense of himself. But he didn't do that. He stuck to business just the way, I suspected, his father would have.

"I don't care what you do for me and I don't care what you think of me. What I want to know is whether you are going to give the house to Riitta and Tom."

"Tom?"

"Doctor Kukka. He's the guy who's in love with her."

There was a brief pause and then, "I thought that was Erik Sundback, my mother's lawyer."

"She loves Tom, not Erik. He's younger. He provides healthcare free of charge for the residents of the lighthouse and a lot of other people, too. Tom and my mother are saints and they deserve something."

"Do you picture me as their fairy godmother?"

"Why not? You owe her a happily ever after."

"One that costs me more than five million? What happens if I say no?"

"I guess I could push you off the gallery."

I grimaced and put my fingers in my ears. When I removed them, a few minutes later, I was relieved to hear Alex laugh, the door close and the sound of Danny's running shoes on the circular staircase. I was just falling off to sleep again when I heard another knock followed by Riitta's voice. It was soft but, for some reason, I could hear every word.

"Is it too late to talk?"

"It's the perfect time," Alex replied. "The witching hour."

I wasn't sure whether it was true delicacy, the effect of my mother's endless lectures on good manners or just plain fatigue but something prompted me to pull the pillow over my face and provide privacy for the long-ago lovers.

It turned out to be an unfortunate decision. If I'd stayed awake, I might have prevented a murder.

CHAPTER 5

The sky was light when I awoke, the sun still below the horizon. I figured it was about five a.m. on the shortest night of the year. There was no sound from next door and I figured Alex had either fallen asleep at his desk or stretched out on the rag rug. After the excitement of the night before, I'd slept like one of the rocks on the tiny island five hundred feet offshore where last evening, Alex and I had lit *Ukko-kokko*, the big bonfire named after the harvest god.

I pulled on some cutoffs and an old tee shirt that read, *906*, which is supposed to intrigue outsiders but, in fact, just refers to the area code in the Upper Peninsula. I scuffed into my red flip-flops and headed down the stairs to the kitchen where I filled bowls of kibble for Larry and Lydia and made the first pot of coffee of the day. Then I let the dogs out back. While I waited for the coffee to perk, I recalled the time I'd spent with Alex out on the lake last night.

The western sun had gilded the edges of pink, fluffy clouds on one side of the sky and, on the other, far off thunderheads had begun to gather, like troops assembling before a battle. It had felt like the calm before the storm, a time out of mind.

According to Arvo's plans, the newlyweds, Captain Jack

and I were to row out to the island to set a light to the bonfire but when the time came, I discovered Jack snoring away in the hammock on the end of the long, front porch and Alex had been kind enough to offer to take his place.

He was, naturally, a great rower, moving the little boat ahead with strong, even strokes. His earlier friendliness had been touched by a little wariness. I knew he expected more questions about the fate of the lighthouse and I decided to confound him by holding my tongue on that subject.

"Did you know there are more than 400 uninhabited islands in Lake Superior?"

He lifted a golden eyebrow and his lips twitched.

"As it happens, I did know that. I grew up here, remember? I spent plenty of time on this island."

I imagined him rowing out here with a girl, a blanket and a picnic and both of them forgetting to eat.

"Mostly when I was much younger," he said, reading my thoughts, "I collected agates and explored the caves. My mother never knew about my boat trips. She'd have had the proverbial cow."

"Did your family own the island?" He nodded.

"Did and does. The island belongs to the light station. I checked on that when I was about twelve."

"Why?"

"I wanted to know what my rights were. And I wanted to name it. I called it Agate Island. You can look it up in the state archives in Lansing."

I squinted at him.

"I thought the Keweenaw meant nothing to you."

"It used to be home. It means nothing now. I told you why I came back."

"You don't like to get fleeced."

"I don't get fleeced," he corrected. "When someone tries it, I make them pay."

"Nobody was trying to take advantage of you here. They honestly thought you weren't interested in the lighthouse."

He rowed in silence for several seconds.

"What are you doing here, Hatti? This is no place to

spend your youth. I don't mean just the lighthouse. What are you doing in the Upper Peninsula? Didn't you ever want to leave?"

I gave him a thumbnail sketch of my history, omitting the tears and the panic attacks and my failure to feed the crickets.

"Unlike you, I had a happy childhood. I love Red Jacket and the people here." That may have been a bit of an exaggeration. My mother and her cronies sometimes drove me crazy. "I'm giving some thought to starting a yarn shop," I said, surprising myself.

"That's a real commitment."

"Well, Pops, my stepdad, has a bait shop and we have a long tradition of hybrid stores. He'd let me sell yarn and knitting supplies along with the worms." I shook my head. "I can't believe I told you that. It was nothing more than an embryonic thought."

"What about your love life?"

"Oh, I don't have one. I'm married."

Once again, the words just popped out. Alex stared at me.

"I hope you're not talking about Captain Jack." He said it with such horror that I couldn't help chuckling.

"No. I was married last year. It didn't work out." Suddenly, I wanted to talk about something else and Alex, bless his heart, seemed to understand.

"So you're serious about the knitting shop? Because if you are and you need funding, give me a call."

"For money?" My voice squeaked. He shrugged.

"That's what I do. I provide startup money for entrepreneurs. I'm an investment banker."

"You'd give me money sight unseen?"

"I'd want a prospectus. You'd be a fool to open a shop without finding out whether there was a customer base."

"I had the idea that we could have knitting classes for kids and set aside one afternoon or evening a week for a knitting circle, you know, like they had in the early days of the American frontier. It could build community."

"Is that something you need? It always seemed to me, as

an outsider, the Keweenaw community was as tight as they come. Probably because everyone is related to everyone else."

"That isn't true," I protested.

"C'mon, Hatti. Tell me you're not related to Riitta."

"Second cousin on my mom's side. But, if you ever took a sociology class, you'd know that community building is always important, especially in this day and age of electronics."

He shrugged. "You could just open a coffee shop for that."

"Knitting is not just a hobby, it's part of our culture. For one thing, mittens, socks, scarves and hats are needed in the Nordic countries and here on the Keweenaw. And creating things by hand is personally rewarding and therapeutic. On top of that, the yarns available these days are beautiful."

He grinned at me. "I'm sold, personally, but let me give you a little free financial advice. When applying for a loan, always stick to the bottom line. A banker doesn't care about building community or finding satisfaction re-creating a centuries-old mitten pattern. All he or she wants to know is whether you can stay in the black."

"Good to know," I said, a little hurt and trying not to show it. "I doubt whether I'll need any start-up money."

He appeared to ignore that.

"I'll give you ten thousand to start."

I cocked my head to one side to look at him.

"Why would you give me that kind of money for my personal goals but you won't relinquish the lighthouse which would benefit all of Copper Country?"

"I told you earlier. I'm not a philanthropist."

A faint bark interrupted my reminiscences and I realized the coffee had finished brewing. I poured a mug and stepped out into the air. There was a faint mist created by last night's storm that turned the pine trees into silhouettes. In just a short time the summer sun would infuse life and color into the landscape but, at the moment, it looked bedraggled and more than a little desolate.

The dogs had disappeared which was unusual. Normally they headed toward the snow fence that separated the lighthouse yard from the waterfront. I figured they'd found something interesting and hoped it wasn't a carcass of a titmouse or a vole. Anyway, I began to circle the house, heading north toward the landward side. The pine trees in the parking area dripped with water from the storm and the sand underfoot was damp enough to leave footprints. The wicker furniture on the porch, including the ladies' canasta table, was still covered with the tarps we'd laid on the night before. There was no sign of life, human or canine, not until I reached the side yard under the tower. Larry and Lydia were pawing at the earth like a couple of warthogs rooting out truffles.

"What have you found," I asked. Neither paid any attention to me.

I knelt to look at the ground but could see nothing but disturbed sand and a few flecks of what might be blood. I figured a seabird had come to grief during the storm and that its body had been carried off by one of the woodland creatures. Then Lydia looked up at me and I saw more of the red substance on her muzzle. It definitely looked like blood.

My first fear was that she'd found a piece of glass in the sand and had cut herself but she didn't seem distressed and I couldn't find any wound. She wagged the puffball that passes for a tail and licked my hand. Larry, meanwhile, had sat back in his most regal position. I met his intelligent eyes.

"What? What is it you want me to notice?"

He turned his gaze to the ground and I followed it.

"I see the blood. Is there anything else?"

Naturally, he didn't say anything. Larry believes in the old adage you can bring a horse to water but you can't make it drink. He's willing to help but expects me to do my own thinking.

"Come on, you ghouls," I said, getting back to my feet. "Let's get in a run on the beach." We headed down to the

shoreline on the other side of a sparse dune and then started
to jog east.

I think they enjoyed it. I know I did. There is nothing
more beautiful than the glitter of the sun on the waves in
the morning. Everything felt fresh and hopeful. I forgot
about the blood on the sand and remembered my
conversation with Alex about the knitting shop and decided
to ask him about it later.

When we got to the oil house, the small square building
that had once housed the fuel for the lantern and was now
home to Captain Jack, we turned around. With the sun
behind us I could really appreciate the dawn. It was like a
colorist transforming the trees to dark green, the water to a
brilliant blue and sky to strips of pink and gold. The vista
reminded me of the ribbon gelatin my late Aunt Greta used
to make for holiday dinners. Each color was vibrant and
lovely and discrete. I'd thought the Jell-o was magic. I
thought the morning sky was magic, too.

I was still smiling at the memory when the dogs and I
bounded up the front porch steps, into the foyer and
through the open paned-glass door into the parlor.

An outraged shriek greeted us and I remembered, too
late, that Miss Thyra Poonjola was scheduled to present
what she called a seminar in this room this morning. Her
lecture, *Lapasat Historia,* or the history of mitten patterns
and their importance in Scandinavian-Nordic culture was,
in Miss Thyra's view, the capstone of the *Juhannus*
celebration. She had arranged for a reporter from *Finn
Spin,* the campus newspaper from nearby Suomi College,
to cover the event and she had spent many hours in
preparation for it.

I stared at the blotches in Miss Thyra's long, sallow face,
and noted that stragglers from her severe bun had escaped
their confines and wisped around her face and I was aghast.
Her small, nondescript eyes were pink from fatigue and the
harsh lines that bracketed her thin lips were as deep as
World War I trenches. She looked both ill and exhausted.

"Miss Thyra, you should go up and lie down," I said. I'd

gotten used to watching for signs of fatigue in the elderly residents.

"Get those filthy mongrels out of here!" She shouted, ignoring my suggestion. "That one is covered in mud." She pointed a long, bony finger at Lydia.

"Not mud. Blood."

The yellowish tone of Miss Thyra's face turned ghost white.

"Blood?"

"At the side of the house. I think it was a seabird." I noticed she was still wearing the high-necked, long-sleeved, black cotton dress she'd worn the day before. "Did you stay up all night?"

She didn't answer immediately. Her flat chest was heaving and she reminded me of a teapot ready to blow its lid.

"*Voi,* Henrikki." I'll admit I was a little shocked at her use of the mild expletive. "Of course I stayed up all night. I had to make sure that everything, *everything,* was perfect for *Lapasat Historia.*" She waved her hand at the beautifully-lettered banner that hung above pocket doors to the dining room and then at the rows of wooden folding chairs she'd lined up in classroom style, after pushing the Victorian sofa and chairs against the wall. Finally, her fingers led my eyes to a length of clothesline she'd rigged above the mantel piece on the fireplace. Some thirty mittens hung from clothespins and it appeared each one was unique.

Looking around the room I was reminded of the Moomins.

When Elli and I were in the first grade, we started to read the series of children's books written by Finnish author Tove Jansson about the funny little hippopotamus-like creatures. In each of the stories, one or the other of the characters had a mission whether it was Moomintroll and his attempt to save his beloved valley, or the whole family's effort to save young Ninny from permanent invisibility or Moominpapa trying to find a way to go live in a lighthouse.

Like the Moomins, Miss Thyra had a mission. She wished to educate people on the importance of knitting patterns as an element of Nordic culture. Elli had a mission, too. Hers was to provide guests with a Victorian-era experience at her bed-and-breakfast. Sofi's was to keep her shop, Main Street Floral and Fudge solvent while she raised her daughter. Providing a home for the elderly was Riitta's mission. Was it my mission to run a yarn market out of Pops's bait shop? It didn't seem very noble. As I scooped up Lydia and headed for the kitchen, I remembered another character, Too-Ticky, and words she spoke in *Moominland in Winter:* "One has to discover everything for one's self. And get over it all alone."

"Halt, Henrikki." Miss Thyra sounded like Heinrich Himmler. "I would like you to wear this for the seminar." She crossed the room and handed me a large bundle that was grayish in color and looked a little like a muskrat that had lost in a skirmish with an SUV. Before I could ask what it was, Aunt Ianthe and Miss Irene entered the parlor from the front hallway.

Both ladies wore summer shirtwaists with polka dots. Aunt Ianthe's dots were bigger, as befitted a bigger person. They were white on a tan background. Miss Irene's dress was blue with a self-belt. Both wore straw espadrilles on their feet and carried white pocketbooks.

"My heavens, Thyra," Aunt Ianthe said, admiringly, "you have turned this parlor into a classroom!"

Miss Thyra nodded her head but said nothing and I thought that my aunt had chosen exactly the right accolade.

"What on earth is that item you are handing to Hatti?"

"It's a *Korsnas* sweater."

"It looks hot," Aunt Ianthe said, a small line between her eyes. "We don't want her to get dehydrated. Don't forget about the baby."

"Of course it is hot." Miss Thyra ignored the absurd reference to the fantasy baby. "The sweater is double-knit to ensure warmth for sailors on the North Sea. It is an excellent example of nineteenth century Finnish knitting."

"It is not a mitten," Miss Irene said, stating the obvious.

"Academic research cannot be constrained by mundane boundaries," Miss Thyra said, with a sniff. "The audience _ and the press _ will find the *Korsnas* both interesting and historical." She looked down her long nose at me. "Please do not wear it with dungarees, Henrikki. A nice wool skirt will suffice."

I considered asking her where I might find a wool skirt in the middle of the summer at a lighthouse but Miss Irene had already launched into a Bible verse.

"Now, when Simon Peter heard that it was the Lord, he girt his fisher's coat unto him (for he had been naked) and did cast himself into the sea. The Book of John."

Simon Peter would definitely have cast himself into the sea if he'd had to wear the *Korsnas* sweater. I began to think, longingly, of the deep, cool, lake. I turned toward the kitchen.

"Hatti, dear," Aunt Ianthe called after me, "we expected to see your bridegroom this morning."

She caught me off guard and the blood seemed to drain out of my head. I sucked in a breath and let it out slowly.

"You mean Jace?"

My aunt looked embarrassed and chagrined. "Oh, no. I didn't mean to remind you about that, then. I was talking about Captain Jack."

I summoned a smile and made an effort to comfort her and divert myself. "Did I tell you how he proposed?"

"Do you mean your real husband," Miss Irene asked.

"Captain Jack," I said, holding the smile. "He asked if I wanted to be buried in the family plot."

"And you said yes?" I nodded to Miss Irene.

"Well, dear, it's all for the best then. And I don't know when Ianthe and I have been so happy. A dear, dear little baby."

"Miss Irene," I said, gently, "the wedding wasn't real. There is no baby."

"Maybe not yet," Miss Irene said. "But soon. Children," she added, "are a gift from the Lord."

CHAPTER 6

I found Riitta in the kitchen squeezing oranges for fresh juice. I could smell *pannukakku* baking in the oven. The traditional oven pancake was a universal favorite. Each of the tables in the dining room had been spread with a snowy, white cloth, settings of Riitta's Finnish flatware and a pitcher of lingonberry syrup. The ladies who came for the lecture on mittens would be rewarded with a late breakfast feast.

I carried the poodle through the swinging door that connects the dining room with the kitchen and headed for the sink where I washed the blood off Lydia's whiskers. As I worked, I explained the incident to my cousin. She nodded but seemed abstracted.

"Hatti," she said, "could you do me a huge favor? When I spoke with Alex last night, I told him I'd send up some breakfast," she said. "If I fix up a tray could you take it up there? I simply don't have time at the moment."

I couldn't help noticing a hint of a blush on her smooth cheeks. "You don't have time?" I repeated her words, turning them into a question.

"Yes, you see, I have to speak to him and it isn't going to be a short conversation. I need to get through this mitten thing first."

"Sure," I said, wondering what I'd missed last night when I'd decided to put the pillow over my ears. "I have to go up, anyway, to search my room for a wool skirt."

Riita knew as well as I did there was no skirt in the room. There wasn't even a closet and, even as she gave me a faint smile in acknowledgement of the absurdity of the request, I couldn't help noticing the shadow in her eyes.

"Is there something wrong?"

"No, no. Well, I don't know. Something's weird."

At that moment, Aunt Ianthe, trailed by Miss Irene, burst into the kitchen.

"Oh, Hatti, dear, you have Lydia. My goodness, you are giving her a bath?"

I realized, belatedly, I was still holding the wet poodle.

"She got some, uh, mud on her nose," I said, changing my story to suit my audience. "I'm just cleaning her up." I put her down on four feet and she shook, vigorously, flinging drops of water in all directions, an action that sent the ladies fleeing back through the door to the hall.

"You got your sweater wet," Riitta said, eyeing the *Korsnas.*

"Yep. That's probably not going to make it more comfortable."

A few minutes later I knocked on the closed door of the watch room. Well, I didn't precisely knock. Since my hands were full with the tray, I just said "knock, knock." I grinned to myself, expecting him to reply, "Who's there?" When nothing happened I set the tray down and rapped on the door. Again, there was no response. This time, like Goldilocks, I opened the door and went inside. And, just as in the fairytale, no one was home.

The windows were open as was the sliding glass door onto the railed gallery that surrounds the tower and I could hear the squawking of the seagulls and the rush of the waves. Sunlight flooded the light keeper's study which made it toasty warm. It dazzled off the green-shaded banker's lamp which Alex had left on. I automatically pulled the little chain and noticed a pair of horn-rimmed reading glasses folded next to it. He must have gone downstairs to grab a nap on a vacant bed, I thought. It was a pity about his breakfast. I'd have to eat it myself.

Except I couldn't. Not until I'd checked over the edge of the railing. I forced myself to walk out onto the concrete gallery. Fear of heights was new for me but none the less intense because of that. I gripped the railing and forced myself to look down at the sand below. There was nothing there. Even so, I realized my heart was galloping a mile a minute and my whole body was shaking.

I dropped into the rocking chair just because my legs felt like rubber. At least, I thought, he hadn't plummeted off the tower. Neither had he skipped town, unless he'd done it without his glasses and the navy blue windbreaker hanging on a hook near the door. He had to be downstairs or out for a walk. I wanted to wait for him to come back, to exchange a few words, to bask in his sun-god-like beauty but it was getting late and Miss Thyra would be looking for a whipping boy. Or girl. I changed clothes and returned to the parlor wearing the closest thing I had to a wool skirt–a pair of Seersucker shorts–and smelling of mothballs and wet dog.

"Henrikki!"

I heard the outraged squeal as soon as I stepped off the walnut staircase. Miss Thyra was in the corridor, fists jammed into her waist, a furious scowl on her sharp features. Her small eyes were focused on my shorts. And her skin looked green.

"Miss Thyra, you need to go upstairs and lie down."

"Nonsense! What I need, Henrikki, is a clothespin."

I looked over at the dozens of mittens hanging from the clothesline and then at the clothespin bag on one of the sofas nearby. The bag wasn't empty.

"I've counted the clothespins and there is one missing," she said, defensively, observing my gaze. "It must be somewhere in the cellars."

In the cellars? The clothespins, along with the washer and dryer, belonged in the main basement. Since the other cellar was used only for storage I couldn't imagine how a clothespin, even one with an adventurous spirit, could have breached the connecting door and found itself marooned there.

"Would you please go down and find it? Check both cellars."

It was an odd request. Some might say idiotic. But it seemed to me that Miss Thyra was working herself into a full-blown nervous breakdown and I thought it would be better to humor her. Also, I knew it was cool in the cellars and the *Korsnas* sweater felt like a woolen straightjacket.

I agreed and headed down the corridor to the cellar door which is across from the kitchen in the back of the house. The cellars were large and built of concrete blocks with dirt floors. Each was lit only by a hanging lightbulb, a situation Riitta had intended to remedy as soon as she got permission to use Johanna Marttinen's trust fund.

The open wooden steps to the cellar, combined with the high window and dim light always made me think of Poe's *Telltale heart* when I came down here. It seemed like an excellent place to stash a body, behind the utilities or the furnace. There was a pegboard full of tools and shelves of household products, detergents, toilet paper, paper towels, and staples like peanut butter and canned fruits and vegetables. Since I had been down here several times doing bedsheets and other laundry, I was surprised at the goosebumps on my arms. At least I thought there were goosebumps. I couldn't see them under the sleeves of the abominable sweater.

I scoured the surfaces and the freshly swept floor. No clothespins. I decided to go into the second cellar, in part to be thorough, in part because I didn't like the way panic was beginning to work its way up my digestive tract. I told myself I was being ridiculous. What on earth did I expect to find down here? I pushed open the door and strode past the disused cistern in the middle of the floor and across the room to the long-abandoned coal chute that stretched from the high window into a bin below. The bin, which was usually filled with scrap woodchips, was empty because a few days earlier, Captain Jack and Danny had taken all the wood they could find out to the island for the bonfire. Nevertheless, I peered inside.

I'd been right about one thing. There was no wood in there. Unless you counted the wooden clothespin.

A chill ran up my spine underneath the heavy sweater as I stared at it.

"Geez Louise," I whispered. "How in the heck did you get there?"

By the time I returned to the parlor Miss Thyra's face was shining with sweat and she'd developed a tic in one eye. She looked like she was about to have a stroke. Was it nerves? I hurried over to her, the clothespin displayed on my outstretched palm. Maybe this would help.

She stared at the item then back at me.

"Where did you find it?"

"It was in the coal bin, of all places. Miss Thyra, let me find Doc for you. You're not well."

"I'm fine. Just a headache. A migraine, I think."

I'd had a couple of migraines since my return from the nation's capital. They were no fun.

"We should postpone the lecture," I said, "I'll talk to Riitta."

"No!" Her voice was sharp, shrill and definitive. "No, Henrikki. The people are outside. After the lecture I will go upstairs and lie down."

I made a mental note to speak with Tom as soon as I saw him. He'd given me something called Verapamil and it had worked wonders.

The women from Red Jacket began to arrive in full force. Riitta greeted them at the door and ushered them into the parlor. Everyone was talking about the great scandal of Johanna Marttinen's son coming back to take over the lighthouse. There was one stranger, a short, snub-nosed adolescent with a lip ring who, I guessed, because of her age, her short, purple hair and her Grateful Dead tee shirt, was from the college paper.

"I'm Garcia," she said, "just the one name." She looked over at the clothesline. "What's with the Three Little Kittens display?"

Miss Thyra frowned. "I am expecting Miss Tiffani Tutilla who has promised to write a piece about my seminar, *Lapasat Historia.*"

"Lapa what?"

"The history of mittens," I said.

"Oh, well Tiff's got a hangover and, anyway, this story falls on my beat. We're not interested in mittens. I'm here about the body."

CHAPTER 7

"Body?" An ugly color rose from Miss Thyra's neck to her cheeks.

"A dead body," Garcia confirmed. "We got an anonymous tip that someone found a corpse at the foot of the lighthouse," she said. "I'm the cops reporter so I came to check it out."

A violent shudder ran through Miss Thyra's thin body. I put a hand on her shoulder and turned her toward her other guests.

"A misunderstanding," I said, soothingly. "Why don't you greet everyone and I'll take Garcia here into the kitchen for coffee."

"I'll take a white mocha macchiato with a shot of whipped cream, lactose free," the reporter said.

I looked at her. "You understand this is a lighthouse, right?"

"Sure. The lighthouse with the body. I heard it was under that balcony thing."

"It's called a gallery," I explained, "and I can assure you there's no body underneath it. I was out there just a short time ago but I'll be happy to take you out there if you'd like to take a look."

We exited through the back door and I showed her the

spot with the roughed up sand. Unfortunately, there was still a little blood in evidence and she pointed it out.

"Most likely a bird or other small critter. You say you got a call this morning? Was it a man or a woman?" She shrugged.

"Tiffany got the tip and called me. In any case I can't reveal a source."

"It just seems odd that if someone had found a body, he or she wouldn't have called the sheriff's department."

Garcia finished the sip she'd taken of her black coffee. "Unless," she pointed out, "the source is the murderer."

It had to be a prank. There was no body. I stared at the disturbed sand.

"Why is the sand dry in that one area? Was there something covering it all night?"

That, of course, was the sixty-four dollar question. Why was the sand dry?

"I don't know," I admitted. "But I've got to get back inside for Miss Thyra's seminar about knitting. If a body turns up, you will be the first to know."

Garcia sent me a thoughtful look.

"If it's all right with you, I'll stay and write about the mittens, okay?"

I pushed aside the ungrateful suspicion that she just wanted to stick around longer in case a corpse happened by and thanked her.

"Miss Thyra would appreciate that," I added.

We found the would-be professor standing behind her makeshift lectern, her lecture underway.

"Mitten patterns," she said, "are artistic expressions of a culture expressed in practical terms. We study them to differentiate between the cultures of the Scandinavian and Nordic countries." She looked at Garcia who had set her cell phone to record, and then at me. I gave her a thumbs up.

"Most of the patterns celebrate the weather, nature, the seasons, Christmas and that sort of thing. Occasionally you find something more sinister." She held up a black mitten

embellished with an evil-looking octopus. "This is *Torsas,"*
she said. "A creature from Finnish mythology."

Sofi and Elli and I had been brought up, not just on
Lutheran tenets and the Moomins, but on the *Kalevala,* the
book of Finnish mythology. *Torsas* was a creature that
lurked in water waiting to devour badly behaved children.
Just a mention of the creature was enough to keep us away
from the lake for weeks. Especially if we had been badly
behaved.

"Knitting has always been part of the Nordic culture,"
Miss Thyra said. Her voice sounded strong enough,
although she was still abnormally pale. "For one thing, in
such a cold climate it was always important to have plenty
of mittens, stockings, hats and scarves. Girls were taught to
knit at a young age. By the time they were married, they
were supposed to have knitted enough stockings to last
their lifetimes. Patterns for stockings and mittens were
passed down within families and neighborhoods. Small
variations in those patterns make it possible to identify their
geographic roots." She moved to the clothesline and
removed three mittens.

"This Norwegian snowflake is more intricate than the
Icelandic snowflake. And this Latvian snowflake is the
most detailed of all."

"Pass them around," Ronja Laplander said, "We want to
take a closer look."

Miss Thyra frowned, torn between reprimanding the
interruption and pleasure at the interest shown by the
listener. I got up, took the mittens from her and began to
pass them around. As I did so, I couldn't help wondering
whether she'd used the wandering clothespin, after all.

Aunt Ianthe asked about a mitten featuring a brightly
colored daisy-like flower.

"It's called *porjus,"* Miss Thyra explained, "from
Swedish Lapland. This one," she held up a red mitten with
intertwined lattices, "is called *Paivatar,* after the Finnish
sun goddess."

The reference made me think of the Finnish sun god I'd

rowed out to the island with last night. I wondered if Alex had awakened and returned to the watch room and I had to repress a nearly overwhelming urge to go find out.

"Wildlife is another subject of many mitten patterns," Miss Thyra said. "Here is a mitten from Latvia with a soaring eagle. Flowers are another popular subject. This pattern of stylized climbing roses has an interesting history. Back around the turn of the last century, there was a famine in the old country and a number of Finnish orphans went to live in workhouses. One of those workhouses was in Arjeplog in Northern Sweden. The girls were taught knitting and other household skills, the boys, woodworking. This knitting pattern was created by the girls at Arjeplog with influence from the Swedish Laplanders who lived nearby. It is, in effect, a hybrid or Finnish-Swede mitten, an example of cross-culture knitting."

"Couldn't you call the Arjeplog pattern, Swedish-Finn," Riitta asked. I wondered if she had Erik Sundback in mind. We all knew that he was part Swedish, but as Arvo liked to say, we never held that against him.

Miss Thyra looked gratified by the question and as if she would like to answer it but I noticed the knuckles on the fingers gripping the lectern had turned white and, once again, I intervened.

"Excuse me for interrupting," I said, as Miss Thyra frowned at me, "but there is really no one more qualified to speak on this subject than our own Arvo Maki, who has just arrived. Perhaps you would allow him to explain the Finnish-Swedish overlap."

It seemed Miss Thyra would. She nodded and Arvo made his way to the front of the room. He surveyed the crowd with his customary wide, friendly smile. Everyone on the Keweenaw loved Arvo even my mother who, however, occasionally pointed out that he was unnaturally jolly for a mortician.

"The relationship between the Finnish people and their nearest neighbors, the Russians on the east and the Swedes on the west, has always been somewhat fluid," Arvo began. "Not always by choice. Russia has been aggressive toward us. There has been war with the Swedes, too, and at one time, for a long time, Sweden held dominion over Finland. As Miss Thyra mentioned, famine affected the populations of the two countries and, sometimes it resulted in permanent relocation.

"The term Swede-Finn, refers to a minority Swedish-speaking population in Finland. At present it is about five percent, but it has been higher in the past. We like to say the Swedes have come to live in the superior country." He grinned. "For the most part there is harmony but there is also rivalry. For example, there is no agreement on what name to give the minority population. The Swedes refer to themselves as *Sverigefinnar,* which means, Swedish-Finn while the Finns call them *Ruotsinsuomalaiset,* or Finnish-Swedes." He smiled at the audience.

"It cannot be so easy for the Swedes living in Finland," he added. "There has always been competition between the countries. There is an old saying that the Finn likes to win, but more than that, he likes to beat the Swede." He stopped to chuckle at his own joke. "The Swede-Finns are not our enemies, though. Some are our friends. One such is Erik Sundback, the lawyer from Houghton, who has helped us with legal issues at the lighthouse. Erik is in a sailboat race down on Keweenaw Bay and I wish him luck. Unless, of course, his opponent is a Finn."

The lame joke got a little chuckle. Miss Thyra, refreshed by a sip of water, judged it was time to take back the podium. She cleared her throat.

"Rivalries between countries," she said, "do not extend to knitting. As you can see, there are many beautiful patterns that, taken together, tell of a rich cultural history in the Nordic countries."

I would never have pegged Miss Thyra as an ambassador for world peace and I thought her closing remark deserved applause. Apparently everyone else felt the same. She looked gratified and, for the first time that morning, she did not seem agitated. She really had been nervous about the presentation.

When the applause had ended, Aunt Ianthe got to her feet.

"Thyra, you have inspired us. We all want to do more knitting and we want to learn the patterns you have shown us here. I hereby declare that we hold a weekly knitting circle. It can meet here at the lighthouse or in town at one of our homes or the church. We'll call ourselves the Wednesday Night Knitters."

"Not Wednesday," Mrs. Edna Moilanen said, "that is choir practice and potluck. And Tuesday is Ladies Aid." She should know since she was the long time president of that esteemed organization.

"And not Monday," Mrs. Sorensen, the pastor's wife said, "that is committee night."

Diane Hakala, co-owner of the pharmacy with her husband, suggested Thursday and everyone agreed until Ronja Laplander, owner of the Copper Kettle Gift Shop, pointed out that Thursday night was for the Martha Circle at church.

I got to my feet at that point.

"We don't have to choose a night right now, but I would like to tell you about my plans. I intend to sell knitting supplies and yarn at the bait shop. If Pops is agreeable, I've even got a new name. We'll call it Bait and Stitch."

After the initial excitement died down, Arvo excused himself to go home for Sunday dinner and everyone else sat down at the cloth-covered tables in the dining room to feast on *pannukakku* and coffee. Most everyone. Garcia left and Miss Thyra excused herself and went upstairs. There was plenty of gossip to catch up on especially for Aunt Ianthe and Miss Irene who had been out at the lighthouse for a week. I listened carefully, hoping to solve the mystery of who had called the college paper with the mysterious tip.

Mrs. Edna Moilanen took the lead. Every small town has its social register and Red Jacket was no exception. Mrs. Moilanen, a well-upholstered widow in her late sixties, enjoyed a position at the top of the social pyramid. Her power derived not from her age or the fact that she had been born in Red Jacket or even that her late husband had been a deacon in the church and an assistant manager at the local mine. Mrs. Moilanen's status came from the fact that for more than twenty years she had maintained her hold on the office of president of the St. Heikki's Ladies Aid, the most prestigious, most dignified, most important post among the church basement crowd.

Like most of the women in Red Jacket, Mrs. Moilanen has her short, gray curls washed and set weekly at Myrna's Beauty Salon and, except for church and other special occasions, she dresses in a pair of polyester slacks and polo shirts embroidered with seasonal designs, like Christmas trees, pumpkins for fall and bunnies for spring. During the winter, she trades the polo for a collared sweatshirt but the idea is the same.

Mrs. Moilanen poured lingonberry syrup on her wedge of pancake and prepared to hold forth.

"Ianthe," she said, "you and Irene must meet the new girl in town. She looks like an angel. And sings like one, too. So lovely is her voice, isn't it, Janet?" Mrs. Moilanen appealed to the pastor's wife, Mrs. Sorensen, for support.

"Just like an angel," the pastor's wife confirmed. "You will appreciate her voice, Irene. She's never off key, is the thing."

I glanced at Aunt Ianthe and noted a slight stiffening of her spine. Mrs. Sorensen had no way of knowing that she'd nearly put her foot in her mouth. She, alone of the women at the table, had not been in Red Jacket twenty years earlier during what Pops sometimes referred to as the potential continental divide. After a lifetime, the friendship between Aunt Ianthe and Miss Irene had been threatened when the church organist decided to retire to Lake Worth, Florida with her husband and the post opened up.

Miss Irene, as the town's piano teacher, was the obvious selection and it never occurred to her or anybody else that Aunt Ianthe, a primary school teacher, had musical ambitions, too. When both ladies turned up at the interview with the then-pastor, he had to do some quick thinking and the result was a solution as neat as Solomon's. Neater, because it did not involve slicing a baby in two. The pastor suggested that Aunt Ianthe, who has never been a fan of sharps and flats, would play all the hymns written in the key of C, while Miss Irene would take on all the rest, including that jewel in the crown, *Be Still My Soul,* by Jean Sibelius.

"You will enjoy the songbird's fine voice, too, Ianthe," Mrs. Moilanen said, demonstrating one of the reasons the arrangement had held for twenty years. The community didn't just tolerate my great aunt, they appreciated her. "Her name is Liisa Pelonen and she has had to transfer to Copper County High because the school at Allouez closed. She needed a place to stay in town and Arvo and Pauline invited her to live at the funeral home."

"What about her parents?" Aunt Ianthe was deeply interested in the tale.

"She has only a father, a hermit who lives alone near Ahmeek. He will probably welcome the solitude. In any case, Arvo and Pauline have gone to town decorating a room all in pink for the girl. It is such a happiness to them to have a daughter in the house at last."

"Liisa Pelonen is not Arvo's daughter." Resentment echoed in Ronja Laplander's deep voice. Ronja, who is short and squat with straight dark hair is the mother of five hopeful daughters all of whom resemble her. "Arvo and Pauline are acting foolishly," she added, with a touch of venom. It did not take long to find out why.

"Liisa," Mrs. Moilanen said, perhaps with some idea of punishing Ronja for interrupting her story, "would make the picture perfect St. Lucy."

"Pah!" Ronja's wide face flushed a dull red and her small, dark eyes narrowed. She shook a stubby finger at the Ladies Aid president. "This girl cannot be St. Lucy. She is an outsider. It is Astrid's turn this year."

The honor of playing St. Lucy in the yearly parade and pageant is as highly sought after in Red Jacket as head cheerleader in Texas. Even though the choice is ostensibly

made by the youth of St. Heikki's, there is a kind of
unspoken pecking order that is usually observed. It wasn't
an absolute that Astrid Laplander would be chosen this year
but it was likely and clearly, Ronja was counting on it. The
thing is that Arvo reserves the right to make the ultimate
decision about anything remotely municipal and if Liisa
were as lovely as advertised, he would be sorely tempted to
choose her to represent the community. And, of course,
Ronja knew all that.

"Well, as far as I'm concerned, it should be Astrid this
year," said Diane Hakala, the pharmacist's wife who could
afford to be generous as her only daughter, Barb, had held
the crown last December. Ronja's face relaxed until Diane
added, "or, maybe Meg Linna."

"Meg Linna?" Ronja's practically spat out the name. "No
way. She is only half Finnish!"

Diane shrugged, as if tired of the subject. "Edna," she
said, "tell Ianthe and Irene about Claude."

Claude, who belongs to Ollie Rahkonen, sexton at the
Old Finnish Cemetery and all-around handyman, is a
reindeer. Once a year he pulls the sleigh in the St. Lucy
parade. Otherwise he grazes and molts and provides
companionship for Ollie. Aunt Ianthe's forehead wrinkled
in concern.

"What about Claude?"

"He's been sick," Mrs. Moilanen explained. "Off his
feed, you know? Ollie took him to see the midwife."

I choked back a laugh. The midwife is my friend Sonya
Stillwater who, when she arrived in Red Jacket two years
ago, thought she would be promoting women's health and
delivering human babies. She had adapted gracefully to the
multiple-hats rule and she regularly treated sore throats,
sewed up split lips and bandaged bloody knees.

"Did Dr. Sonya cure Claude?" Miss Irene asked.

"She told Ollie to feed him milk-bread and scrambled
eggs until his stomach settles down but it was Einar who
really cured him." She smiled at me. "He told Ollie to put
Claude in the sauna."

She pronounced it sow-na, the approved Keweenaw usage. Sauna is the first line of defense in our community for practically any illness. If it doesn't work, coffee is next followed by Vic's Vapo Rub. If none of those cure you, as Pops says, it's time to head to the marble orchard.

"We have some health news, too," Aunt Ianthe said, soberly. "Flossie Ollanketo collapsed last night on her way to sauna." There were several gasps and exclamations of dismay. "Doctor Kukka gave her some medicine," my aunt reassured them. "Flossie is still asleep but he says she will be all right."

"So she ate too many sausages last night?" Ronja Laplander put the question.

Aunt Ianthe shook her head. "She had a heart palpitation and I know why. She was upset about the lighthouse."

"What about the lighthouse?" The question came from Edna Moilanen.

Aunt Ianthe and Miss Irene exchanged a glance. Miss Thyra stared down at her untouched plate of food.

"You haven't heard about Johanna Marttinen's son coming back?"

"Of course I heard," Edna said. "What of it?"

"He came to claim the lighthouse and the money that goes with it," Aunt Ianthe said. "The retirement home will have to close."

CHAPTER 8

The guests finally left around noon and Aunt Ianthe and Miss Irene went upstairs for a rest while I helped Riitta clean up the dining room and the kitchen.

When the last plate had been washed and dried and returned to the cupboard and we'd sponged off the counter tops, Riitta poured two cups of fresh coffee and handed me one. She leaned against the island in the center of the kitchen.

"Hatti, you have a good head on your shoulders."

"There are those who would disagree with you," I said, lifting my cup to take a sip. She didn't smile.

"I'd like to run something by you." I nodded. "Last night I went up to the watch room to talk to Alex. As you've probably figured out, we knew each other years ago and I thought I would see if there was any way I could convince him to let us have the lighthouse." She held her cup between her hands as if she craved the warmth. "It was pleasant. We reminisced a little, talked about stuff."

"Danny?"

Her eyes shot to mine. "Oh, so you figured that out, did you?"

"It's kinda hard to miss. They look like matching sun gods."

She sighed. "Danny figured it out, too. I should have told him years ago instead of making up a fictional dad. Alex had said he would never come back but I was always afraid he might change his mind. I didn't want to risk a custody battle or any unpleasantness. I didn't want anyone to find out."

"But Johanna knew, didn't she?"

Riitta nodded. "Like you said, it was hard to miss the resemblance. We didn't talk about it but I figured that was why she decided to support my dream of making the lighthouse a retirement home for the disenfranchised."

"It was probably why she gave Alex a year to come back," I said, remembering my conversation with him. "She hoped he'd come back and find his son."

Riitta's eyes widened. "I hadn't thought of that but it makes sense. You know, he wasn't even angry with me. He just said he owed me and wanted to make reparations."

I wondered if she knew about Danny's visit to his father but decided it wasn't my place to mention it.

She wrapped her arms around her waist.

"Here's the thing. He told me he was giving me the lighthouse and the money. He said he had made a bundle and that I deserved some of it for raising Danny alone. He said he'd never miss the trust fund money and that he had no intention of ever coming back to the Keweenaw, so he wouldn't miss the lighthouse, either."

"Wow! Riitta, that's huge! It means you and Tom and Mrs. O. and Miss Thyra and Captain Jack can stay here. And you can afford to do the renovations to house more elderly people. Aren't you excited?"

"Oh, yes. Of course. And Grateful. But, Hatti, there's something weird. He told me about his plans last night but this morning when I woke up, he'd changed his mind."

"What?"

"There was a letter shoved under my door." She pulled a folded envelope out of the pocket of her white slacks and handed it to me.

The typed letter was addressed "To Whom it May

Concern" and signed by Alexander Martin with yesterday's date. I read it aloud:

"This is to state my intention of transferring the ownership of the Painted Rock Lighthouse along with a trust fund of five million dollars to the Copper County Board of Commissioners. The building is to be used in perpetuity as a retirement home for indigent seniors. The trust fund is an endowment to support the retirement home and is to be administered by the presently constituted County Lighthouse Commission."

I looked up from the letter.

"Your name isn't in it." She shook her head. "It isn't what he told you last night." She shook her head, again. "But it amounts to the same thing, right?"

"Oh, yes. It doesn't matter at all. He stipulates that the commission should continue to run it and Arvo, Erik and I are the commission. It doesn't change anything. It's just weird, is the thing."

"Have you talked with him about it today?" She shook her head again.

"That's why I wanted you to take his breakfast up to him. I knew that when we got to talking it would take awhile."

"Riitta," I said, suddenly remembering, "he wasn't up there. I left the *pannukakku,* figuring he was down in the bathroom or taking a nap somewhere. The food was probably cold when he got back," I added, apologetically. "As far as changing his mind, I wonder if he wanted to take the burden of ownership off of you. I mean, if you decided you didn't want to operate a retirement home, say, if you got married or moved away, you would have to get out from under the responsibility of the lighthouse and the retirement home."

"That's probably right," she said, slowly. "I guess I'll have to ask."

"What has it been like to see him again," I asked, suddenly curious.

She smiled, faintly.

"He's just as handsome as ever. More, really. But there's

a hardness under the surface, you know? A kind of meanness. It may have been there before and I was too young to notice. Or, it may have developed during his years in business."

"Or, maybe you notice it now because you're comparing him with Tom, who hasn't got a mean bone in his body."

At the mention of the doctor's name, her pretty face went blank and she ignored my comment.

"I guess if I want to know what he was thinking, I'll have to go to the source," she said. "And there's no time like the present."

"I think I'll take the dogs out."

"Oh, Hatti, would you walk down to the oil house? It isn't like Jack to miss pancakes. Tell him to come on up and I'll make him a new batch."

I was happy to do it. One of the fascinating things about the world's largest fresh water lake is the way it changes with the seasons and with the time of day. On a hot, sunny summer day in the early afternoon, the deep blue of the lake challenges that of the sky and the richness of both shades almost hurts your heart. I hurried outside, anxious to see the lake at its most regal but as I started up the yard to the dune, I realized I'd lost the dogs. I turned around to whistle to them but the sound died on my lips and I knew my view of the lake would have to wait.

Larry and Lydia sat like a couple of sphinxes, one on each side of a figure that had, very recently, been human, but wasn't any longer. Garcia's anonymous tipster had been right.

I felt a blast of grief echoed in Larry's mournful bay. The body was facedown, tanned arms spread out, golden hair gleaming in the sunlight. Long lashes protected the unseeing turquoise eyes. The regret that swamped me did not include surprise and I realized I'd known, ever since I took his breakfast up to the empty watch room. I'd known it would end like this. I'd fought the knowledge but I'd realized Garcia's information was accurate. I cursed to myself. How was I supposed to tell Riitta?

CHAPTER 9

It occurred to me, belatedly, that I should check for a pulse. But when I touched his exposed neck and watched his head flop like a flower on a broken stem, I hastily withdrew my fingers. He'd clearly plummeted from the gallery. There appeared to be a nasty gash on the side of his head, too, as if he'd hit a stone when he'd fallen to earth. Only there wasn't any stone. Not an accident, then. I realized I'd never considered that it was an accident, anymore than I thought it was suicide. Alex Martin had come into our little world and shaken things up enough to make someone push him off the tower. There were lots of questions, such as, when was he pushed? Why were his polo shirt and khaki pants damp? Had this happened during the night, perhaps even before the start of the rain? If so, where had the body been when the dogs and I came out here before dawn?

But all those questions could wait for an investigation. The single, harsh, horrible truth was that Alex Martin had returned home to die and that the Keweenaw had experienced its first murder in the twenty-first century.

My cheeks were wet and my eyes stinging and I had one dog under each arm hunkering against me, providing comfort before I thought about calling the cops. It took three tries to punch in 911.

The phone rang and rang. And rang some more. I wondered why the sheriff's department didn't have an answering machine and concluded that it was because they were supposed to answer each and every emergency call. But they weren't answering this one. I started to count the rings and got to eleven when a familiar voice apologized.

"Hello, hello, oh, I'm so sorry about the delay! I was down the hall in the little girl's room. So, what can I do you for, then?"

"Mrs. Toukolehto?" The woman had been our primary grades Sunday school teacher twenty years earlier. "Are you the sheriff's dispatcher?"

"Well, I am for just the moment, dear. Justin Erkkila's over to Embarrass, Minnesota visitin' his daughter and I'm holding down the fort so to speak. Who is this?"

"Hatti," I said, "Hatti Lehtinen. I'm out at the lighthouse."

"Oh yes. I ran into Ianthe at the hardware last week. She told me your dad was sending you out there on account of the crickets."

I couldn't help contrasting this, the second example today of the efficiency of our grapevine, with the fact that a 911 call could go unanswered for long minutes. And then something occurred to me.

"Mrs. Too, earlier this morning did you get an anonymous phone tip about a body at the lighthouse?"

"I don't know, dear. Let me check my log sheet." She was silent for a moment. "No. No tip. Just a fender bender over in Lake Linden and Mrs. Saarinen calling from Hellmuth to say Samson was up the tree again and could we get him down. Why are you calling? Did Larry wander off?"

I felt an ominous foreboding as it came to me how woefully ill-equipped we are to handle a murder investigation.

"No. Larry's fine. The fact is, there's a body at the lighthouse." I knew it sounded melodramatic but, geez Louise, it was only the truth. "We've had a sudden death."

"I'm sorry to hear it! And on *Juhannus,* too. Good gracious! It's the old lady isn't it? Flossie Ollanketo? Jeanie Lasker over at the pharmacy told me Doc Kukka just renewed the old lady's heart medicine and he wasn't his usual self. Looked upset as if he was afraid it would be the last time. So her heart finally gave out, eh?"

"It isn't Mrs. O. I mean, she did have a kind of heart attack last night, but she didn't die. It's someone else. Could you send the sheriff out right away?"

"Someone else? That other old lady? The one who's supposed to give the mitten talk today? Or is it that old man who takes care of the Fresnel lens? I've wondered if it wasn't too much for him climbing up to the top of that tower to clean up the beacon."

I interrupted her in a way that would have had my mother washing my mouth out with soap if I'd been younger.

"Mrs. Too. Listen to me. It's a man you don't know. I think he's been murdered. Please send the sheriff immediately with the, uh, vehicle for transporting bodies." I wasn't sure whether the sheriff's department had such a vehicle but figured it would be prudent to ask.

"Well, Henrikki, I can't do either one of those things. The wagon's got a broken axle. Sheriff's driving his Corvette today. Anyhow, he's down at the diner. It's Sunday, you know, and that means fresh *pannukakku.* I could send Ollie Rahkunen over in his pickup."

I shuddered, thinking of Alex Martin bouncing around in the back of Ollie's old Chevy.

"Never mind about Ollie. I'll get Arvo to bring the hearse. But you're going to have to interrupt the pancake breakfast. This appears to be a case of murder."

I should have hung up immediately but I wasn't thinking fast enough and my old Sunday school teacher launched into what had long been her favorite subject.

"Henrikki, I know why your marriage broke up. You are still in love with Waino. The two of you were always meant to be together and providence has brought you back at just the right time. I ran into Hilda Aho at Shopko and she says Waino is between girlfriends. The one he was seeing has gone off to a Luther League Convention up in Duluth."

Luther League Conventions were for high school students and I should have been more shocked than I was that Waino was dating someone that age. He had already been over six feet tall and built like Paul Bunyan when, during the summer between sixth and seventh grade, he and I had decided to skip a Vacation Bible School lesson on Lepers and spend the morning playing spin the bottle in the cloak closet. Mrs. Too had found us and, perhaps out of guilt, she'd always believed we were "predestined" for one another.

"This is the perfect time to look him up, Henrikki. Strike while the iron's hot."

"Thanks for the heads up," I murmured. "Mrs. Too, I've got to go now. Don't forget to send the sheriff." I hung up as three people approached. Tom Kukka looked grim and Danny Thorne had his arm around his mother.

Somewhere in the back of my mind it registered that none of them seemed surprised. Had they known Alex was dead?

Tears slid down Riitta's face. Tom asked Danny to take her back inside and return with a blanket and I asked him to ask Arvo to drive back to Red Jacket and return with the hearse. Then I watched Tom's careful examination of the body. When he'd finished, he covered Alex's remains with the Hudson Bay blanket Danny provided.

"When did you find him, Hatti?"

"Just now. Well, within the last fifteen minutes or so. What do you think happened?"

"Swan dive off the tower. He's got a broken neck. That would've killed him. Or it might have been the deep gash in his skull. I'd say he landed on a rock."

I nodded. "If there was a rock. There's none here now."

"Suspicious."

"Yep."

Tom squinted up at the tower and seemed to be doing some calculations in his head.

"Unlikely to have been an accident," he said. "He may have gone out on the gallery during the storm but he grew up here in the lighthouse. He'd have known how to handle the weather conditions. Besides, the body is a little too far away from the tower for it to have been a straight fall."

"Suicide?"

Tom shook his head. "Most suicides want to get a running start. There's no place up there for that. And why should he commit suicide. Hell, the guy had everything in the world to live for."

"You can't always tell what's going on in somebody's mind."

"True, but he couldn't have brained himself with a rock. We'll find out in the autopsy."

"Tom," I said, swallowing hard, "Can you tell what time he died?"

"It's a bit murky because of the heat of the day. The rule of thumb is that you lose 1.5 degrees of body heat per hour after death but there are plenty of variables, including age, physical shape, clothing, and, of course, the environment. It's getting on for ninety degrees out here so the temperature drop would be slow. He's down to 94.1 but he coulda started low. I'm guessing death was at least three hours ago. Probably longer."

"I hate to bring this up, but his clothes are damp, which probably means he was out in the storm and the body wasn't here when the dogs and I came out this morning."

Tom Kukka's wide, cheerful face lost most of its color.

"What are you saying?"

I stared into his honest blue eyes.

"I think the body was moved."

He uttered a soft curse.

"If you're right, there's no way to pass this off as an accident or suicide."

"So it's murder?" My voice sounded thick. "Do you think it's someone we know?"

"Yep. Gotta be," he said. He didn't look happy. He stared at me. "Hatti, you sleep up in the tower. Did Danny go up to see him last night?" I nodded, reluctantly.

"And so did Riitta."

"Well, hell," he said. He glanced at the lighthouse. "If the body was moved, and it's a big if, it would have been hidden somewhere."

"I know. I was thinking about that. What about the cellar?"

Tom looked at me. "What makes you suggest that?"

"For one thing, there aren't many other places. For another, it would be relatively easy for a strong person to hoist the body into that wheelbarrow," I pointed to the cart on the backporch, "to wheel it over to the window which would have been opened from the inside, and to dump the body down the coal chute."

"But why?"

"Yeah. I don't know. Maybe to establish an alibi? You said trying to pinpoint the time of death depends on body temperature. What better way to mess up that calculation by keeping the body in a cooler place then returning it to the hot yard?"

"But there'll be other indications in an autopsy," he argued. "Stomach contents, for instance."

The stomach contents wouldn't include that yummy fresh *pannukakku* Riitta had sent up to him. I felt a tidal wave of sadness.

"There is one problem with the coal chute theory," I said, knowing I had to be honest, "Miss Thyra sent me down there to look for a clothespin and there was no body there then. And speaking of Miss Thyra," I continued, suddenly remembering, "she's complaining of a migraine. I thought you might give her the Verapamil you gave me last week."

"I'll check on her as soon as we get through this."

CHAPTER 10

The fire-engine-red Corvette swept up into the circular driveway and skidded to a stop in front of the lighthouse. A tall, skinny kid with a thatch of flame-colored hair that made him look like a lit matchstick unfolded himself from the passenger's seat. He slammed shut the car door then circled to the driver's side as the vehicle began to buck like a bronco. We heard a series of groans and muttered curses. Finally, an individual emerged and headed toward us across the lighthouse lawn.

Sheriff Horace A. Clump had always reminded me of Humpty-Dumpty before the fall, not just because of his barrel-like proportions but because his heavy, bulldog jowls seemed to melt into his shoulders. He had no discernible neck which made it a challenge for him to turn his head from side to side. In fact, he didn't. Clump was known for keeping his eyes straight ahead, choosing the most direct, easiest path to his goal. A lot of folks thought he was lazy. A lot believed he was parsimonious. He kept getting re-elected, anyway, even last year after he'd decided to replace the sheriff's department wooden-sided station wagon with the low-slung sports car, a singular choice for a law officer whose principle duty was to rescue snow-stranded motorists.

Clump's point, when asked, was that the sports car had saved Copper County both time and money because nearly all abandoned driver calls were referred to Arvo Maki whose hearse was the heaviest vehicle in the county and who was willing make the rescues free of charge.

Clump waddled across the lawn toward us, his flabby cheeks the color of eggplant in the early afternoon heat. His small, beady eyes sparked with irritation. He was breathing like an out-of-shape runner at the end of a race.

I was so focused on the sheriff, I had barely noticed the matchstick deputy at his side so I was taken by surprise when the latter spoke to me.

"*Hei*, Hatti. Remember me? I'm Ellwood Lantti."

I did remember him. He was the much younger brother of one of my classmates at Copper County High.

"Sure," I said. "How is Annemarie?"

"Pregnant," he said. He swallowed and I watched his Adam's apple bounce up and down like the mercury in a thermometer. That reminded me of watching Tom taking the corpse's body temperature and I felt a chill, despite the ninety-degree weather.

"Huh. This her third?"

"Fourth."

There seemed to be nothing to say to that. Everyone my age was pregnant, just had been or was about to be.

"I didn't know you were the sheriff's deputy."

"Yep."

I wondered how long Ellwood would last in that position. Clump was known for going through his deputies as if they were paper towels. I introduced Tom to the sheriff and Ellwood and then the deputy knelt down to remove the blanket.

Clump glanced at the body, stuck his thumbs into the straining suspenders that held up his uniform pants, and glared at me.

"What in the H-E-double hockey sticks happened here?"

"He's dead," Ellwood said.

"Well, hell, boy. I kin see that. I wanna know how he died. And when."

"The victim is Alex Martin from Los Angeles," Tom said. "He was the son of Johanna Marttinen who owned the lighthouse. She died last summer. Martin has lived in California for twenty years but he came home yesterday to claim the property, just in the nick of time. If he had waited one more day, the lighthouse and a trust fund was to go to Copper County for use as a retirement home."

Doc had Clump's attention. "Go on," the sheriff said.

"I've examined him and have determined that he died from injuries due to a fall from the lighthouse gallery."

"Accident," Clump said. He sounded relieved. And why not? An accident would not require either the energy or resources that would be needed for an investigation.

Tom shook his head and gave Clump the same reasoning he'd given me.

"Suicide, then."

"I don't believe so for a number of reasons, including the fact that somebody bopped him on the head with a hard object."

"Well, shoot-a-dam-mile," Clump said, annoyed. "Why in the Sam Hill would somebody kill the feller?"

Tom and I exchanged a look and he spoke.

"No one here would do it. Folks were upset about possibly losing the lighthouse. We've got a number of elderly people living here already. But it would have taken someone young and strong to overpower a man in the prime of his life. It couldn't have been anybody at the lighthouse."

"And yet," Clump said, "the feller's dead."

"Sheriff," I said, hastily, "Tom doesn't know this, but Alex Martin changed his mind about the disposition of the lighthouse last night. He decided to let the county have it to use as a retirement home. So there was no need for anybody here to kill him."

It wasn't until I'd finished my explanation that I realized I'd boxed Tom into a corner by admitting he didn't know about the change in circumstances.

Clump removed his wide-brimmed hat and swept his arm

across his sweat-streaked forehead. The bushy, salt-and-pepper eyebrows contrasted with the smooth bald egg of his head. Both eyebrows tipped up, like a drawbridge opening.

"He leave a note?"

"You mean a suicide note," I asked.

"No. A Valentine. Of course I mean a suicide note."

I swallowed an angry response. "He left Riitta Lemppi a letter. She'll show you. It outlines his plans for the lighthouse."

Clump's small eyes squinted at me.

"What're you doing out here, anyways?" Clump's voice was hostile and, since he had no reason to resent me personally, I figured his attitude was directed at Pops with whom he'd had more than a few run-ins. "I heard you was running your daddy's worm shop in Red Jacket."

I appreciated the fact that neither Tom Kukka nor Ellwood brought up the unfortunate cricket incident. I was able to tell Clump that I had accompanied my aunt and her friend and had stayed to help out Ms. Lemppi, who was my second cousin.

The sheriff cursed, softly. "Everybody on this damn peninsula is related to everybody else. It ain't healthy." He asked for the names of the inmates of the retirement home and I listed them. Even though there were only eight of us, he lost interest long before I finished.

He asked Tom the usual questions, why he was there, what time the deceased had died, and, to my surprise, why the deceased was barefoot. It was a detail I hadn't noticed. When he'd finished he turned to Ellwood.

"Got a real smorgasbord of suspects," he said. "You've got your work cut out for you talkin' to 'em all. Come on, now, and help me get back into the car."

"What about the autopsy," Tom asked.

Clump glared at him. "Have to wait until one of coroners gets back from vacation."

In Copper County we don't have a full-time medical examiner. Four doctors, a pediatrician, an obstetrician and two general practitioners, share the duties of a coroner which, as previously noted, do not often arise.

"Talk to everybody in the lighthouse," Clump said to Ellwood. "Get their alibis. I'll be back after Sunday dinner."

I watched Ellwood shoe-horn his boss back into the Corvette. When he returned, I left him and Tom to stand vigil until Arvo returned with the hearse while I went inside. Riitta and Danny were in the kitchen, the former standing at the sink, gazing out the window to the backyard and the latter leaning against the refrigerator, his arms crossed over his chest, a scowl on his face. Tension was high. They both turned to look at me.

"Tom says it was murder. Someone hit him then pushed him off the gallery. His neck was broken in the fall."

Danny cursed and Riitta made a little choked sound. Her light summer freckles stood out against the extreme pallor of her face and purple crescents underlined her large, blue eyes.

"It doesn't make sense," she said, in a small voice. "Who would have wanted to kill Alex? He'd promised to give us the lighthouse. Nothing was going to change."

"What?" Danny's one-word question exploded in the room like a Roman candle. The obvious surprise in his voice made Riitta wince and me, too. He hadn't known about the gift. "What are you talking about, mom?"

"I talked to Alex last night," she said, her arms folded across her waist as if she were cold. Her back was hunched. "He promised me the lighthouse. Everything was settled."

"When did you talk to him," Danny asked, "what time?"

"I think it was around midnight."

Footsteps in the corridor made Danny speak quickly, urgently.

"Until we find out what time Martin was killed, don't tell that to the cops or anybody else."

Ellwood stepped into the kitchen and I introduced him to mother and son. When I'd finished, he turned to Riitta and said, in a low-key, polite voice, "don't tell me what?"

CHAPTER 11

M y cousin was saved from answering, not by a bell, but by Aunt Ianthe who came hurrying down the backstairs calling, "Riitta? Oh, Riitta, dearie, where are you?" She stepped into the kitchen with Miss Irene right behind her, spotted her quarry, and gave a fulsome sigh of relief.

"*Voi,* I'm so glad to find you. Thyra has a migraine headache, you know, and we thought Doctor Kukka might have something to help her. I imagine she got it from staying up all night preparing for the seminar."

Ellwood's hazel eyes widened. "This Miss Thyra stayed up all night? Maybe she knows what happened. I'll need to talk to her."

"Oh, yes, yes, of course," Aunt Ianthe said. "But could it wait until she feels better? There's no great hurry then, is there? You know, dear, a little lemon juice on those freckles would do wonders for you. We used it on Hatti when she was a girl and look at her now."

It was true that the freckles that marched across my nose had faded somewhat but I doubted it had anything to do with the lemon juice. I smiled at the two old ladies.

"Something has happened that you should know about," I said, quietly. "Alex Martin is dead."

"*Voi!* That golf course man? But he was so young."

"It wasn't a natural death," I said, gently. "He fell off the lighthouse tower."

"Someone hit him on the head and pushed him off the tower," Danny struck in. There was a raw note in his voice. He had obviously abandoned discretion."He was murdered by someone in the lighthouse."

We were all standing in the room, some with arms crossed, others with jaws dropped. It must have looked like a stage set to Erik Sundback. He'd let himself in through the front door but had entered the kitchen from the corridor. He wore a red-and-orange Hawaiian print shirt, a pair of white shorts and white canvas boat shoes and his face, reddened by the sun and the wind, was the picture of good health and bonhomie. He moved easily across the room and took Riitta's hands in each of his.

"Oh, my dear, I'm so sorry," he murmured. "I was out on the boat but came just as soon as I could. I wouldn't have had something like this happen for the world but who could have known? No one's ever before fallen from the tower."

He obviously believed it was an accident.

"Excuse me," Ellwood said, demonstrating a fine alertness, "I'm Ellwood Lantti from the Copper County Sheriff's Department and I'd like to know how you heard about the, er, incident."

Sundback grinned at him.

"I'm a nosy son-of-a-gun. I've got a police scanner on my sailboat and I heard the 911 call Hatti made. As soon as I realized it had happened here," he looked, meaningfully, at Riitta, "I got back to shore as quickly as I could and headed up here. I called the department from my car. That's when I found out the accident victim was Alex."

"Murder victim," Tom Kukka said, entering the room. His normally friendly voice dripped with ice and his eyes were focused on the hands holding Riitta's.

"Murder?" Erik sounded both shocked and a little offended. "That's pure nonsense. Who would want to murder Alex Martin?"

Arvo entered from the back door.

"Loaded up and ready to go," he said. "Dang. We haven't had a body in that morgue in I don't know how long. Not this century. Plenty of bodies back in the day, of course. Lots of conflict among the miners." He looked older and tired, especially in contrast to Erik. "Murder. It's a bad business."

"Fret not thyself because of evildoers, neither be thou envious against the workers of iniquity," Miss Irene quoted. "For they shall soon be cut down like the grass and wither as the green herb."

"Providence, Irene?"

Miss Irene looked at her friend. "Someone wanted Mr. Martin dead and he is dead. Surely, that is providential for the killer."

Suddenly, Riitta's practical good sense reasserted itself.

"Tom," she said, "you must go up and see about Miss Thyra's headache and check on Flossie. I'll put together a light lunch for each of them and bring it up." She looked at me. "Hatti, you get the ladies settled in the parlor with a cup of tea. They can talk to the deputy."

"Oh, no, dearie," Aunt Ianthe said, "we want to help, too. We'll make some little sandwiches for Flossie and bring them up. You go on with the good doctor."

A short time later, Aunt Ianthe, Miss Irene and I carried the sandwiches up to Mrs. Ollanketo, along with a carafe of coffee and a glass of water. The door to her room was open and she was propped up against a bank of pillows. The white curls that would normally have been secured by bobby pins, were disheveled and, for once, there was no twinkle in her blue eyes.

"We've brought you some lunch, Mrs. O.," I said, with what I hoped was a bright smile. "And some company. Aunt Ianthe and Miss Irene and I have missed you."

"I'm an old sleepyhead," she said. She spoke in the familiar monotone but her voice had lost some volume and vigor. "I'm glad to see all of you."

The tray was the kind with the little legs and I set it up

across her lap and invited the other ladies to take the two available seats in the room.

"I'll just go see if Miss Thyra needs anything," I said, looking at Mrs. Ollanketo so she could see me. Her lips pulled into a little line and something flared in her eyes.

"Don't go away, Hatti. I want to speak to you."

I assured her I'd be right back. I found Doc out on the landing near the antique table where he kept his bag. He was wearing plastic gloves and filling a syringe. Miss Thyra's door was closed.

"That stubborn old woman refuses to take the Verapamil," he said, darkly. "Anyone can see that she's in pain but she's determined to be a martyr."

"Let me guess. She told you that if God wanted her to be in pain who was she to gainsay his will?"

"You've heard that before." Tom almost chuckled. "I've heard it, too. It's the kind of thing my maternal grandmother used to say when she had a guilty conscience about missing church or letting her temper slip. Think that's what it is with Thyra? She killed Alex Martin and now she thinks she deserves a headache?"

I knew he was teasing but the words shocked me and the breath caught in my throat.

"You don't mean that, do you?"

"Why not? Thyra Poonjola was one of those who'd have been displaced if the lighthouse was sold. She's as good a candidate as anyone."

"What about moving the body? She's pretty old." The tight expression faded from his eyes.

"You're right, of course. I don't seem to be myself today. I don't know when I've been so off balance. Anyway, I talked to Flossie earlier. She's going to get a second dose of Digitalin in a few minutes but she said she said she wanted to speak to you."

"I know." I crossed the landing and ushered the other ladies out of the room. Then I went over to the bed and sat on the side of it. "I'm sorry we didn't get to take that sauna last night, Mrs. Ollanketo. We'll have a raincheck as soon as Doc Kukka gives us the okay."

"I've had a lot of sauna in my life," she said, her voice overloud, as usual. "Doc told me about Alex Martin, Henrikki. Is it true that someone pushed him off the tower?"

"I'm afraid so. But I don't want you to worry about it. The sheriff's deputy is a nice young man. You can meet him when you wake up." I smiled at her.

"Do you know who did it?"

I thought it was an interesting way to phrase the question. Not, 'does anyone know who did it' but more personal, as if she knew the culprit's identity. But, surely, that was impossible.

"Nobody knows yet. But we'll find out."

Her eyes looked past me out the bedroom door onto the landing. Tom, Arvo, Erik and Danny were gathered there, speaking in low tones.

"I want you to do something for me, Hatti," she said. "There is a blue mitten in the bottom drawer of my bureau. Can you get it?" I found it easily, as it was the only one with a blue background.

"This is a match to the green Arjeplog mitten, isn't it? Miss Thyra told us the green background was for women, the blue, for men. It's beautiful. Did you make it?"

"Yes. I want you to give it to Thyra."

Suddenly, I understood. Mrs. Ollanketo had slept through the history of mittens. She didn't know it was over. "Oh, I don't think," I started to say, then stopped. What harm could be done to let her think she was contributing to Miss Thyra's success?

"Of course I'll give it to her," I said. "As soon as she wakes up from her nap."

The old lady sank back onto the pillows but she didn't seem especially relieved. Her face looked older than I'd ever seen it. She appeared weary and resigned.

"Say your goodbyes," Tom Kukka said, entering the room with a poised syringe. "Flossie here is going back to dreamland for a few hours."

I kissed the old, withered cheek, then headed back up the circular staircase to my room. Since I didn't know when

Miss Thyra would wake up, I didn't want to carry the mitten around for hours. The watch room door was open and there were voices coming from inside it, so I joined them.

"Geez Louise," I said, as I recognized Erik Sundback. "You're Voldemort."

"What?"

"The dark lord from Harry Potter. He has the power of teleportation. Didn't I just speak with you, seconds ago, down in Mrs. O.'s room?"

Sundback laughed a little ruefully. "I've only been here a minute or two. Figured I'd better take a look around since it seems like this is where it happened. And then my friend, Ellwood here, joined me. It's so hard to believe that just last night Alex was in here, working. There are his glasses," he pointed to the pair on the secretary, "and his windbreaker. But where are the papers he was working on? And where are his shoes?"

"He was barefoot," I recalled.

"It's an interesting point. I spoke with the sheriff on the phone. He said the shoes were missing." He chuckled, suddenly. "Well, what he actually said was 'the corpus is barefooted.'" He looked around the small room. "If that's true, shouldn't the shoes be here?" And then he noticed the mitten in my hand. "You expecting a change in the weather?"

I explained about the Arjeplog mitten from Swedish Lapland.

"Mrs. Ollanketo slept through Miss Thyra's presentation this morning. She thinks it hasn't happened yet and wanted to contribute something of her own."

"So the mitten is half Finnish, half Swedish," Erik said. "Like me." I nodded.

"Arvo made that point this morning." Sundback grinned, ruefully.

"From now on my name will be synonymous with workhouse mittens," he said. "At least it will keep me on the minds of the ladies but only as a hybrid."

"Hybrids are good things up here," I reminded him. "You get to enjoy all the cultural perks of two countries." Erik laughed at that.

"I was raised in a series of foster homes," he said. "None of my foster parents were much interested in cultural customs including birthdays and Christmas."

"I'm sorry," I said, feeling a flash of quick sympathy. He grinned at me again.

"I survived. And now, at the ripe old age of fifty-three, I'm ready to start exploring my heritage."

"Why now?"

"It's never too late for that," he said, lightly, "any more than it's too late to fall in love." He didn't pause and I figured the subject was closed. "I'm concerned about Mrs. Ollanketo. Does doc think she'll be all right?"

"She's got congestive heart failure," I said. "One of her symptoms is an occasional irregular heartbeat. In an extreme situation, the beats become so far apart that the heart is not pumping enough blood to the brain and the patient faints. That's what happened last night when we were crossing the lawn to get to the sauna. She just collapsed."

Erik frowned. "Any way to prevent that from happening again?"

I shrugged. "Avoiding stress and over exertion. Tom asked me after it happened whether she was upset about something. She'd just seemed tired. She was, of course, much more upset this afternoon when she found out about Alex Martin's death but then, anyone would be."

"Poor lady." He shook his head. "Well, I'll let the two of you get back to sleuthing. My suggestion, set up an interview spot, maybe the parlor. You can close the doors to the foyer and the dining room and have some privacy to talk to people there. I'll be around in case Riitta needs anything so don't hesitate to ask if I can help."

CHAPTER 12

"Nice guy," Ellwood said, after the lawyer had left. "He's been a huge help to my cousin and Arvo. He's handled all the legal stuff and paperwork. And you know how excitable Arvo is. Erik has been kind of a yin to his yang. A voice of reason." And then I remembered the shocking, frightening moments in the middle of the festival when Mrs. Ollanketo had slumped against me throwing us both to the sand. "And he was a rock last night. Mrs. O. fell on top of me and they got her onto her back with her feet elevated while Doc ran up to the lighthouse to get a syringe. And then Alex and Erik carried her up to her room."

Ellwood frowned. "Did anything happen to upset her on the walk to the sauna?"

"Nothing traumatic. There were dozens of folks around eating and drinking, singing and dancing. There were kids with sparklers. It was busy and loud but that wouldn't have bothered Flossie Ollanketo. She's completely deaf but she can read lips as far as twenty feet away."

"Could she have lip read a conversation that upset her?"

I pictured the scene on the lawn. It had been a typical small town festival, the kind you see depicted in an Americana jigsaw puzzle, complete with lighthouse and beach and a maypole. I'd noticed half a dozen groups of two or more people.

"I guess she could have," I said, slowly. "Everyone was out there except the older ladies from the lighthouse and Captain Jack. I remember seeing Riitta and Tom and Arvo and Danny and Erik. Alex surprised us by taking a sauna and he'd just come out of it when Mrs. O. fainted. I don't think there's anything in that, though," I said. "She'd been shaky throughout the walk and her breathing had gotten rougher. She did tell me she had taken a sauna every *Juhannus* of her adult life and she implied this would be the last. She may have been thinking about her mortality."

Ellwood said nothing for a moment.

"Sundback likes your cousin Riitta."

I nodded. "I hadn't really noticed that before. Tom Kukka has proposed to her repeatedly but she refuses to marry him, I think, because she feels she's too old for him."

"Maybe she doesn't love him."

It was a chilling thought. Poor Tom.

"Hatti, where was Erik Sundback last night?"

"He left about eleven thirty to drive back to his condo in Houghton. Tom left at the same time to go to the hospital in Hancock."

"Did you see them leave?"

I laughed, suddenly. "They stopped by the kitchen to say goodnight. Not to me, so much, as to Riitta. I assume they left via the front door since it is closer to where the cars were parked. By then the wind was howling, thunder crashing and lightning flashing. It was not a great night to be out."

"What did you do after that?"

"I went upstairs and went to bed. With the dogs," I added.

"Did you see anybody else the rest of the evening?"

I didn't answer immediately as it dawned on me what he was doing.

"You're interviewing me here and now?"

He shrugged. "You had the room next door to where it all

happened and we're up here now. I thought maybe you'd remember something important."

A wave of nausea rippled in my stomach. I'd been aware, on some level, that what he said was true but I hadn't expected to have to tell him what I'd heard until I'd had a chance to think about it. But that wasn't the way it worked, was it? My testimony was only useful if it came from my raw memory. I just prayed my raw memory wouldn't implicate anyone who was innocent. I told him about overhearing Danny Thorne speaking to Alex.

"He sounded angry?"

There was another wave of nausea and I ground my teeth. I was aware, suddenly, that there was perspiration on my upper lip.

"I should probably tell you that Danny had just discovered that Alex Martin was his biological father. The same was true for Alex. I think Danny went to see Alex to try to convince him to relinquish his claim on the lighthouse and trust fund. He said Alex owed Riitta for the years of single parenting."

"Holy wha," Ellwood said, using a strong Yooper expletive. "That's a motive, all right."

I jumped to Danny's defense.

"There was no need to kill him. Alex agreed to give up his claim on the property."

"You heard him tell that to Danny?"

"No," I said, before I spotted the trap. By then it was too late to take back my words. "I heard Alex tell that to Riitta. She came up to see him after Danny left."

"What time was that?"

"Twelve," I said, miserably. "The Witching Hour."

And that's when I remembered something else. Something that had truly shocked me at the time but which I'd forgotten because of everything else that had happened.

"The words witching hour reminded me," I said, suddenly. "Chakra Starshine and her friends were on the beach last night. She's the new yoga instructor in Red Jacket and she's also a Wiccan. She and her coven were celebrating the summer solstice, and they were doing it skyclad."

"Skyclad?"

"Dressed in only the sky."

"You mean, naked?" I nodded.

"Could they have killed Alex Martin," he asked.

"Why would they?" He shrugged.

"A ritual sacrifice. Maybe they couldn't find a goat. Maybe Mrs. Ollanketo lip read a conversation about that."

"I don't think so. They were farther down the beach. And, I'm sure they all went home when the storm started."

Ellwood appeared to think.

"Hatti, when Mrs. O. spoke to you just now, did she ask you about the future of the lighthouse?" I shook my head.

"Wouldn't you think that would be the first thing on her mind? I mean, if Alex Martin had claimed the place, he'd have torn it down and sold the land, right?"

"I see what you mean. I think Mrs. O. was more worried about Miss Thyra's lecture."

We headed down the circular stairs and I told Ellwood about the contradictory evidence of the damp clothing, the disturbed sand and the blood, and the anonymous tip about a body.

He scratched his head. "Sounds to me like somebody's trying to confuse us," he said. "First thing we've got to do is find out when the rain started. By the way, I sure appreciate your help in this. I've never investigated a murder before."

I was pleased that he wanted me.

"I haven't either but I did spend a year at law school, of course, it was mostly torts and contracts. And then during the last few months I wasn't really paying attention."

"Attention deficit disorder?"

"Nope. Love. It didn't end well."

"I'm sorry," he said, sympathetically.

"It's okay. I've watched enough *Law & Order* episodes to muddle my way through this."

"All I really need you to do is give me some background

on all these folks. You know them better than I do."

That took the wind out of my sails.

"Sure. I think I can handle that."

As we headed down the hallway to the glass-paned doors that open into the parlor, I figured we'd have to clear away the folding chairs and Miss Thyra's banner and the mittens to turn the place into an interview room.

But while we'd been upstairs, even though it was midsummer and as far away from Christmas as you can get, the house had been visited by a *tonttu,* which is a mythical elf who helps out in the household. I gazed at the smiles on two wrinkled faces as Aunt Ianthe and Miss Irene welcomed us into the lecture hall-turned-tearoom.

Make that plural. *Tontut.*

CHAPTER 13

The rows of folding chairs and the lectern were gone. The mittens still hung by the chimney but they weren't bothering anybody. The Victorian sofas and chairs were still pushed against the walls and center stage was occupied by a card table and four chairs which would have served perfectly as an interview room except for the white, lace tablecloth spread across it and the Arabia china, cups, saucers, plates and teapot of blue cornflowers on a white background.

There was a crystal bowl of roses in the center, crystal flutes filled with pink lemonade and a plate of crustless sandwiches, fruit and shortbread cookies.

I took a quick peek at Ellwood, afraid he'd be annoyed at the interference with his investigation, but he just looked appreciative. And hungry.

"No reason you should have to interview people on an empty stomach," Aunt Ianthe said, with a grin. She and Miss Irene took their places across the table from one another, leaving the other two seats to the deputy and me. "Tea, anyone?"

"Thank you," Ellwood said, pulling out a chair for me. "It seems to me we should interview the two of you first."

"Oh my goodness, Irene," Aunt Ianthe said, enormously pleased. "We're suspects!"

"Witnesses," Ellwood corrected, helping himself to a sandwich. "Everybody is just a witness."

"For thou shalt be his witness unto all men of what thou hast seen and heard," Miss Irene quoted, passing a jug of cream. "Acts of the Apostles."

Ellwood consumed three sandwiches in record time and then pulled out his cellphone. I held my breath, wondering not whether but when Aunt Ianthe would reprimand him for ill manners but he surprised me by admitting it.

"I'm not making a call," he said, apologetically, "I'm looking up what questions to ask. You see, this is my first murder investigation."

The confession drew the immediate sympathy of both ladies.

"Ellwood," I told them, "is the younger brother of Annemarie Lemppi. You must remember her. She had the piano lesson just before Elli's on Wednesday afternoon."

"Of course," Aunt Ianthe said, happily. "Red hair. It reminded me of the burning bush." She looked at Miss Irene. "You always used to say she had so much potential."

Ellwood, his eyes still focused on his phone, snickered.

"My mom used to say that about her all the time. She had potential in ballet. She had potential in math. She had potential in confirmation class. The trouble was, she was only interested in boys."

"A sad but common circumstance," Miss Irene said. "She, like so many students, met her Waterloo in Hanon."

The reference was to C.L. Hanon's *The Virtuoso Pianist,* a thick compendium of finger strengthening exercises that resemble a swarm of black ants on every page and represent a form of torture to all but the most dedicated piano students.

I thought, not for the first time, how the life of a small town piano teacher must be full of disappointed hopes.

"Deputy," Aunt Ianthe asked, "do you think Mr. Martin was killed by a passing stranger or someone in the house?" I could hear the anxiety in her voice and knew that she, as much as I, hated the thought that someone we knew, someone who was part of our community, could have crossed the line that separates human being from murderer.

"We're going to find out," Ellwood said, gently. "And we're going to do it by the book. I've found a website. *Ten Steps to Solving a Murder.*" He grinned at me. "We'll just skip the parts about making sure the victim is dead, drawing a circle around the body with tape and go straight to the interviews and the timeline."

"Timeline?" Aunt Ianthe sounded bewildered but intrigued.

He nodded. "Once we know when death occurred, the alibis will flow from there. Now, when did you last see the deceased?"

Aunt Ianthe shivered and the tea party notwithstanding, I knew the reality of the crime was beginning to set in.

"We saw him on the beach last night during the festival," she said. "Irene and I were watching from the front porch. He had gone into the sauna and he came out again. Someone brought him a beer. I think it was Arvo. The two men were talking when Flossie had her attack and fell on Hatti. We saw Alex Martin rush to help Flossie and then, after awhile, he helped carry her up to her room, then."

Ellwood nodded. "That's perfect. That's exactly what I want. So that was the last time you saw him?"

"Oh, no. We saw him a little later down on the porch during *revontulet,* the Northern Lights. He didn't stay there the whole time. I don't know where he went after that."

I took a sip of tea to keep myself from blurting out where Alex Martin had been. I'd have to tell Ellwood at some point but this testimony wasn't supposed to be about me.

"Miss Irene? Is this the way you remember it?"

"Oh, yes. It was just like that."

"Can either of you think of anyone who would want to harm Mr. Martin?"

Aunt Ianthe pursed her lips.

"No one was very pleased about the golf course. So there's that."

"He hadn't been a very good son," Miss Irene said.

"Honor thy father and thy mother, you know."

"He hadn't been a very good father, either," Aunt Ianthe said, in a sorrowful voice. "He did not even know about Danny until yesterday. When do you think he was killed?"

"That's what we're trying to determine," Ellwood said, emptying his teacup. "That's why we have to ask everyone in the house to describe the last time he or she saw him."

"Oh, my land," Miss Irene said, suddenly. "I have lied to the police."

"Irene!"

"Oh, my goodness. I'm so sorry. I have something to add to my confession."

"Your statement, Miss Irene," I said, gently. "You didn't do anything wrong." Her large, pale blue eyes turned to me.

"Oh, yes, Henrikki. I misled the deputy. I did not see Mr. Martin after the Northern Lights but I heard him."

"No, no, dear," Aunt Ianthe said. "We were asleep. You must have had a dream."

"You were asleep," Miss Irene corrected. "I had gotten up to visit the rest room." A faint color flushed her cheeks. "The backstairs comes out right by our room and on my way back to bed, I could hear two people talking in the stairwell."

"What time was this?"

"After eleven thirty."

"You recognized Alex Martin's voice?"

"Not his voice, precisely. The man was whispering."

"Whispering to whom, Miss Irene?" She looked at me.

"A lady. I thought it might be you, Henrikki."

I stared at her. "It wasn't me."

"Then, perhaps it was Riitta." Miss Irene's voice trembled. "I do not wish to get her into trouble. The two of them may have met to talk about Danny."

I shook my head. "I don't think it was Riitta. Not at quarter to twelve. Danny came to see Alex about that time and Riitta came to see him fifteen or so minutes later. I didn't listen to his entire conversation with Riitta but the beginning of it sounded as if they hadn't spoken earlier."

"You say you didn't listen to his conversation with Riitta," Ellwood said. "Does that mean you did listen to the one with Danny?"

Too late I realized I'd trapped myself. Luckily, he didn't press me and I knew it was because of the presence of the ladies.

"What I heard Alex Martin say," Miss Irene continued, "was that he was glad she _ Madame X _ had come to see him. I got the impression they had known one another in the past."

"Could it have been Miss Thyra?"

Miss Irene's lips twitched. "No, Henrikki. No. I may be a spinster but I have read my share of romantic novels. I would never repeat the words but suffice it to say Mr. Martin was not speaking with Miss Thyra."

Ellwood and I exchanged a look over the teapot.

After the ladies had left we discussed the statement but could come up with no identity for Madame X.

"Let's take it back a step," Ellwood said, finally. "Where was Alex Martin during the Northern Lights?"

"It doesn't have anything to do with the murder."

"Tell me, anyway."

I stared at Annemarie Lantti's little brother. He was logical and thorough and the thought crossed my mind that he was unlikely to fail to fulfill his potential.

I shrugged. "He was in my bedroom. With me."

Ellwood's hazel eyes focused on me for a long moment.

"But you're not Madame X?"

"I'll tell you the whole story. It's not really very interesting."

It had been a private moment and I didn't want to talk about it but I knew that, if the positions were reversed, I'd have expected Ellwood to fill in the blanks for me.

"Everybody else was out on the porch. I'd gone up to my room and, for whatever reason, Alex had followed me. Or, maybe he'd just decided to get busy with his work and then he realized he wasn't the only one in the tower. I'm pretty sure I'd closed the door but all of a sudden he was there so

I guess he just walked in. Why not? It's his lighthouse. I was sitting on the bed faced away from the window and he thought, not unnaturally, that I was afraid of the lights. Some people are. He gave me the scientific explanation, you know, that they're caused by explosions on the surface of the sun and that solar flares, filled with charged particles, shoot toward earth where they crash into storms in the earth's magnetosphere."

"And that those collisions allow the particles to break free and propel themselves in the directions of our poles," Ellwood said, finishing the explanation. Anyone who lives as close as we do to the Arctic Circle knows the basics about aurora borealis. "Then what?"

"Well, he'd misunderstood. I'm not afraid of the lights. It's just that a year ago, after our wedding, my husband and I did a canoe trip on the Au Sable River down at Grayling. We camped out on the banks and one night we got a magnificent display of *revontulet.*"

I was silent, recalling the vibrant colors, hot pinks and fuschia and wisps of mint green. I'd told Jace the light were called *revontulet,* or fox fire because they're caused when the arctic fox uses his tail to sweep snow up into the sky. I'd known he'd debunk the Finnish myth and he had, all the while sifting his fingers through my long, thick, wheat-colored hair.

"Let me tell you the real story, wife," he'd said. "After the Creator finished making the earth and went to live in the north, he wanted to leave a sign for his people to let them know he was always watching over them so he built large fires. Their reflections from the sun formed the Northern Lights."

I'd gazed at him. "I thought you didn't believe in any myths, not even Ojibwe legends."

"I don't," he'd said, loftily. "It just so happens that this one is true."

"The lights brought back memories," Ellwood said, bringing me back to the present. "You weren't frightened. You were sad."

"Yes. Alex seemed to understand. He just sat next to me on the bed until the thunderheads drove the lights away. Then he went into the watch room and I went downstairs to cover the porch furniture and help the picnickers pack up their cars to leave."

"What time was that?"

"Around eleven."

"Hatti? What did you hear Alex Martin and Danny say to each other?"

"Danny asked him to give the lighthouse and the trust fund to Riitta so that she and Tom Kukka could make a home for the indigent elderly on the Keweenaw."

"How did he ask?"

"You mean was he polite? Come on, Ellwood. Danny's a nineteen-year-old boy."

"I'm nineteen, myself. I can't imagine being civil to the man who'd abandoned my mother."

"You're right, of course. He was loud. He said Alex owed Riitta."

"Did he threaten Alex?"

"No." Technically, I suppose, that was a lie but even though Danny had mentioned pushing Alex off the tower I knew he hadn't meant it.

Ellwood thrust long, thin fingers through his carroty hair.

"We need to find out what time the rain started. I'll call the National Weather Service."

"Leave it to me," I said, glad to be finished with the topic of Danny. "I'll call Einar at the bait shop. He knows everything there is to know about the weather."

"Okay. Great, then. Listen, can you hold down the fort here for an hour? I've got to run down to Chassell."

Aunt Ianthe and Miss Irene re-entered the parlor just as he was completing his sentence.

"Why are you going to Chassell, dear," Aunt Ianthe asked.

"To pick up my mom. There was a box lunch today after church at St. Peter and Paul's."

"Ah," Miss Irene said, knowingly. "That's why we never

see you at St. Heikki's. You're Missouri Synod."

Since Ellwood was without wheels, I gave him the key to my Jeep. I figured it was the least I could do even if he was Missouri Synod.

CHAPTER 14

During my week at the lighthouse, I'd discovered the best (and only) way to ensure privacy was to duck into the first floor powder room. Once inside I punched the number of Carl's Bait Shop into my phone. The endless rings gave me a distinct feeling of déjà vu. Where in the heck was Einar? Sure, it was a Sunday afternoon but our main street shops stayed open on the weekend during the tourist months and, anyway, unless he was in the sauna, the shop was Einar's real home. I pictured him perched on the high stool near the cash register, his shiny, pink head bent over the knots he was making in fishing line.

Why wasn't he answering the phone?

Frustrated, I disconnected and punched in another number.

"Main Street Floral and Fudge," my sister said, in a crisp voice. "Specials today on carnations and salted caramel."

"Sofi, is there something wrong with Einar? He isn't answering the phone."

"He never answers. He doesn't hold with the telephone. I expect it's the talking. You're the shop manager, how come you don't know that?"

"I haven't had any reason to call before. What do you mean he doesn't hold with the phone?"

"He thinks it's lazy. He says if someone wants to buy bait they can come into the shop. Of course he says it in fewer words."

Normally, I'd have laughed at the eccentricity. Not today.

"Well, I need to speak with him."

"Is this about Alex Martin's death? They're saying it's murder. Is that true?"

If there's one thing we excel at on the Keweenaw, it's the grapevine, which is kind of counterintuitive when you consider how many Finnish-American men begrudge every syllable. For the most part (with the exception of Arvo) communicating is left up to the women.

"That's what it looks like. I don't know who or why. Not yet."

"What do you need from Einar?"

"Alex's clothes were damp when I found him but the sand underneath the body had been dry for hours. I need to know what time the rain started."

"Hang on, hang on. Why do you need that," she asked, emphasizing the pronoun. "Isn't the sheriff's department investigating?"

I explained about Ellwood and told her I'd been favorably impressed with Annemarie's teenage brother.

"Wait a minute. I still don't understand why you're involved in this. You're supposed to be out there helping Riitta and Ianthe and Irene, not playing Inspector Clouseau."

"I'm just helping Ellwood keep the players straight."

"So what does the rain have to do with that?"

"We, that is, Ellwood, needs to know when the body came off the tower. He figures it happened before the rain started and I told him Einar is more accurate than the National Weather Service."

"So you're helping him collect data, too?"

Her lack of confidence hurt but, in light of the cricket fiasco, I couldn't really blame her. I changed the subject.

"Oh, by the way, Annemarie's got a fourth bun in the oven. We probably shouldn't mention it to mom." Our mother missed no opportunity to remind both of us that she expected more grandchildren.

"Like she won't find out," Sofi said. "Anyway, since neither of us is in a functioning marriage at the moment, this probably isn't the time to turn up pregnant." She paused. "Look, Hatti. I didn't mean to hurt your feelings. I just worry about you."

"I'm fine. There's no danger to me and I really can be useful to Riitta and the old ladies." I didn't tell her about Mrs. Ollanketo's attack or the fact that I was getting a little worried about Captain Jack who hadn't shown up for the pancake breakfast. "Can you get Einar on the phone for me?"

"Yep. One last thing," she said, and I heard her moving through her shop to the back door which led to the alley. "I know you're smart, Hatti. And normally you have good judgment."

"But these aren't normal times, right?"

"Not for the reason you think. This isn't about the crickets. You're loyal to a fault and I'm afraid you won't see the forest for the trees, you know? Remember, if Alex was murdered, somebody did it. And, almost certainly, it's someone you know. Don't just blindly trust everybody."

"You make me sound like the village idiot."

"Well, if the shoe fits."

"Thanks, big sis." I spoke dryly but, in fact, I knew where she was coming from. She'd trusted her husband and he'd let her down and then she had to relive the same experience when Jace ejected me from my marriage. "I'll take everything with the proverbial grain of salt."

She must have been walking and talking because I suddenly heard her say, "it's Hatti," and then I heard Einar's adenoidal breathing through the receiver.

"*Hei,* Einar. How's it going?"

He grunted.

"I've got a question about last night's storm. Do you know what time the rain began to fall out at the lighthouse?"

"Twelve forty-six."

"Thanks," I said, and found myself speaking with Sofi.

"Did you get your answer?"

"Yep. And in three words. Two, if you consider the hyphen. Think it's a record?"

"I know it's not. I've had plenty of conversation with Einar in which he has uttered, *joo* or *ei* (yes or no) and several in which he just grunts, which I guess, counts for no syllables at all."

I left the peace and solitude of the powder room to step into the midst of a boxing match or, at least, the timeout when the competitors had retreated to their separate corners. Riitta, arms folded across her chest, stood at the window staring out into the sunlit afternoon while Tom Kukka sat on one of the stools at the island, staring through the open swing door into the dining room. I didn't think he saw the tables and chairs. There was a crease between his eyebrows and a frown in his light blue eyes. The tension and the anguish in the scene smacked me between the eyes. I cleared my throat.

"Ellwood's got to run an errand. We'll pick up the interviews when he gets back. In the meantime, I thought I'd take the dogs down the beach to check on Captain Jack. Everything all right here?"

It was an absurd question. Things were clearly not all right but whether it was because of the murder or the old disagreement about marriage, I had no idea and, if the latter, it wasn't my business.

"Thanks," Riitta said, as if I'd offered to do her a favor. "Please tell Jack I'll make a fresh batch of *pannukakku* if he comes up to the house." She produced a ghastly facsimile of a smile and excused herself. When she'd left the room I looked at Tom.

"Can you tell me what's wrong?" He sighed, heavily.

"She's afraid Danny will be arrested for killing Martin."

"Why?"

"He was in shock from learning the identity of his father. He's young, impulsive and strong. He believed Martin owed his mother the lighthouse and he intended to get it for her."

"I know. I heard him talking with Alex shortly before midnight. But then he left and someone else came."

"Who?"

I hesitated before continuing. "Riitta," I said, knowing it wasn't something that could be kept secret.

"Riitta didn't kill him," Tom said.

"I know. Danny didn't kill him, either."

Unless Danny went back. Neither of us voiced the words but I had no doubt we were both thinking them.

CHAPTER 15

I focused on the timeline as I corralled Larry and Lydia and headed out the back door. If I was right and Alex had fallen onto dry sand and covered it all night and through the thunderstorm, there was a very small window of time in which the murder could have occurred. It must have happened after Riitta left him and before twelve forty-six, which was probably half an hour or less. If only I hadn't pulled the pillow over my head!

The thirty minutes had to accommodate more than just the murder. Alex had told Riitta he was giving her the lighthouse and trust fund but after she left, he changed his mind, wrote a letter outlining his intention of giving the whole kit and caboodle to the county, delivered the letter to her bedroom on the second floor and returned to the watch room in time to die before the rain started. I wondered how often real-life detectives encountered the problem of too many incidents for a small time frame. It seemed like an embarrassment of riches. The problem was that I needed to clear both Danny and Riitta, which meant I needed another viable suspect and it had to be someone Alex trusted enough to accompany out onto the gallery.

I walked, slowly, deep in thought, while the dogs raced on ahead. Well, raced is probably the wrong word. Larry ambled and Lydia scrambled a few steps then stopped to dance around in a circle before scrambling a few more steps. As I reached the fence that separates the lighthouse yard from the lakeshore, I gazed at the water. The mid-afternoon sun in the bluebird sky had turned it to turquoise, the color of Alex Martin's eyes. And Danny's.

A sudden shout pierced my chest like a bullet at close range.

"Umlaut!"

For a split second I couldn't seem to suck any air into my lungs or any sense into my brain. It was Jace's nickname for me. Intellectually, I knew it wasn't my husband, that he couldn't, wouldn't be here on the Keweenaw but emotionally, it felt like schrapnel. I took a deep breath and turned to see Max Guthrie striding toward me across the sand.

"Hatti? Are you all right?" He sounded concerned and I realized I wasn't smiling. I made an effort to lift the corners of my mouth.

"Hey, Max. Good to see you!"

It sounded as forced as it felt and what made that particularly galling was that I really was glad to see him. I really liked Max. More than liked, actually. This business of reacting to a nickname like a third-grader getting blasted with a dodgeball was part of the haunting of the almost ex-husband but there was no way to explain that.

Max had appeared out of nowhere last year. He'd bought the abandoned fishing camp Namagok located between Red Jacket and the Copper Eagle Reservation, and reopened it. He and I had bonded over bait. He was tall, broad-shouldered, loose-limbed and moved like a young man, but the effects of forty years of hard living showed on his rugged features. Max was as craggy as the Marlboro Man and his dark hair, liberally streaked with silver, emphasized the deep tan of his complexion. I especially liked the long, vertical creases in his lean cheeks and the glitter in his chocolate brown eyes. He was that rare combination of a man's man and a guy who liked women and, therefore, understood us.

There were those among my friends, specifically my Pollyanna-ish cousin Elli, who thought a romance might develop between Max and me. Sometimes I thought she was right. Then there were the times, like now, when I let my husband's defection poison the well of my life.

"I guess you heard what happened out here."

He nodded. "Mysterious death. Probably homicide. That's why I came. Thought you could use some back up."

"Me? Why would I need back up?" His grin was pure male and it reminded me that for six months I'd been living like a nun.

"Are you trying to tell me you haven't jumped into this hornet's nest up to your pretty neck? I know you better than that."

"You think my neck is pretty?"

"Definitely. And worth preserving."

"Well, thanks, but I'm not a kid. I can take care of myself."

Max had bent over to rub the soft skin behind Larry's ear with one hand and the curls on Lydia's neck with the other. Both dogs had their eyes closed. Max looked up at me.

"I know you can. But this isn't a TV show, Hatti. When a real person commits a murder it's either because he's a sociopath or desperate. Either way, everybody involved is in jeopardy. Where were you heading when I startled you," he asked. I told him about my errand to the oil house and he invited himself along. "Want to tell me about it?"

I realized I did. Max, along with a magnificently male body, had a good brain. I wanted to tell him what I knew. I wanted to get his thoughts about that crowded half hour last night before the storm.

I started at the beginning with Alex's arrival during the faux wedding.

"He had come back at the eleventh hour to claim the lighthouse and it was like someone throwing a hand grenade into a Sunday school picnic. The festival continued but tension and anxiety swirled around like smoke from the barbecue. One old lady had a seizure. Several people, including me, tried to talk Alex into relinquishing the lighthouse so it could be used as a retirement home."

"Did he agree to that?"

"Basically, yes, but there's some disagreement about how and when. He met with several people last night up in the watch room in the tower and, at this point anyway, we think he was hit with a rock or something and pushed off the gallery around a quarter of one. Before that, there was a parade of people in and out of the room."

"You've learned a lot."

"Bits and pieces. And some of it is contradictory." I told him the theory about the body being moved. "That doesn't make sense and yet, Alex's clothes were damp and the sand under the body was dry. None of it makes sense, especially not the part where he agreed to let us keep the lighthouse but he was killed anyway."

"Sounds like somebody didn't get the memo."

"Yep."

"Some of this will get untangled with the autopsy," Max said, soothingly. "At this point, it's important to collect all the evidence and all the statements and then you can put everything together and sort it out. Is there anybody you suspect? Is anybody acting out of character?"

I contemplated the question before I answered.

"You know, there is someone. Miss Thyra Poonjola. She's generally sharp-tongued but never sickly and all day she's looked like moldy cream cheese and complained of a migraine. And this was her big day. She gave a lecture on mittens and it was so important to her she stayed up all night preparing for it."

Max looked thoughtful. "That might explain her ailments," he said. "Or, maybe, she observed something suspicious in the small hours of the night."

I stared at him. "You mean the murder? You think Miss Thyra is an eyewitness?"

"I don't think you can leap to that conclusion," he said, with a chuckle. "Just find out what she noticed." We walked a moment in silence. "At the risk of stating the obvious, money is usually a pretty solid motive for murder. You might try to find out what happens to the rest of Martin's estate, not including the lighthouse."

It was a heartening thought. It meant we could expand the investigation to Alex's L.A. life and, maybe, just maybe, the murderer would turn out to be someone from the outside.

"Don't count on it," Max said, reading my mind. "The lighthouse is pretty remote. It would have been hard for an outsider to show up and push someone off the gallery without being noticed." He grinned at my woebegone expression. "On the other hand, if you're planning to commit a murder, the Keweenaw is the perfect spot to do it. Very few witnesses, very little law enforcement."

"Great," I said, heavily. "I'll have to tell Arvo. He can start marketing us as the perfect spot for a destination murder."

As we reached the copse where the Wiccans had celebrated the previous night, I remembered something Chakra had mentioned to me.

"Someone told me she'd seen the lighthouse lantern on a couple of weeks ago. It was a weeknight, I think, and the light went on for about ten minutes."

"Captain Jack keeps the antique lens clean, right? Maybe he does an occasional trial run just to make sure the circuits are working. Who saw it?"

"Chakra Starshine. She's the yoga instructor in town. Have you met her?"

"Yeah."

I had to laugh. Of course Max had met her. In a population of less than a thousand people, a six-foot tall woman with silk-like black hair, green eyes that turn up at the corners and luscious lips would not go unnoticed, especially by Max.

"Have you dated her?"

"I'm too old to date, Hatti. We've talked some."

"About downward dog, sphinx position? Plank?"

He took the kidding well. "What did she tell you about the light?"

"She and her consort, Sebastian were out here that night and right after they saw the light go on, a small motorboat docked at the oil house. They watched while Captain Jack and the boat driver carried something from the boat to the cabin. Sebastian thinks they're smuggling cocaine from Canada."

Max laughed. "In a small motorboat? I think it's unlikely. And even if it's true, how does Alex Martin fit into that? He only returned yesterday, right?"

I shrugged. "Maybe he got an anonymous tip. Oh, and that reminds me. Someone called the student newspaper over at Suomi College and told them there was a body at the lighthouse. Only it was hours before we actually found a body."

Max looked thoughtful.

"The tip is interesting. Has to be the murderer. I suppose there's no way to trace the call."

"I'll ask Sheriff Clump," I said, "if I can catch him between meals."

"Like that, is it? Poor Hatti. Well, let's see what Jack has to say."

CHAPTER 16

The oil house, built originally to store the oil that fueled the light source in the lantern and to provide a platform for the long, foghorns that warned ships of the nearby shoals, was small and square and made of stucco with an asbestos shingled roof. The insides had been turned into a cottage some forty years earlier and Captain Jack had lived in it for many years while he did odd jobs for Mrs. Marttinen and kept an eye on the antique lens at the lighthouse.

The metal door was shut and a faded curtain over the front window blocked any view of the interior. Tufts of grass grew unchecked from under the building's concrete foundation. The little house looked as abandoned as any of the dozen and a half ghost towns on the Keweenaw.

I knocked and waited and then knocked again. When there was no answer, Max looked at me.

"Have you got a key?"

My lips twitched at his question.

"You've forgotten our unwritten rule. We only lock our doors if we're going to Florida. Or the hospital. We're way more afraid of locking ourselves out and freezing to death than we are of break-ins. Besides, people are always dropping off hot dishes and plates of bars."

"To Captain Jack?" Max sounded skeptical.

I shrugged. "I doubt there's anything here to steal and, well, we just kind of think it's an affront to our neighbors to lock the doors."

He lifted an amused eyebrow. "Captain Jack is worried about offending his neighbors?" He looked at the lake and the sand and the trees.

I decided it was time to shut down the jokes about our community and reached around him to press down on the door's latch. It opened, immediately. The cabin felt empty. No, more than empty. It felt bereft.

After the brilliant sunshine, the shadows engulfed us. I pulled the chain on the single lamp in the main room that appeared to be both a living area and a kitchenette. Both were sparsely furnished and tidy. A beaten-up recliner occupied the corner with the lamp and there was a bookshelf nearby. A copy of Hemingway's *Old Man and the Sea* sat on the lamp table and next to it was a pair of reading glasses. The spectacles reminded me of Alex and stuck a dagger into my heart. It seemed to me that one of two things had happened. Either Jack had killed Alex Martin and skedaddled, or whoever had killed Alex had also killed Jack. Why I should think that, I didn't know but, in that moment, I found myself believing in plan B.

The kitchenette occupied the back wall and included a small window framed with faded red-and-white gingham curtains, a sink and very short counter that held a toaster oven and a hot plate. A college dorm-room-sized refrigerator was tucked underneath.

"I'd say Jack's a minimalist," Max said into my ear. I jumped. I'd forgotten he was there.

"Did you see this?" Max handed me a half-whittled piece of wood. It was clearly intended to be the Painted Rock Lighthouse and it touched my heart and my nerves.

"Simple arrangements," I agreed, "but comfortable. He takes most of his meals at the lighthouse."

The bedroom occupied the other half of the small house. It was even smaller than my room in the lighthouse, the floor space almost completely taken up with a twin-sized mattress. There was no bedframe, no box spring, only a blue-and-white striped comforter and a pair of pillows that had been placed side by each, as Pops would say. Both pillows were dented, an indication they'd been used recently.

"Interesting configuration on the pillows," I said.

Max sent me an amused glance.

"I'd say, offhand, that two people slept here. Only natural when you consider it was Captain Jack's wedding night."

Except that the old man hadn't shared his bed with his bride.

I picked up one of the pillows with the idea of smelling it but I was distracted when something light and silvery flew through the air and dropped onto the long boards of the floor. I scooped it up and stared at the item on my palm.

"Looks like an earring," Max said, peering over my shoulder at the encircled five-point star. "Have you seen it before?"

"It's a pentacle," I said, grimly, "a Wiccan symbol. I saw it last night on Chakra Starshine. Apart from its mate, it was the only thing she was wearing."

"I think we can assume she was not here with Captain Jack," Max said.

"No. I imagine she and Sebastian decided to shelter here when the storm started. But that means..." My voice trailed off and Max finished the obvious thought.

"That means that Jack never came back here last night." His voice was gentle but inexorable. "That's been likely all along, Hatti. It doesn't mean Jack is the murderer."

But it could mean that. Or it could mean he was dead. I shuddered.

"You've got to face something else, too," Max continued. "If Chakra spent the night here, she had the means and the opportunity to kill Alex Martin."

"But there's no motive." I was ashamed of the pleading note in my voice. I cleared my throat. "There's no motive," I repeated. "No reason for Chakra to want to kill him. As far as I know, she never even met him."

Max poked his head into the mouse hole of a bathroom.

"There's no sink and no shower," he said.

"No need," I replied, absently. "Jack could wash his hands in the kitchen and he'd bathe in the lake or the sauna."

"What sauna?"

"Oh, there's a sauna," I said. "Has to be. There must be an outside entrance."

"Let's go look," he suggested. On the way, he asked the age-old question. "When the rest of the civilized world pronounces the word saw-na, why do you Yoopers make it sound like a female pig?"

"Because in Finnish, every syllable is pronounced with the emphasis on the first. The word is properly pronounced sa-oo-na. When we speed it up, it ends up sow-na."

Max lifted his left eyebrow.

"Apart from the fact that Finns almost never speak rapidly, how do you happen to know that?"

I grinned at him. "You aren't the first outsider who has asked the question. I looked it up. Anyway, no self-respecting Finlander like Jack would live in a cabin without a sauna."

"I have no objection to steam baths," he said, "but I don't understand why it's almost like a religion for some of you."

"It is like a religion," I explained, as we walked back into the sunlight on our way around the little cabin. The dogs, who had waited nearby in the shade, joined us. "It's tradition. Finnish pioneers have always built the sauna first and the homestead second. The sauna is a place that's warm and sanitary. Generations of babies have been born in the sauna. Generations of families have spent their Saturday nights there. In our culture, it's a sanctuary."

He grinned at me. "When was the last time you took a sauna?"

"Three days ago. I went with Mrs. Ollanketo. I'll take her again as soon as she's recovered."

"Lucky Mrs. Ollanketo," he murmured, in a voice that brought the color to my cheeks. "Here's the entrance."

The door to the sauna was fastened with a padlock, which surprised me.

"Apparently Jack doesn't welcome food-bearing, drop-in guests to his bath," Max said. He produced a pocket knife, popped the lock and opened the door into another small space, this one covered with red cedar boards. There was a small stove topped by rocks, a bucket and ladle nearby and a built-in bench called a *lavat* on the wall. There was also a barrel filled with woodchips.

"So this is where the magic happens," Max said. "How hot does it get in here, anyway?"

"Around 120 Fahrenheit," I said. "The tradition is to cool off afterwards in the lake or a snow bank and then go eat a sausage and drink a beer." I flashed on the image of Erik Sundback handing a beer to Alex Martin when the latter had come out of the sauna by the lake. Erik had said he didn't know much about Finnish culture but he'd absorbed more than he'd realized. Or, maybe, he was being a courteous host.

"So the fire is fed with those woodchips and water is poured on top of the stones giving off the steam?" I nodded. "Sometimes the bather hits himself gently with birch twigs to stimulate circulation but I'm guessing all available birch twigs were confiscated for yesterday's *Juhannus* festival." I stopped, suddenly and Max eyed me with concern.

"What's the matter? What's wrong?"

"Danny and Captain Jack gathered up all the birch twigs and woodchips from here and the lighthouse for the bonfire," I said, slowly. "There shouldn't be any woodchips here."

"There must be an explanation," Max said.

My voice shook. "I can't think of one."

A strong arm came around my shoulder and he gave me a little squeeze. And then he began to dig through the chips, scattering them on the floor. He found what he was looking for a minute later. It turned out to be a corrugated cardboard box, about twelve inches by twenty-four and strapped with heavy-duty packing tape which reminded me of *mummi's* dress.

Once again he produced the pocket knife. He had just sliced open the package when we heard *Blow the Man Down,* in a familiar, cheerful off-key whistle. I rushed to the door to greet my bridegroom.

"Jack," I screeched, in exactly the voice I'd have used if he'd been my real husband, "where in the bleepity-bleep have you been?"

He was still wearing the wife-beater tee shirt, the dungarees and the red hat but his eyes were bluer and, by some miracle, he had more teeth. He looked as astonished as I felt.

"Who are you, den?" He asked. "Where's Jack at?"

He looked beyond me at Max and the item Max had extracted from the package in the woodchips. His eyebrows formed a line of thunderheads over his brow and something flashed in his blue eyes as he spoke, accusingly.

"What da hell you doin' wit dat sirrup?"

"Syrup?" I stared at Max who held up a plastic container filled with a mahogany-colored substance.

"Maple syrup, I'm guessing." Max said. "Let me introduce myself and my friend, here. I'm Max Guthrie and this is Hatti Lehtinen. We're friends of Jack's. I assume you are Jack's partner in crime."

"Not a crime," he said, stubbornly. "Just a bizness."

Max shook his head. "We're not here to bust your chops. What's your name?"

"Tavi."

Max nodded. "We are here looking for Jack."

Tavi's eyes narrowed. "In dat barrel?"

"Touche," Max said, with a laugh. "We had heard some gossip about smuggling."

"Not smuggling," Tavi said. "Free enterprise. We get the syrup from Canada and bring it to diners in the U.P. Nobody gets hurt."

I stared at the little man.

"What's the point?"

"Visitors to the U.P. want syrup made here but Canada sugarbush is better."

"I think what Tavi is telling us is that some diner owners put the Canadian syrup in bottles with local labels."

Max had gotten to his feet and joined me. He held Tavi's gaze for a moment. "Putting aside tariffs and taxes and FDA regulations, it isn't honest," he said, quietly.

Tavi struck out his scrawny chin. "Where's Jack?"

"We don't know," I said, feeling another flutter of distress. "Nobody's seen him since last night."

"Give him this."

The little man dug his fist into his pocket, pulled out a wad of what appeared to be low-denomination bills and handed them to Max.

"You should probably hang onto it for now," Max said, gently. "You can give it to Jack when he gets back. Come on. This syrup is heavier than it looks. I'll help you carry it to your truck. How many customers have you and Jack got?"

"Half a dozen."

"Tavi," I said, remembering Chakra's comment, "do you and Jack ever use the lighthouse to send messages."

"Never," he said, decisively. "Hardly ever." He got into the cab of the ancient pickup truck and tipped his cat. "Bye, missus."

"Huh," I said, as we watched the rig drive off down a rutted, unpaved road. "He called me Mrs. How did he know I married Jack last night?"

"He thinks you're married to me." Max's grin made me shiver but this time it wasn't out of fear. Not for the first time I wondered where this relationship might go if I weren't still hung up on my AWOL husband.

We walked back along the lakeshore flanked by Larry and Lydia.

"Is there anything else about this business that you haven't told me," he asked, finally.

I thought through what I'd already said.

"There's the clothespin." I felt a little silly even bringing it up but I explained that Miss Thyra had sent me to the cellars to find it and that I'd found it in a most unlikely place.

"What do you deduce from that?"

"Riitta's the kind of housekeeper who keeps everything in its place and the coal bin was empty because of the bonfire. When I told Tom Kukka about the idea that the body had been moved, he said the killer could have used the wheelbarrow to get it to the window that opens into the coal chute. I can't help wondering if Miss Thyra moved the body and dropped one of her clothespins in the process."

"That would mean that Miss Thyra is the killer, right?"

It seemed absurd. Not only because she was an old woman but because she was a dyed-in-the-wool Evangelical Lutheran. She might be furious with Alex Martin for threatening to deprive her of her home, but she wouldn't have killed him.

"I don't know about that. I do think she knows something. She looks like death warmed over."

"If Miss Thyra had dropped the clothespin when she hid the body of the man she'd killed," he said, hypothetically, "why would she ask you to go to the cellar to retrieve it?"

"Oh, that's simple. Guilt. She wanted me to find the clothespin."

"Why?"

"I think she wanted me to find the body."

"But it wasn't there," he pointed out.

"No." I looked up at him but, for once, there was no amusement in his chocolate eyes. "I think she was surprised that I didn't find it," I said, thinking aloud. "She didn't kill him, Max. I'm certain of that. But I'm afraid she knows who did."

CHAPTER 17

Before Max left he cautioned me.

"It's not a scavenger hunt, Hatti, or a jigsaw puzzle. This is serious business for someone. You've got to be careful."

"Always," I said. "Anyway, there's safety in numbers. Thank you for coming out here today."

"Always," he said, with the crooked smile that had such a devastating effect on female hearts.

Ellwood had returned from Chassell and I found him at the interview table with Riitta and Danny. Tom and Erik were there, too, the former standing by the mantelpiece where the mittens were still displayed, the latter in an easy chair he'd pulled up close to Riitta. Something about the scene struck me as all wrong.

"Is something the matter," I asked.

Riitta spoke first. She turned toward me slowly, as if it required a great effort.

"Hatti, did you find Jack?"

"No. He's not at the oil house. Indications are he hasn't been there since yesterday."

"How can you tell that," Erik asked, pleasantly.

I hesitated. I didn't want to mention the contraband if it wasn't necessary. Why give away Jack and Tavi's secret? I was reluctant to mention the pillows with their indentations or Chakra's pentagram earring, either.

"A faint layer of dust on everything," I said. "The bed didn't look as if he'd slept in it and the place smelled musty, you know, as if the windows hadn't been opened in twenty-four hours."

It occurred to me that I had the makings of an excellent prevaricator.

"Where is Jack?" Riitta's voice trembled and faint freckles stood out on her pale face.

Erik Sundback put a comforting hand on her shoulder.

"He could easily be somewhere sleeping it off. From what I noticed, he consumed more than his fair share of beer last night."

She looked at Tom.

"You know Jack," he said, with an attempt at lightness, "he's happy as a clam sacked out in a hammock or even on the floor. For all we know he could have curled up last night down in the cellar."

"He's not in either cellar," I said. "At least he wasn't at eight thirty this morning."

"Hatti," Ellwood interrupted, "did you find out what time the rain started last night?"

"Twelve-forty-six," I reported. "You can take that to the bank."

"What's all this about the rain?" The question came from Erik. "Is that important?"

"We're working on a tentative theory that death took place before the rain started, that the body was left outside all night then moved after the rain stopped," Tom explained.

Erik looked at Tom as if the doctor had grown two heads.

"But the body was found under the tower, wasn't it? I don't understand."

"It doesn't make much sense," Tom admitted, "but, at the moment, that's what the facts suggest."

Ellwood cleared his throat.

"All right, to recap," he said, "here's what we know so

far. Martin was with Hatti up in the tower until about eleven. After that his movements are unclear until sometime after eleven thirty when Miss Irene heard him speaking with Madame X on the backstairs."

"Madame X?" This time both the doctor and the lawyer asked the question. Ellwood explained about Miss Irene's statement and both professionals continued to look skeptical.

"After that," Ellwood continued, "Martin was in the watch room. At about quarter to twelve he was visited by Danny who demanded that Martin turn the lighthouse and trust fund over to his mother and Doc Kukka on the grounds that he owed Riitta compensation for raising a son, Danny, alone."

I glanced at Riitta and saw that her slim fingers were clenched into a white-knuckled fist.

"The issue was not resolved and Danny left before midnight. So we have approximately forty-five minutes unaccounted for."

"I can account for them." Riitta's voice was clear and steady. "I went up to the watch room to talk to Alex and I was there for some time."

Ellwood's gaze shot to me.

"I heard Riitta and Alex talking," I said. "I know it was twelve because he said something about the witching hour."

"How long was she in there?"

If I lied she'd be safe. The thought flitted across my mind and was instantly rejected. No one would be safe until we got at the truth.

"I thought they deserved some privacy so I put my pillow over my ears," I confessed.

"So you don't know what time she left," Ellwood said.

"That's right."

"What did you talk about with Martin," Ellwood asked Riitta. His voice was gentle.

"Oh, the past, a bit. And Danny. He wasn't angry. He just seemed a little regretful."

"You mean he regretted missing out on watching his son grow up," Erik asked.

She considered that. "It was more that, just for a moment, he wished he were the kind of man who would have enjoyed that. He wasn't. I knew that. That's why I never contacted him."

"Did Martin tell you what he intended to do about the lighthouse?" Erik Sundback had taken over the questioning.

Riitta nodded. "He said he was giving it and Johanna's trust fund to me, that I could use it to house the poor or I could turn it into a casino and brothel. But then this morning I got a letter from him. It was pushed under my bedroom door." She produced the envelope and handed it to the deputy.

"It says here he's transferring ownership to the Copper County Board of Commissioners," Ellwood said, reading from the document. He looked at Riitta. "So you're telling me he changed his mind after talking to you and before getting pushed off the tower, a matter of less than half an hour." She shrugged.

"It doesn't make sense to me, either."

Tom Kukka rubbed the palm of his hand against the back of his neck. His broad face was drawn and there were deep circles under his eyes.

"I feel like we're all getting jerked around here, like a bunch of puppets."

Erik Sundback, more than twenty years older than the doctor, looked younger with his golden tan and his flashing white teeth. He pursued the questioning but in a low key way that shouldn't have been distressing to Riitta.

"Did you talk to anyone after you left the watch room? Did you tell anyone, Danny, for instance, what Alex had said to you about the lighthouse?"

She stifled a small, involuntary cry. "No. I thought about telling Danny and Tom, but Tom had gone off to the hospital and Danny wasn't," she hesitated and rephrased her comment, "and it was too late to bother Danny."

I was certain that each of us knew she'd been going to say that Danny wasn't in his room but, too late, she'd realized that left him without an alibi.

Erik quickly filled in the awkward silence.

"Does it matter so much to you, my dear? Of course that money would make you independent but, knowing you, I imagine you would just use it for the greater good here at the lighthouse in any event."

"No," she said. "No. It doesn't matter to me. Johanna's money was meant for the retirement home and that's how I should have used it no matter what."

"But it's a discrepancy," Tom said, heavily. "One more thing that doesn't make any sense."

"How long were you with Martin," Ellwood asked. I noticed he was making a physical timeline on his notepad.

"Quite a while," Riitta said. I got the distinct impression she was trying to leave a vague answer, no doubt to provide cover for Danny. "Maybe half an hour."

Ellwood gave her a long look but said, "all right. That leaves fifteen minutes or so." He looked at me. "I don't suppose you happened to remove the pillow from over your head?"

"Dead to the world," I said, then winced at the ill-chosen words.

"Well, who have we got?" Erik asked. He looked at me. "We know Miss Thyra was up all night. I think we can rule her out as the killer but maybe she saw something." I nodded. "Tom and I left at eleven thirty, Mrs. O. was upstairs asleep and Ianthe and Irene went to bed at, what time?"

"Eleven-thirty-ish," I said. "Irene heard Alex in the stairwell talking to some unknown woman."

"Leaving that aside for the moment," Sundback said, "what about Captain Jack? When was the last time anyone saw him?"

"He watched the Northern Lights with us on the porch around ten-thirty," Riitta said. "I don't know what he did after that."

"He helped me cover up the porch furniture when the thunder started," I said. "That was around eleven."

"All right," Erik said. He'd gotten to his feet and was pacing around the room, his hands behind his back. "That leaves his whereabouts unknown from, say, eleven fifteen last night until now."

"Not quite." Danny's voice was higher than usual but it didn't waver. "Jack was up in the tower later than that. I saw him."

"You mean when you went to see Alex at eleven forty-five," Ellwood asked. Danny shook his head.

"No. I'd gone back downstairs but I wasn't satisfied with the way we'd left things. I wanted to talk to him again." He had to have heard Riitta's harsh intake of breath but he didn't look at her. "I wanted to see him, again," he said, simply.

CHAPTER 18

"You mean Martin, don't you," Erik asked, in the hushed silence. "Just to be clear."

"That's right."

"But when you were up there, you saw Jack?"

Riitta's fingers were pressed against her lips in what, I knew, was an attempt to keep from crying out. She was frightened to death about what Danny would say.

"I'd better tell you the whole story instead of answering a lot of piecemeal questions. I went back upstairs around twelve fifteen but before I could knock on the door, I realized there was someone in the watch room with Martin. It was my mother." His handsome face twisted. "It was the first time I'd heard the two of them together." And the last time, I thought. "It felt kind of surreal."

"Did you consider joining them," I asked.

"Yeah. But I didn't do it. I figured they–she–didn't need the complication. I didn't eavesdrop or anything," he said, glancing at his mom. "I stood back in that little recess by Hatti's room and waited."

"So you didn't hear anything," Ellwood asked.

"Only what they said to one another when she left and that was because the door was opened."

"What was it?" I wasn't sure who asked the question. We

were all straining forward, fascinated at the account of the interview between the star-crossed lovers.

"I know why my mother wrote her will as she did," Martin said. "She wanted me to come back to the Keweenaw. She wanted me to see you and to find out about Danny."

"What did Riitta say to that?"

Danny's eyes were still on his mom.

"She agreed. I got the feeling she'd figured that out a long time ago."

Tears were coursing down Riitta's cheeks. Tom and Erik were behind her and didn't see. Danny came around the table and gathered her into his arms. After a poignant moment, he sat down again.

"All right," Erik Sundback said, "how does Captain Jack come into all this?"

Danny accepted a tissue from me and wiped his nose.

"Jack was there, too."

"In the lightkeeper's study?" Erik sounded thunderstruck. (I should probably point out, somewhat belatedly, that the lightkeeper's study and the watch room are different names for the same place).

Danny nodded. "I listened to my mom go down the circular stairs. When I couldn't hear her footsteps anymore, I headed for the watch room door intending to knock but before I could, the door opened and I heard Alex Martin speaking. He said, something like, damnation, Jack! You scared the life out of me. What the hell were you doing up there with the light?"

"And what did Jack say," Ellwood asked.

"He said he was cleaning the lens and he didn't want to interrupt the reunion."

Riitta released a small groan. "Does everybody know about my former relationship with Alex?"

I figured it was a rhetorical question.

"So that's when you saw Jack," Ellwood said, getting back to the point. "What time was it?"

"After eleven thirty. He headed down the circular staircase."

"And then you went in to see your father?" Erik asked.

Danny shook his head. "No."

Riitta perked up. "You changed your mind?"

"Not really. It's just that someone else was coming up the steps to see him."

Once again we were all leaning toward Danny.

"Who?"

Danny shook his head. "I couldn't tell. I heard Jack's footsteps stop and then I heard Jack say something about it was good weather for ducks, and then I heard two sets of footsteps, Jack's going down the stairs and the newcomer coming up the stairs."

"But you must know who it was," Erik said. "You must have seen him or her on the landing."

"I didn't. I pressed myself flat in that little alcove. I didn't want to be seen. I don't know why."

I thought I understood. Danny had felt self-conscious about stalking the father who had abandoned him all those years ago. He didn't want to be seen and he'd had no idea that he might have interceded in a murder.

"The person coming up the stairs may have been the murderer," Ellwood said. "Did you get any impression of whether it was male or female? Young or old?"

"Only that I thought Jack didn't know the person very well. I mean, that duck remark was the kind he'd make to someone he wasn't comfortable with, you know?"

"Wait a minute," I said, "what about the note under Riitta's door? If the newcomer was the murderer, Alex would have had no chance to deliver it."

"He might have given it to Jack," Tom said. "He might have asked him to slip it under Riitta's door on his way home."

"The problem with all of this," Erik said, "is that there's no one left. Unless someone from the outside slipped into the lighthouse."

"I can't think that Jack would have just walked past a complete stranger," I said. "He's very protective about the lighthouse in general and the lens in particular. He'd have wanted to strip search somebody he didn't know."

"At least that's one question we'll be able to get the answer to," Erik said. "All we have to do is ask Jack."

At that moment, the silence was shattered when the front door opened. My heart lifted but quickly sank when the new arrival turned out not to be Captain Jack but Sheriff Clump.

He was a virtual mountain of sweat-soaked aggravation. He removed his hat, rubbed an arm against the moist peak on the top of his head and glared at us for a moment, his purplish cheeks expanding and contracting like a pair of bagpipes.

"Awright, deputy," he said, finally, "I hope to Hades you're ready to take somebody downtown." By downtown he meant the single cell in the one-story, cinderblock building in Frog Creek that is the Copper County Sheriff's Department. The cell's only use is as a drunk tank or an emergency bed for someone who got stranded in the snow. Locals never mind staying there because the food is provided by Vesta Raatikainen, Clump's mother-in-law, who happens to own the local diner, the Lunch Box.

I looked at Ellwood, curious about how he'd handle the question. His response set me back on my heels.

"I'm arresting Danny Thorne," Ellwood said. "As a person of interest in the murder of his natural father, Alexander Martin."

At that announcement, Riitta screamed, Tom shouted, Erik tried to pour the oil of common sense on the hysterical waters, and Danny just stared at the other nineteen-year-old in the room. One comment stood out above the others.

"Okey-dokey," Clump said. "Cuff 'im, deputy."

"We gotta Mirandize him." I knew he was referring to the law officer's responsibility to advise a suspect of his right not to incriminate himself before questioning. I was pretty sure Clump had forgotten about that if he'd ever known it.

"Hell's bells!"

"It's no problem, sheriff. I've got a copy of it here on my phone. I'll read him his rights." He scrolled down. "You have the right to remain silent. Anything you say could be used against you in a court of law..."

"Hold on," Erik Sundback interrupted. There was so much authority in his voice that Ellwood stopped short. "Surely this is premature. You have no reason to suspect this young man. He has been straightforward with you about his actions and there is no evidence to suggest that he was the killer."

"It has to be him," Ellwood said, simply. "There's nobody else it could be. He maybe have told the truth about everything else but there was no unknown person coming up the tower after twelve thirty that night. There was only Danny Thorne. He made up that stuff about Captain Jack to throw us off the track. He went back into the watch room with Alex Martin. Martin would have gone out on the gallery with him. He wouldn't have suspected his own son. Emotions got the better of the younger man, he hit Martin with a rock or something, then pushed him off the tower. Case closed."

In the midst of my horror, in the midst of my disbelief, I had to admire the young deputy. What he said fit the facts. What he said made heartbreaking sense. I couldn't even look at Riitta, who had gotten to her feet and turned into Tom Kukka's arm. But Tom moved her aside.

"Danny's telling you the truth," he said, to Ellwood. "He heard someone coming up the stairs. He heard Jack speak and the other person murmur a response. He heard the newcomer knock on the watch room door and enter it and subsequently, kill Alex Martin. Cuff me," he said, quietly. "Read me those Miranda rights. I'm your guy. I killed Alex Martin."

"Criminently," Clump roared.

"But what's your motive," Ellwood asked. "Why did you kill him?"

"I could tell you it was because he'd threatened to take away the lighthouse which is life and death to me because it allows me to work with Riitta but it wasn't even that noble. I saw the attraction between Martin and Riitta.

They'd been together. They shared a son. For all I knew, they'd get together again. He deserved to die for what he'd done to her all those years ago but the fact is, I didn't kill him for that. I killed him for the oldest reason in the book: jealousy."

"So where's the rock?"

Tom turned to look at me. "What?"

"The rock. The one you used to conk him on the head. What'd you do with it?"

"I threw it in the lake," he said.

"What about your alibi of going to the hospital at eleven thirty?"

Tom's blue eyes narrowed on me.

"I lied about that. I drove part way then turned around. I parked out under the trees and sneaked back into the lighthouse through the back door." He paused, and added as an afterthought, "almost got caught by Miss Thyra."

"Seems like you're awful eager to take the blame for this," the sheriff said. "The boy's got a better motive."

Tom Kukka stared Clump directly in the eye.

"I love Riitta Lemppi," he said, simply. "Everyone knows it. And everyone knows that I've proposed to her repeatedly and she's always turned me down. There's nothing that means more to me than she does. I killed to keep her. It was a risk but I took it and I'm not sorry."

CHAPTER 19

A fter a brief, shocked silence, everybody spoke at once. Danny was on his feet saying, "that's a lie! He's just saying that to keep me from being arrested!"

"My dear friend," Erik Sundback said, "surely you want to reconsider your words. Let me get ahold of a top-notch defense attorney for you before you give a statement."

"Hells, frickin' bells," Clump said, over and over. "Cuff, 'im, deputy."

"Tom," I said, with a reproachful look.

Ellwood was fumbling with the handcuffs attached to his belt. I was pretty sure he'd never used them before.

"Listen, deputy," Tom said, "I can save you some time on the Mirandas. I don't need to hear them. But I need a favor. Could I speak with Hatti privately for a moment?"

Before he could answer, Aunt Ianthe and Miss Irene tripped into the parlor. The former noticed the handcuffs and beamed at Ellwood.

"Did you catch the culprit then, dearie?"

"Let judgment run down as waters and righteousness as a mighty stream," Miss Irene said. "I think that is the most famous passage from Amos."

"Amos who?" Clump stared at her.

"Amos was a grower of sycamore figs as well as a shepherd."

Tom jerked his head toward the dining room and I followed him.

"I don't believe you," I said, in a low voice, when we'd reached the relative privacy of the next room. "You couldn't kill a fly. And how on earth did you move the body if you were still at the hospital?"

Tom waved my words aside.

"I need you to check up on the old ladies. Miss Thyra refused to take Verapamil and so she's had no remedy for her migraine. If she's vomiting or running a temperature, I want you to get her down to the hospital in Hancock. The same thing for Flossie. She should be all right after two injections of Digitalin and all that rest but if her heartbeat's too fast, I want her looked at, too. You know how to take a pulse?" I nodded. "And, listen, especially with Flossie, if you need an ambulance, call one. Or get Arvo to drive you down in the hearse."

"Why did you confess? It's just going to give cover to the real murderer."

"Danny Thorne's a good kid who deserves a chance. Can you imagine what it would do to his life if he were arrested for killing his own father?"

"What if he did it?"

"I don't think he did but it doesn't matter. An arrest would wreck his chances. And it would kill Riitta."

"And you don't think this will hurt Riitta?"

"I know what I'm doing, Hatti. You have to trust me. Take care of my patients?"

"What about Riitta?"

The lines that bracketed Tom's mouth, deepened.

"She's got Danny and Sundback. She'll be all right. I just hope the same is true for Jack."

The actual, physical departure of the entourage reminded me of the Keystone Cops. There was no room in the Corvette for a prisoner, so after Ellwood shoehorned the sheriff into the driver's seat and waved him on his way, he had to borrow my Jeep to drive the suspect to jail.

After they'd left, the house became very quiet. Erik

Sundback went upstairs to the watch room to make some phone calls and Danny went out for a run. Riitta disappeared and Aunt Ianthe and Miss Irene sat down on the sofa in the parlor, knitting in hand. I joined them but, for the first time in a week, I could find no joy in either the craft or the company of the old ladies. The sheriff had the wrong man in custody and it was up to me to find a way to prove it. The thing was, I couldn't immediately decide what to do. After a few minutes of pacing around the parlor, I excused myself. There was one person in this house that had both the intelligence and the experience necessary for this situation. I climbed the stairs to talk to him.

The eastward-facing watch room had been brimful of light in the morning. Now, after three o'clock, the sun had dropped into the western quadrant of the sky which meant the rays laid a path along the wooden floor and left the upper half of the room in shadow.

The attorney was sitting at the antique desk leafing through a stack of papers. There was a laptop next to him. He appeared busily productive but he flashed me a warm and welcoming smile when I appeared. I knew I'd been right to go to him. He was the only one around here still acting like a rational human being.

"What do you think of this crazy business," he asked, indicating that I should take the rocking chair which I did.

"The murder itself or the confession?"

"Take your pick. I guess I meant Tom. He's got an overdeveloped sense of protectiveness. If the boy pushed Alex we can make a case for a momentary impulse."

"What about the head wound?"

"Oh, the rock? Well, Alex could have fallen on it. If someone did move the body, presumably they moved the rock, too."

I nodded. I thought the case came down to that. Who had gone up to the tower with a rock in hand? And why had he or she hidden the body then resurrected it?

"There's no accounting for the thinking of a murderer," Erik said, reading my mind. "Their brains are wired differently from the rest of humanity."

"You don't believe that any of us could kill given enough provocation?"

"Oh, I think any of us could kill. I even think any of us could murder. But I think it takes a certain kind of individual to conclude that there's no other way out of a problem than to kill someone. It's anathema to our upbringing, for one thing." He grinned at me, "and for some cultures, to our faith."

"And yet, it seems like in this case, somebody was desperate enough to kill Alex Martin. And, possibly, Captain Jack."

It was the first time I'd said that aloud and just saying the words triggered an onslaught of nausea. I clamped my teeth shut and hoped the feeling would go away.

Erik swore. "I hope not," he said, quietly. "I hope to hell the old man is okay." I felt a rush of affection for the attorney and wound up asking him a question that was uppermost in my mind.

"What are your intentions toward Riitta?"

One sandy-colored eyebrow quirked up and I braced myself for a well-deserved set-down. It was none of my business. But he winked at me.

"Strictly honorable, Hatti, but I'm not sure I should tell you before I ask her."

"You want to marry her?"

He laughed and lifted a shoulder.

"I've avoided the state for a long time but who could meet her and not want to marry her?"

"But what about Tom?"

He seemed to take some care with his answer.

"It seems to me that's between the two of them. It's my impression she doesn't intend to marry him, that she's never intended to marry him."

"I don't think she'll marry anybody else while he's in the clink," I said.

"You know as well as I do that's temporary. Tom didn't kill Martin any more than I did. He left the lighthouse with me at eleven thirty p.m. We'll find the real killer, Hatti, and this nightmare will be over."

Except for Alex, I thought. And, possibly, except for Captain Jack.

"Did you come up here for a specific reason? Not that I'm not happy to see you. You've got a good head on your shoulders, Hatti. Riitta is lucky you chose to spend a few weeks here this summer."

"I wanted to get your opinion of the letter. The one Alex slipped under Riitta's door. Did you get a look at it?" He nodded. "What did you think, I mean about whether it was legitimate?"

His eyebrows lifted.

"Looked like it to me. Typed on a laptop, probably, signed and slipped into an envelope with her name on the outside in his handwriting."

"The name on the envelope was printed."

He looked surprised. "Was it? Good heavens, you're really turning into a detective. In any case, the signature looked real and it had a businessman's attention to detail." I nodded. "What makes you question it?"

"Mainly the timing. When would he have had time to write and deliver the letter?"

Erik stroked his chin. He had a heavy jaw, one that complemented his broad face and his slightly jutting brow. When I looked past his age, I could see that he was a handsome man.

"It wouldn't have taken long to write the letter," he said, after a minute.

"But there was no time to deliver it. The timeline accounts for nearly every minute of the three-quarters of an hour after midnight."

"Well, we don't know what happened after Captain Jack passed the man on the circular stairs. Alex may have excused himself for a minute and gone down to deliver the letter then. Or, and this is more likely, he had the letter ready and he gave it to Jack with instructions to deliver it to Riitta's room."

"I thought of that."

"We'll have to ask Kukka whether Jack had the envelope in his hand."

I stared at Erik Sundback. "Tom won't know. He didn't see Jack on the stairs."

Sundback slapped his forehead and groaned.

"You're right! I'm confusing reality with fantasy. Maybe Danny got a glimpse of Jack." I shook my head.

"He was back in the alcove, remember? He didn't actually see Jack."

Erik's lips twisted. "Good thing I'm not representing anybody in all of this. Sorry, Hatti. I didn't help you much. I do think the letter's legit, for what my opinion's worth, if only because of the signature."

"Erik, if the courts decide the letter represents Alex's wishes and the county gets the lighthouse and the money, will you remain on the lighthouse commission?"

"Absolutely."

"Because you want to marry Riitta?"

"Because it is an obligation I've assumed and it has turned into a duty. Because it was my late client, Johanna Marttinen's wish. And, because, I want to marry Riitta."

"Thanks." I got up to go.

"Something's bothering you."

"The lighthouse and money will go to the county just as we thought it would yesterday at this time. Nothing's changed except one man is dead and another is missing. It all seems so pointless."

"Murder's out of tune and sweet revenge grows harsh," he said.

"Shakespeare?"

"Romeo and Juliet."

Since Alex Martin and Riitta Lemppi had been, in effect, star-crossed lovers, that quote seemed apt. Sort of.

"Erik, what do you think really happened?"

He frowned. "The truth? Between you and me?" I nodded. "I'd say this thing has youthful passion written all over it."

I grimaced. "I was afraid you'd say that."

CHAPTER 20

I rested my elbow on the open driver's side window and Larry rested his chin on the passenger side. Lydia stood on her hind legs in the backseat, her paws on the window sill. Her white fluffy ears had turned into twin zeppelins.

Since Ellwood had borrowed my Jeep, I was driving Riitta's SUV. The shocks were newer and better than mine, not that it made any real difference to the dogs. Or me, either.

I just wanted to get away from the lighthouse and driving on the Keweenaw in the summertime is pure pleasure. The major roads are bare of snow and other vehicles. And they're either lined with columns of pine-tree sentinels or with wide fields of green grass that create a bucolic pleasure.

The Keweenaw Peninsula is almost as beautiful and untouched now as it was two hundred years ago before mining companies had made it the world's number one supplier of pure copper and logging companies had cut down its old-growth forest of white pine trees. We were like some reverse civilization. Industrialization had come and gone but it hadn't left us unscathed.

The good news was we had a very cosmopolitan look for a tiny town buried in the north woods. We had our gothic architecture, including St. Heikki's, our historic opera house, complete with columns, cupolas and a golden dome and we had a couple of blocks of storefronts that could have come out of Charles Dickens's London. Oh, and as Arvo likes to point out, the abandoned mine shafts have turned into excellent habitats for bats.

The bad news was that our lovely fields were covered with poor rock leftover from the mines, tailings from the stamp mills, piles of slag from smelters and tree stumps. Underground the earth had been carved away leaving water-filled chambers that posed a threat to hikers. And then there were the waters. Waste products from the years of mining polluted our streams, rivers and lakes from the Keweenaw waterway down at Houghton to Torch Lake.

I wasn't thinking about any of those things though, as I turned off U.S. Route 41, the highway that connects Copper Harbor at the top of the Keweenaw with Miami, Florida. I drove down Tamarack Street into Red Jacket and, instead of turning down Calumet to my parents' home, I made a left onto Third Street. A moment later I was downtown, parallel parking on Main Street in front of Carl's Bait. The Gone Fishin' sign was in the window so I knew Einar had left for the day. The canines and I got out of the Jeep and entered the shadowed shop.

It felt oddly like home. I'd always loved the long wooden floorboards, the pressed-tin ceiling and the bay window where Pops and Einar have a couple of rods and reels on display. The shop had so much potential. I caught my breath on a laugh as I remembered Miss Irene's words about Annemarie Lantti. But it was true. The place was quaint, historical and perfectly suited to the display of yarn and other knitting products. And the fact that shoppers would be browsing the selection of brightly hued wool and cotton alongside the coolers of mealworms and minnows would just provide local color.

As I contemplated my fledgling plan, I felt a surge of the old enthusiasm I'd always enjoyed until my marital disaster. I crossed to the backroom and unearthed the huge ceramic ashtray I'd made for Pops ten years earlier at Lutheran camp. Though a lifelong nonsmoker, he'd kept the monstrosity. That's just the kind of stepdad he is. Anyway, I filled the bowl with water for the dogs, considered and rejected making a pot of coffee for myself, and, instead, poured water for myself into a cracked ceramic mug. As I drank, I thought back to my first day as summer manager of the shop, three weeks earlier. I'd wanted to show Pops I was interested and because he'd given me a free hand, I'd immediately ordered an office water cooler and paper cups. Einar had gone ballistic and had, in taking me to task, used up his quota of words for the month.

"You want to *pay* for water? Are you crazy? Water is free! And paper cups, too? Who do you think you are, then? The Queen of England?"

Sheepishly, I'd canceled the order.

I wandered out to the front room and gazed around. The shop was sparsely furnished. The rods, reels, baskets and nets, bait bags and fishing tackle were displayed on tables or hung on the wall amid pictures of proud fishermen holding their catch. I imagined where I'd put the antique furniture I intended to find at local flea markets or, more likely, in local attics. An old-fashioned tall boy in one corner, a dry sink in the center of the room to display buttons and needles and what crafts people call sundries. A bank of cubbies along the far wall, where the yarns would be displayed according to weight and color. I imagined the ruby red, emerald green and winter white wool traditionally used for Nordic patterns next to bins of baby yarn, including pale blue, peppermint pink, lemon yellow and mint green. We could gather here for a knitting circle. We could hold workshops. The first one would be dedicated to Miss Thyra's Nordic mitten patterns.

I knew that, at least Yooper women, would not be put off by the coolers full of live bait. The room had a friendly presence. A positive aura.

Aura. It was that word and the fact that my right hand slid into my pocket and touched the pentagram that brought my wayward thoughts back into sharp focus. All at once I realized my subconscious had led me to Red Jacket for a very specific purpose.

As I was driving the three blocks to Heart and Hand Wellness Studio, I remembered something else, too. I'd promised to tell Garcia if a body showed up. I paused at the only stoplight in town and wrote her a text. *Body at lighthouse. Alex Martin. Investigation underway.* It was only the bare bones but I wasn't willing to tell a reporter about Tom Kukka's arrest, even if it was just the *Finn Spin*. I was still sitting there when my phone buzzed. I checked the caller I.D. and picked up.

"Sonya," I said, truly pleased to hear from one of my best friends.

"Hey, Hatti," she said in her low, pleasant voice. "I've missed you! I wanted to come to the *Juhannus* festival but I've been tied up on the rez with a very nervous first-time mom. I heard something that might interest you."

My heart jumped. Was this about Chief Joseph Night Wind, the grandfather-in-law I'd never met? Was it about Jace?

"Did you know that your victim, Alex Martin, was married to someone local?"

"What?" Once again my mind jerked back to the present. "I didn't know he was married at all. And how did you know about Alex Martin?"

"Oh." She sounded half embarrassed. "I ran up to the market to get some ice for the family I'm with and I ran into, uh, Max Guthrie. He mentioned the death and the fact that you were investigating it."

"Max?" My antennae perked up. "Max was out on the rez? He told me he had to get back to Namagok."

"Oh, I think he was just gathering supplies," she said, vaguely.

I didn't respond to that. We don't have a huge number of shopping options on the Keweenaw but there are at least two markets closer to Max's fishing camp than the rez, including the Shopko on Lake Linden Road and the Gas & Go in Red Jacket.

"Anyway, here's what I heard from one of the old men who gather at the community center every morning to drink coffee and watch the entertainment shows. It seems that Alex Martin was married to a Hollywood starlet."

"Was or is?"

"Don't know that. They kept the whole thing very secretive. Don't even know whether it's true but it probably is. Anyway, the two weren't together very long. They separated about six months ago."

An old, familiar pain sliced through my heart.

"I know this is hard for you to hear," Sonya said, sympathetically. "The parallels and everything. Here's the important part. The wife was Stella Ransom. She had a leading role in a sit-com called 'Marrying Mr. Wrong.'"

"Prophetic," I said, as lightly as I could.

"Yep. After the separation she left the show and came to the Keweenaw, Hatti, where she opened a yoga studio under the name of Chakra Starshine."

CHAPTER 21

Heart and Hand, Chakra's yoga studio, was located two blocks farther down Main Street from the bait shop and on the opposite side in a stand-alone shop front. Over the years of my life the space had been home to a bicycle repair shop, the Keweenaw Dairy, a tobacco store, a hockey equipment emporium and (very briefly) a Christian Science Reading Room. It was not an ideal location since it was two blocks away from the real action in town which included the diner, the hardware store and the pharmacy across from the bait and fudge shops and Ronja Laplander's Copper Kettle, but it was quaint with its small balcony on the second floor and the leaded glass windows in the bay of the first floor.

I pulled in behind Chakra's vehicle, a late-model, cream-colored Escalade and felt a little flicker of self-disgust at my puny observational powers. It had never occurred to me to wonder how a yoga instructor in the U.P. could afford a luxury car. Was the money from her acting career or from her marriage?

The studio was closed according to the neat, script sign on the lower pane of the front-door window. The front room, where we spread out our mats to do downward dog and sphinx and humble warrior, was dark but I could see light filtering in from the backroom which was divided between an office and a kitchenette. I asked Larry to keep Lydia from jumping out the open window, then I walked down the narrow driveway that led to a detached garage. Next to the back entrance to the building was an outside staircase to the second floor apartment occupied by Chakra and, I presumed, Sebastian. Had he known about his girlfriend's marriage?

The back door stood open, only a screen separating me from the empty kitchenette where I had, from time to time, shared a post-plank cup of tea with Chakra. We'd talked about self-defense techniques and how they could be incorporated into yoga moves. We'd talked about my emotional distress and ways to use yoga and other wellness techniques to overcome it. Chakra had never spoken about her own relationships and I, to my shame, had never asked. I'd failed her as a friend. Had she come to Red Jacket to exact revenge on a faithless husband? Would it have helped to talk to someone (me)? Had the upshot been that she'd pushed Alex Martin off the gallery of the lighthouse? The voices clamored in my head and I had to breathe purposefully to still them enough so that I could eavesdrop on the conversation inside the studio.

"I'm leaving," Chakra said, in a firm voice. "I didn't want to just disappear. You deserve to know. But the fact is, I'm going back to California."

"Because Martin's dead." Sebastian sounded bitter.

"Because my business here is finished. I told you in the beginning this was temporary, Seb. I needed closure and now I have it."

I winced. The question was, how had she achieved that closure? I put my ear right up against the screen and tried to quiet the loud thudding in my chest.

"I thought we had something together."

"We did. I'm fond of you, Seb. We were together for six months which is longer than my marriage lasted. I'm not about permanency, you know. When something's over, I move on. Everything about the Keweenaw is over for me. Including you."

"I don't think you realize what you owe me," he said, in a statement that was eerily reminiscent of Danny's charge to his father. "I helped you get accepted in town. I helped you start the studio, get it painted and up and running. I helped you find the coven."

"I know. I'm grateful."

"Not grateful enough to stay."

"I can't stay, Seb. You know that. We've done things that, well, you know what we've done."

"Exactly," he said. "So what about me?"

There was a short pause and I felt a flicker of panic. What if they had finished talking and were coming into the kitchenette? Indecision gripped me but I stayed put. Information was more important than potential humiliation, I thought, but my insides quivered.

"You would be smart to move along, too," Chakra said, finally. "Go somewhere new."

"But not with you."

"No. Not with me."

He uttered her name in a hoarse whisper and then he roared into the kitchenette and slammed open the screened door with enough force to have broken my nose if I hadn't jumped clear. He evinced no interest in my presence as he blasted a path to the garage. A moment later, the battered, pablum-colored Oldsmobile that must have been the hand-me-down of a grandparent, backed down the driveway. He caromed off the brick wall of the studio then bounced over to scrape the side of the pawn shop next door.

Apparently, no one had ever taught Sebastian to look over his right shoulder while in reverse.

"He's an atrocious driver even when he isn't mad." I hadn't heard Chakra's footsteps and her voice made me jump. "One of the many reasons I had to bring our association to a close. You really shouldn't leave your pets in the car on a day like this, Hatti. They'll melt in the heat." She opened the screened door and I saw Larry and Lydia drinking from a bowl on the floor.

"How did they get in here?"

"I let them in while you were circling the house. Don't worry, it's only water," she said, correctly interpreting my frown. "I haven't poisoned your dogs."

She was dressed today in a sophisticated outfit, a long, silky sleeveless gray vest over a fitted camisole that emphasized both her slender waist and generous bust and in smoky gray tights that shimmered and drew attention to her long, well-shaped legs. The dramatic dark hair feathered down her shoulders and back and was held off her face with a pair of Jackie-Onassis-type sunglasses and she wore a heavy, gold bracelet on one slender wrist and a diamond as big as the Fresnel lens at the lighthouse on the third finger of her left hand. She looked every inch both the Hollywood starlet and the pampered wife of a very wealthy man. But she was neither one nor the other now.

"You're wearing wedding rings," I said.

"I'm entitled. I'm a widow or haven't you heard?"

I ignored the sarcasm and fought a feeling of intimidation. I needed some answers. I stared at her.

"Did you kill him?"

"Why should I?"

"I understand he was worth a lot of money."

"That's true. Something like a hundred million. I signed a prenuptial agreement when I got married. I get a settlement in the case of divorce or death."

"How much?"

"Ten million."

"Not too shabby."

She looked at me for a long minute.

"Were you thinking about money when you married?"

"No."

"Were you thinking about it when you separated?"

"No."

"I was making good money on my own, Hatti. I didn't need to marry a rich man, nor did I need to inherit money. I'd have paid ten million dollars if it would have made the marriage work out."

"What did you mean when you said you were looking for closure?"

She sighed. "Come sit down and I'll explain it over a cup of herbal tea." It would be my second cup of tea that day and, as I've mentioned, I'm a big-time coffee drinker. I must have sighed because she grinned, suddenly. "Forget the chamomile-slash-dandelion root. I'll make a pot of coffee."

A few minutes later the dogs were stretched out on the cool, linoleum floor and Chakra and I faced one another across the small table. The coffee was excellent and reviving. I explained that I wanted to talk to her, not because I am inherently nosy (which I am) but because I was trying to help Ellwood Lantti investigate Alex's murder.

"I didn't kill him," she said, giving me the most important piece of information first. "I was obsessed with him, but I guess you've realized that. I worked in his office for a bit before I got my acting break and I just fell for him, hook, line and sinker, you know?" I nodded. "Of course, you know. You felt that way about Jace, didn't you? As if you'd been broadsided. I don't know whether it's love," she said, looking over at Lydia, who'd rolled onto her back, her little paws in the air. "It's some kind of alchemy. It makes you willing to give up everything you are just to be with that person. And when it's over, you'd give up everything all over again to get it back.

"Alex liked me. He was comfortable with me. He agreed to marry me because I wanted it so much but he was honest right from the start." She paused. "I tried to be that way with Sebastian and you saw how well that worked out. Anyway, we agreed to try marriage and a family and if it didn't work, to go our separate ways with no hard feelings."

"A family? Do you have children?" She shook her head.

"That didn't happen which was probably just as well. We lived together for one hundred and seventy-one days."

"Wow. That's almost exactly the same length of time Jace and I lived together."

"Yeah." She laughed, but there wasn't any amusement in the sound. "I don't know where they got the idea of the seven-year itch. Seven months is more realistic. Anyway, I accepted his suggestion that we separate but I couldn't seem to stop thinking about him, to stop fantasizing about what our lives should have been. I'd gotten into yoga and I spent all my time at the studio. At least, all the time I wasn't trying to get him on the phone or arrange a meeting in person. He eluded me. I went to a yogi who prescribed a deep trance and, long story short, I saw a vision of meeting Alex, only it wasn't in L.A. It was on the Keweenaw. So I came out here."

"Let me get this straight," I said. "You moved to Red Jacket, opened a studio and waited around just hoping he would come back here someday?"

"It wasn't quite that stupid. I knew his mother had died and that she had property. I figured the odds were that he'd come back. And after I got here, I liked it. It's so different from southern California, Hatti. I mean, a hundred-and-eighty degrees different. Even before he showed up, I started to heal."

"And then he actually came back." She nodded, her hands wrapped around her coffee mug.

"As you know, the coven was out on the lakefront during the festival. I went over to buy a lemonade from one of the vendors and when I turned around I saw Alex heading for the sauna. He looked exactly the same, tanned and golden and he had the same old gleam in his turquoise eyes. He saw me, too."

I could picture it. I leaned across the table in my eagerness to hear what came next.

"He showed no surprise just said he was glad to see me and asked me to come up to the tower if I could get away."

"Yikes. Did you?"

"I slipped away from the others after the Northern Light display and, yes, I went to see Alex."

"Did you use the backstairs?" She nodded.

Well, that was one question answered. Chakra Starshine

was definitely Miss Irene's mysterious Madame X.

"What happened in the tower?"

Her lips twisted. "Pretty much what you'd expect. But that was only part of it. When I'd seen him down in the lighthouse yard, I'd felt gobsmacked by the same old shackles of breathless attraction and obsession. But after we got together, it was like they fell away. I could look at him as a person who was separate from me. I could see that he wasn't perfect and that I could enjoy him and walk away. I was free."

"Sounds like a miracle."

"You sound cynical, Hatti, but it was a miracle. The unhealthy bond was broken."

"And you left him alive?" She nodded.

"You know I did. I left at about eleven-forty. He was alive after that, wasn't he?"

"Yes." It crossed my mind to wonder how she knew that. "Where did you go afterwards?"

Chakra shrugged her elegant shoulders.

"It was thundering and lightning and I'd left my car in the pines near the lighthouse. So, like the rest of the coven and everybody else on the beach, I went home."

I felt broadsided by the lie and my feelings must have shown clearly on my face.

"What's the matter, Hatti?"

"I believed you. Every word. It was a great story. The thing is, it isn't true." I put my hand in the pocket of my shorts and pulled out the earring to show to her. "You spent the night at the oil house. You and Sebastian."

A dull red color flashed on her cheeks. It was, I thought, the first time I'd seen Chakra embarrassed.

"If you didn't go back to the lighthouse and kill your husband, why the lie?"

She looked over at the dogs for a long minute and then she sighed.

"You want the truth? Sebastian knew I was going to see Alex. He was jealous and I prearranged a meeting at the oil house with him for afterwards. I was about to dump him and, unfortunately, I know all too well what that feels like."

"So it was a pity tryst?"

"You could call it that."

"I'm not sure that's what the sheriff will call it."

She winced but didn't argue.

"Chakra, how did you and Sebastian know the oil house would be vacant last night?"

"I arranged that, too. Earlier, when I saw Jack on the beach. I asked him if we could use his place that night, for a fee. He was very gracious. He said he didn't mind. He had somewhere else he could stay."

"Did he say where?" She shook her head but I still felt better. Jack's reason for not returning home last night had had nothing to do with Alex's murder. If, that is, I could trust Chakra's word.

It occurred to me, not for the first time, that a murder investigation involved a lot of lies that had nothing to do with the principle event. Everybody had something to hide.

CHAPTER 22

I wanted to believe Chakra was telling the truth about her activities last night. Heck, I wanted to believe she was telling the truth about her release from the obsession about her husband. But there was no getting around the fact that she'd lied about spending the night in the oil house. A totally unnecessary lie, surely. Unless she'd sneaked back up to the lighthouse an hour after she'd left it to push Alex Martin off the tower.

But what about Captain Jack? Had he made his now famous duck remark to Chakra? Or had he made it at all? Had Danny lied, too? And where was Captain Jack?

Questions about the murder buzzed around my head and overlaying them all was the question about closure. If I could come face to face with my husband for just an hour, would I, too, be free to let go of the hopes I'd had for a life with him? Could freedom be as simple as looking into someone's eyes and recognizing, finally, that the light that had been there for you, had burned out?

I parked Riitta's SUV among the pines and followed the dogs to the lighthouse. It was nearly seven p.m. and there were still hours of daylight left but the sun's rays were slanted now and the angle created a kind of mist that made the landscape look like something out of a storybook. The faded stone of the building took on a rosy hue against the azure sky and the square tower looked less like a factory smokestack and more like the turret of an enchanted castle. It felt almost as if I were coming home after months of a sense of displacement. I thought I had understood why this place was important to Miss Thyra and the others. Now I actually felt it.

Riitta and Tom had made the lighthouse a sanctuary.

Lost in my thoughts, I didn't notice the man leaning against the newel post on the front porch steps until he called to me.

"Hey, Max," I said, pleased to see him. "You didn't call me Umlaut."

His grin was slow and devastating. I wondered how it was possible he was still single.

"I got the feeling you didn't like it, that maybe that particular expression had other associations for you."

"Hmm. So now, in addition to all your other talents, you're psychic?"

His grin widened. "Everybody's got a past, sweetheart. Even me. Anything new in the investigation?"

I told him about Chakra.

"She told you she was married to Martin?"

"Oh, no. Sonya Stillwater told me. She said she got it from one of the old men out on the rez who got it from a Hollywood gossip TV program. She called because you told her I was investigating the murder. She said she ran into you at the market on the rez." I waited for him to explain that but he didn't.

"Huh." We'd sat down on the top step on the front porch. Normally on a summer night as fine as this one, the old ladies would be playing Canasta at the card table and Jack would be napping in the hammock. Tonight we were alone.

"So you've got the hour between eleven and twelve accounted for with Chakra and Danny, and then Riitta visited Martin at midnight."

"Right. Oh, and I forgot to tell you, Tom Kukka confessed that he'd gone up to talk to Alex between twelve-thirty and twelve forty-five and that he pushed him off the gallery."

"Why?"

"He killed Alex because he was jealous. He thought Riitta was falling in love with him again."

"Hatti, I know as well as you do that Tom Kukka didn't kill anybody. Why did he say he did?"

"He's trying to shield Danny. I gather Riitta is afraid he might have done it and I have to admit you could make a good case for it. All we have is his word that he heard Jack on the steps talking to someone else coming up the stairs. Even Erik thinks this whole business looks like the result of a youthful impulse."

"He's right. And yet, there are aspects of it that show brainwork. The moving of the body, for instance. Why would someone go to the trouble to hide it then put it back? The autopsy results will give a fairly accurate time of death. There was nothing to be gained by that except delay." I nodded.

"And there is the weird story about Alex changing his mind about the disposition of the lighthouse and writing that letter. And then there are the shoes."

"The shoes?"

"Alex's. They weren't on the body and they aren't up in the watch room. So where are they?"

We were sitting, shoulder to shoulder and he looked down at me.

"You've got pretty good instincts about this," he commented.

"I don't know. I totally believed Chakra. Even when I caught her in a lie, I tended to believe the rest of her story." I told him the business about the oil house.

"Well, at least it's good news about Jack. He must be holed up with a friend somewhere. Listen, I think you should trust your instincts."

Was he talking about the murder or about whatever this thing was between us? He'd turned back to gaze out toward the lake and all I could see was his craggy profile. I couldn't read his thoughts.

"Maybe," I said, as a sudden thought struck me, "it wasn't Chakra. Maybe it was Sebastian who killed Alex."

Max shook his head. "Martin didn't know him from Adam. He'd never have welcomed him into the watch room or turned his back on him to go out onto the gallery. It has to be someone closer. Someone like his wife or his son or the mother of his son."

I winced and winced and winced, again.

"I hope to H-E-double hockey sticks that you're wrong."

"Take it one step at a time, Umlaut." He winced when he said it which made me laugh. "Listen, I've got a friend here from the west coast and he's got his heart set on visiting Hemingway's Big Two-Hearted River. We start at zero-dark-hundred."

"He's a Nick Adams wannabe?"

"The river is there," Max said, using a dramatic voice to quote from Hemingway. "The grasshoppers were all black."

"He felt he had left everything behind," I quoted back at him. "He was happy."

Max grinned. "A genius writer."

I waved him off then took the dogs inside. Despite my worry about Jack and Tom and everybody else, I felt better. I felt less alone in this nightmare. And, I felt like a re-read of Hemingway.

"Hello, dearie," Aunt Ianthe said, coming to meet me in the foyer. "Riitta, Danny and Erik have gone into Frog Creek to visit dear Tom. Irene and I have put out the doggies' dinner and there are sandwiches, egg salad, for you in the kitchen, along with a pot of fresh coffee."

I kissed my aunt and thanked her.

"Hatti, dear," she said, "Irene and I are a bit worried about Flossie and Thyra. Should they be sleeping so long?"

"I'll go up and check on them both," I said, with a stab of guilt. I'd left that too late. "Tom seemed to think they would both be right as rain by tonight. I think you can anticipate a few hands of canasta."

"That would be nice, dearie," Aunt Ianthe said, with less

than her usual enthusiasm. I got the feeling she was humoring me, as if she knew that I was desperate to get back to some sense of normalcy. The ladies love canasta but that passion had been eclipsed by the murder and Tom's arrest. "You know, Irene and I can't help worrying about Captain Jack. Do you think we should phone in an APB?"

"An APB?"

"All points bulletin," she explained. "They do it all the time on *Law and Order: Special Victims Unit.*"

"That's probably a good idea," I said, choking back a chuckle. "I'll talk with Ellwood next chance I get."

I was aware of a profound sense of fatigue as I made my way up the main staircase. It seemed as if this day had gone on forever already. As I knocked on Mrs. Ollanketo's door, I found myself uttering a silent prayer that she was all right. And then I remembered she wouldn't have heard a sledgehammer much less my knock so I lifted the latch of the unlocked door and walked in.

The old lady was sleeping on her side, her face turned away from me, her white curls foaming above a blanket drawn up to her neck. There was no sound at all in the room. Not a breeze from the open window, nor a gentle snore. I felt uneasy and I approached the bed with some reluctance, laying a couple of fingers against the soft folds of her neck. The touch confirmed what I'd instinctively feared. The flesh was cool, flaccid. Life was extinct. For a moment, I stood there in the silence of the room and thought about the difference between sleep and death. They were similar but, at the same time, oh, so different.

I'd felt the difference, the emptiness, as soon as I'd stepped into the room. She was gone. She'd never take another sauna. I could feel emotion trying to grab hold of me and I resisted it. I thought about the cycle of life in the matter-of-fact words of the *Moomins.*

"When one's dead, one's dead. This squirrel will become earth all in his time. And, still later on, there'll grow new trees from him, with new squirrels skipping about in them. Do you think that's so very sad?"

I did think it was sad. Unbearably sad. My knees buckled and I buried my face in my hands and sobbed.

When I had cried until my chest hurt, my eyes were swollen and the bedclothes were soaked from my tears and my running nose, I felt cold fingers on my exposed upper arm and heard a familiar voice speaking with unfamiliar gentleness.

"Get up, Henrikki. There are things to do, then."

I sniffled, struggled to my feet and faced the other patient I had neglected.

"This is my fault. I went into Red Jacket this afternoon and she died. I should have been here. I should have checked on her."

"That's blasphemy, Henrikki," Miss Thyra said. "It wasn't your fault. Flossie was an old woman with a bad heart. Don't you remember your catechism? God decides when it is time to come home. God and only God."

I sniffed. "Do you think God decided it was time to hit Alex Martin with a rock and push him off the lighthouse tower?"

She frowned at me. "I don't want to hear any sass from you, young lady. Now get up, wash your face and put your shoulders back. This is no time for moping. We have to be practical. That is what's needed now."

I wasn't fooled into thinking she was unaffected by Mrs. Ollanketo's death because I recognized the typical stoic attitude that I see all the time in our community. Don't give in to emotion. Get on with the work at hand.

"I'll go get Doctor Kukka," she said. I clutched her arm.

"He isn't here, Miss Thyra. He's in jail over in Frog Creek. He confessed to killing Alex Martin."

Miss Thyra's long, narrow face paled and her nondescript eyes seemed to grow bigger as she stared at me.

"He never did that."

"I know." I told her about Danny's story of Captain Jack speaking with someone on the circular staircase. "Sheriff Clump thought Danny was lying, that he was the last one to visit Alex and he was about to arrest Danny for murder.

Tom stepped in to prevent that." I remembered, belatedly, that I was supposed to be taking care of Miss Thyra. "How's your migraine, by the way?"

"Fine. I'm fine." She didn't look fine. She looked green. I peered at her.

"Are you sure? I understand you refused to take the Verapamil."

"I don't hold with drugs. Everything passes. My headache passed."

In my opinion, she looked far from well. Strands from her scraped back hair had come loose and drifted around her long face and the lines in that face were as deep as crevices in dried mud. There was a barely concealed expression of panic in her eyes and the bony fingers of each hand clasped and unclasped each other. Still, I didn't think she was in pain and really, there wasn't much I could do for her.

"If Doc Kukka isn't here," she said, all business, "we will have to get someone else to look at the body and sign the death certificate. Call the sheriff, Henrikki."

I suppressed a smile. "Before or after I wash my face?"

Her small eyes narrowed on me.

"Oh," I said. "I almost forgot. Mrs. O. wanted me to give you something. I'll be right back." I headed up the circular stairs, retrieved the mitten and returned. "She'd forgotten that the seminar was over. She wanted you to have this blue Arjeplog mitten to go with the green one."

I don't know what I expected. Maybe a softening of the eye. Maybe a tear or two in appreciation of the thoughtfulness of her late friend. I did not expect to see her sallow face turn sheet white or to see an expression of sheer terror in her pale eyes. The expression didn't remain. After a minute, her color returned and she appeared almost normal.

"Thank you," she said. "As you say, Flossie must have gotten confused about the seminar. All right, now. Wash your face and call the sheriff."

Aunt Ianthe and Miss Irene, wondering what was

happening on the second floor, arrived on the landing and I tried to console them as they found out about Flossie Ollanketo's death. They and Miss Thyra brought chairs into the room and alternately reminisced and cried and it was some time until I could slip out onto the landing to make my call to the sheriff.

Doc Kukka's black bag was still sitting on the hall table. He'd left it open when Ellwood had handcuffed him. I glanced inside at the ubiquitous Vics Vapo Rub, the stethoscope and the little hammer, rolls of bandages, gauze pads, Betadine antiseptic, plastic gloves, eyewash, a glucometer to measure blood sugar, a regular thermometer and one in a container labeled, "rectal thermometer" which, I knew he had used this morning to try to determine the time of Alex's death. I felt a sudden knife thrust of sadness about the two losses. And then my eye fell on an unused syringe and my amusement faded.

Doc had prepared two syringes for two patients. Only one of the patients had taken hers. She'd lived while the other patient had died. Why hadn't the Digitalin saved Mrs. Ollanketo's life? Was the heart damage too severe? I hated the idea of reporting this to Doc. He would blame himself. I gritted my teeth, punched 911 into my phone and prepared to wait.

CHAPTER 23

"Nine-one-one," the male voice said, crisply, answering on the second ring, "what is your emergency?"

I was momentarily speechless with shock. I had a sudden vision of Mrs. Touleheto splayed out on the floor with a knife in her back while the murderer answered the phone.

"Hello? Do you have an emergency?"

At that point I recognized the voice and let out a breath of relief.

"Erik? Is that you?"

"Hello, Hatti." The lawyer chuckled, softly. "Not the person you were expecting? Mrs. Touleheto is in the ladies room. Or, maybe, she ran out on an errand. I've forgotten what she said. I was here so I answered. Is this an emergency?"

His question reminded me of why I'd called. I explained it.

"It may have been a natural death," I finished, "but someone should come and see."

"Well, damn," he said, without heat. "What a damn shame. Poor old lady. I imagine you'd just call Maki if it weren't for our murder. I'll dig up the sheriff and get back out there as soon as possible. Everybody else all right?"

When I responded that we were fine but shocked he sighed again. "I'm not looking forward to breaking this to Riitta. She's going to take it hard."

Tom would take it hard, too. An instant later, he echoed my thought.

"No one would blame Doc Kukka," he said. "The man was just doing his job. The Digitalin should have worked for her. I guess we'll never know whether the Verapamil would have worked for Miss Thyra since she refused it."

"How do you know that?"

"What? Oh, Doc handed me her syringe to rinse out in the sink. There was no way to recycle it so down the drain it went. I washed out the syringe and left it on the side of the sink. I imagine Doc washed his out after he injected Mrs. O., too. They should both be there. In the little hall bathroom."

I crossed the hall and looked in. Sure enough, two empty syringes lay on the sink surround.

"Hatti?"

"What? Oh, yes. They're both here. Miss Thyra is fine, by the way. She seems to have recovered. Thanks, Erik."

"See you soon."

I wondered what we'd do without the attorney. He always seemed to be around when a level head was needed. I was glad to let him corral Clump and handle the next steps in Mrs. Ollanketo's death.

The ladies were still sitting vigil with Flossie's body so I sat on the top step of the stairs and looked up both medications on my cellphone. If someone had asked me why I was doing it, I wouldn't have been able to articulate an answer. Not, anyway, until I'd read through online descriptions and discovered they were eerily similar.

Digitalin, a natural remedy made from foxglove, was a stimulant that had long been used to jump start a recalcitrant heart. Verapamil, on the other hand, was synthetic and fairly new. It, too, worked on the heart, but it was intended to relax the heart muscles and blood vessels. Two medications with opposite effects. If both were administered to the same patient, they would cancel each other out. I continued to sit on the top step so long that the dogs finally found me and nosed their way under each of my arms.

"I don't know what I'm worried about," I finally said, aloud. "There is no reason I can think of for anyone to want Mrs. O. to die." I tried to expand my thinking on that. Could she have been a threat to someone? Say, to Alex Martin's murderer? I didn't see how. She wasn't very mobile and she couldn't hear at all. And then I thought about the Arjeplog mitten and Miss Thyra's odd reaction to it. Had Mrs. O. observed something suspicious? Was the mitten intended as a clue? Surely not or Miss Thyra would have said something.

Unless, of course, Miss Thyra was afraid. Or implicated. I kept going back to that.

I heard my aunt call my name so I got up and went into the room of death.

"Irene's going to do a Bible reading, dear," she said. "In honor of Flossie." We stood in a circle, not touching. I expected to hear something comforting, like a verse from the Beattitudes or the Twenty-Third Psalm. But Miss Irene selected a verse from Revelations:

"And I looked and behold a pale horse: and his name that sat on him was Death, and Hell followed with him."

There was no remonstrance from Aunt Ianthe or Miss Thyra and that's when I knew that all three ladies suspected foul play in Mrs. Ollanketo's demise. I had no chance to ask them, though, because we heard the front door opening and then Tom Kukka was pounding up the steps and into the room.

"Oh my god," he said, looking at the remains of his late patient. "Oh, my good god."

Ellwood, on his heels like a well-trained herding dog, stared at the body, too. Then he looked at me.

"What's the story here, Hatti? Did you find her like this? Did you touch her?"

"Just to check for a pulse," I said.

Ellwood looked at Tom.

"Did you expect her to die?" He shook his head.

"It could have happened any time. Her heart was weakening and it took longer to recover after each attack. But, no. I didn't think this would be the time but it was. And I wasn't here."

I caught Aunt Ianthe's eye and, to my shock, she understood my unspoken message.

"Deputy," she said, taking Ellwood's arm, "I could use your help with something down in the kitchen. Would you mind? It won't take a moment."

He didn't want to go. He knew he shouldn't go. What if this was a crime scene? And yet his nineteen years of training to be polite and helpful with his elders held firm and he descended the staircase with my aunt.

"Tom," I said, in a low voice, "do you think there's any chance this wasn't natural causes?"

"What? What are you saying, Hatti?"

"I looked up the two medications, Digitalin and Verapamil. They are contraindicated. Do you know what that means?"

"Yes. I'm a doctor, remember?"

"What if Mrs. Ollanketo got the Verapamil instead of the Digitalin?"

"That couldn't have happened. Not by accident."

"No. I know. But what if it wasn't by accident?"

He looked utterly bewildered. "Are you accusing me of murder?"

"Of course not! I'm just saying what if."

"What if what?"

"What if Mrs. O. knew something about Alex Martin's murder, Tom? What if she had to be silenced?"

He shook his head. "It isn't possible. She collapsed last night before any of it happened and she hasn't been out of this room today except to visit the bathroom. How could she know anything?"

"I've been thinking about that. Remember right before she fainted? We were walking across the lighthouse yard toward the sauna. There were dozens of people here and everything was loud and chaotic but that wouldn't have bothered Mrs. O. On the other hand, she'd have been able to lip-read a conversation, right?"

"I guess so."

"Maybe she saw something compromising."

"Like what? You think she saw someone announce his or her plans to kill Alex Martin?"

I shrugged. "Something like that."

He didn't dismiss the idea right away. That was one of the many things I liked about Tom Kukka. He never reacted defensively.

"So who was out there?"

"Pretty much everybody. I remember seeing you and Riitta talking over by the dock and Arvo and Danny speaking with Patty from Patty's Pasties. And then Arvo took a couple of beers to Erik Sundback and they talked, and when Alex came out of the sauna, Erik handed one to him and they talked some more. Oh, and I saw Danny speaking with Captain Jack, too."

Tom seemed to think about that and then shook his head.

"I don't see how any of those conversations could have compromised anyone. I mean, if someone intended to kill Alex, he or she wouldn't have announced it. I'm inclined to think that was a spur of the moment thing in which case Flossie could have known nothing about it."

"There is one thing," I said, and told him about the blue mitten for Miss Thyra. "What if Flossie was trying to pass along a message?"

"Like what? If you go out to play in the snow you must keep your hands warm?"

I threw him an affectionate grin.

"You have so little imagination. What if the mitten is a clue about the identity of the murderer or the motive?"

"What did Miss Thyra say?"

"She said Flossie must have forgotten the lecture was over."

"Well, there you have it. If the mitten were a clue, Thyra would have said."

"Yeah. I was afraid you were going to say that. Are you positive Mrs. O. couldn't have gotten the wrong medicine?"

"As sure as I can be. I handed the Verapamil to Erik and asked him to pour it down the sink. I watched him go into the bathroom and I heard the water go on. When I took the empty Digitalin syringe in to wash it out, the empty Verapamil syringe was sitting right there on the sink surround." He glanced over at the open bathroom door. "They're still there."

Hurried footsteps coming up the stairs turned out to be Riitta, who had arrived in a different vehicle. She rushed into the room, took one look at the bed, slapped her hand across her mouth and moaned. Tom moved as if to comfort her but he was too late. Erik Sundback came up behind Riitta and pulled her against him.

Tom dropped the arm he'd extended and moved closer to me. I glared at him, irritated that he was just giving up the field.

"I am so sorry, my dear," Erik said, in a low, soothing tone. "If it's any comfort to you, she died painlessly and of natural causes."

I looked at him, sharply and Ellwood, who'd returned, said, "unfortunately, we don't know that for sure. We'll have to do an autopsy."

Sheriff Clump, who was making his way slowly up the steps, stopped midway and howled.

"By the great horned spoon! Another dagnabbed autopsy? You people are going to break the bank!"

Arvo, who was behind Clump, assured him that he would transport the body to the morgue, thus saving the county a few pennies and within an hour, Mrs. Ollanketo left the lighthouse for the last time.

Before that, though, Riitta made coffee and we cut up and served bowls of freshly cut strawberries and plates of date-nut bars. Tom, who had only been allowed to return home because he was needed to issue a death certificate, was to return with Ellwood to the jail. He stood at the dining room window and stared out at the twilight. I brought him a cup of coffee and then stayed.

"What are you thinking," I asked.

"About what you said. If there was a mistake with the syringes, it was mine. It's possible that she's dead because of me, Hatti, because I had my mind on other things."

"You mean Alex Martin's murder."

"Worse. I was worrying about the attachment between Riitta and Sundback."

"She isn't serious about him."

"It's not such a bad idea," he said, heavily. "He's a decent guy and he's loaded. He could do a lot for Danny. She's already made it clear she doesn't want me. But I can't believe I was so preoccupied I'd have mixed up the syringes."

"I don't think it was a mix up, Tom. If Mrs. O. got the wrong medication, I think it was one hundred percent deliberate."

His blue eyes were bleak.

"In either case, I'm the one who injected the syringe. It comes right back to me."

CHAPTER 24

I finally got to bed, bookended by Larry at my feet and Lydia's muzzle on my shoulder. I couldn't seem to stop thinking although it wasn't very productive. Everything kept going around and around in my head, like a taped recording of Bob Seger singing *Running Against the Wind* over and over while you endure an hour in a dentist's chair.

The first death had shocked me. The second one, stunned. What was happening to us? Was it possible there was more than one individual involved? Or had Mrs. Ollanketo known something? All at once I knew this was no coincidence. These crimes, and they were crimes, were connected. Someone wanted Alex Martin dead and by some mischance, Mrs. Ollanketo had found out about it. Did that mean Captain Jack was dead, too? Or was he hiding out? Was there still time to save him? And what about Miss Thyra? If the blue mitten was a clue, was she at risk?

I was still wide awake when the moon had risen high enough to cast a spill of light across my bed. It seemed like a signal and it gave me the courage to make a move. A very bold move. I twisted this way and that, angling myself out of the vise created by the two dogs. I was wearing my usual sleeping garb of a nightshirt from Ronja's store printed with the slogan: *London, Paris, New York, Ishpeming,* so I took a moment to pull on a pair of panties, too. Then I descended the circular staircase as noiselessly as I could, cast a glance at the closed door to Mrs. Ollanketo's room, stepped in front of Miss Thyra's door and knocked softly. Very softly. All the bedrooms except mine were on this level and the last thing I wanted to do was wake up Riitta, Aunt Ianthe, Miss Irene or Danny. Erik Sundback had insisted on staying and he was sacked out somewhere. When I'd gone to bed, Riitta had been trying to convince him to sleep in her room while she slept downstairs but, my guess was that he'd wound up in Mrs. Ollanketo's room. Erik struck me as one of those lucky people who is not bothered by superstition or an excess of sentiment.

The first knock went unanswered. A second, slightly louder knock went unanswered, too, but I knew Miss Thyra was in there and I strongly believed she was not asleep. I am pretty familiar with the Lutheran conscience.

As I was standing there, shivering from the cold and from the temerity of what I was about to do, it occurred to me that most of the rooms in the lighthouse did not lock. I made a mental note to encourage Riitta to use some of the trust fund money to install new locks while, at the same time, feeling glad they hadn't been installed yet.

I turned the knob of Miss Thyra's door and stepped inside.

"Henrikki," she growled, but I thought I detected, under the annoyance, a certain amount of relief. Evidently she did not think I was the murderer. "What do you want at this hour?"

There was a nightlight on the bedside table, one of those old-fashioned lamps that has a bulb in the top and a globe underneath. It was the globe that cast enough light for me to see my quarry and vice versa. Miss Thyra's hair was encased in a hairnet that reminded me of one of the characters on *Laugh-In.* She was wearing a white nightgown that reached her chin and her wrists and, I had no doubt, fell to her ankles although I couldn't see her ankles because she remained in bed. There was dignity in her straight back but she looked like what she was: trapped. She repeated her question. It's not easy to infuse a whisper with a sense of indignation but she did a pretty good job.

"Miss Thyra, I think you know something and I want you to tell me what it is."

"What on earth are you jabbering about?"

"You were up all night preparing for the seminar. You must have seen people coming and going on the main floor of the lighthouse. Maybe you even saw the body. I mean, it would have been perfectly visible from the dining room window."

"That's absurd," she snapped. "I was occupied with my own preparations, my own thoughts."

"Don't try to pull the wool over my eyes," I said, borrowing a phrase from my late *mummi.* "You are capable of doing more than one thing at a time. I believe you noticed something relevant to Alex Martin's death. Moreover, I think the blue mitten from Mrs. Ollanketo was intended as a clue. What I can't understand is why you are reluctant to tell anyone what you know or suspect."

"There's nothing to tell," she snapped. "Go back to bed and let me get some sleep."

"Why did Flossie want you to have the Arjeplog mitten?"

"She slept through the seminar. I told you that. Or, rather, you told me. She got disoriented. The blue mitten is companion to the green one and she wanted me to have both."

"You knew she had the blue one, didn't you? Why didn't you ask her for it if it was so important to the lecture?"

"Contrary to what you seem to think, Henrikki, I am not Superwoman. If I thought of it at all, I thought one Arjeplog mitten was enough. Flossie was the one who came up with the idea of two."

I shook my head. "I don't buy it. That mitten meant something to Mrs. Ollanketo and she knew it would mean something to you. What are you hiding, Miss Thyra? What are you afraid of?"

She sat up very straight in her bed.

"What am I afraid of? Oh, let me see. I am afraid of old age. I am afraid of poverty. I am afraid of being homeless. I am afraid of being alone. You can't understand any of that because you are young. If you are not happy, you have only to go somewhere else, to start over. An elderly person does not have that option, especially an elderly person without means. I have no choices. Flossie had no choices, either."

I stared at her, the truth of what she was saying triggering a sense of horror.

"Flossie knew something, didn't she? She couldn't easily tell anyone what she knew because of her hearing and her loud voice." A truly horrible thought came to me. "Did she know she was at risk? Geez Louise! Did she use her last few minutes in a heroic effort to get a message to you? Did she know she was going to die? Miss Thyra, you have to tell me. She can't have died in vain."

"You are overly dramatic, Henrikki. I have no idea what Flossie knew." She paused, and then said, grudgingly, "she certainly had *sisu.*"

"What does the blue mitten mean?"

"Your guess is as good as mine."

"Roses," I said, remembering the pattern. "Rows and rows of stylized roses. Climbing roses, too, like the kind you'd find on a trellis or a garden wall. Red with yellow centers, aren't they? Roses. Leaves, petals, stems, thorns."

I stopped and stared at Miss Thyra. "Thorns. Was Mrs. O. trying to point the finger at Danny Thorne?"

"You see why I did not want to talk about it," Miss Thyra said, quietly. "What is the good of convicting a young man like Danny? We don't know whether he is guilty but an accusation from the grave is very powerful and he had means, motive and opportunity. If you insist upon sharing this theory, Henrikki, this will be on your head."

She spoke with such gravity, such dignity that I had nothing to say. Of course I didn't want to injure Danny Thorne and, by extension, Riitta. Miss Thyra was right. There was no way to know for sure what Mrs. O. had been trying to say. It wasn't up to us to interpret the mitten.

"I'll let you get back to sleep," I said, heavily. She made some kind of inarticulate sound and I left her room. It wasn't until I was back in my dog-filled bed that I remembered I'd intended to ask her about the clothespin.

"Well," I said to Lydia who had snuggled up to my chin, "it'll give me something to look forward to in the morning."

CHAPTER 25

When I opened my eyes, the morning rays of the sun played across my quilt. The dogs had jumped ship sometime in the night and I was alone in my pleasant cocoon. For the first few seconds, I felt cozy and safe. And then I remembered the murder. And the mitten. And Danny.

The atmosphere of peace and comfort dissipated. What I needed to do, first thing, was see if Captain Jack was back at the oil house. I slipped on a red, paisley halter, stepped into my cutoffs and tied on a pair of red sneakers. Then I attacked my hair, briefly, with my brush. The tufts stood up and out to the sides. I looked like a starfish.Time to chop it off again.

I wondered how Max and his Hemingway buddy were doing this morning and figured they were having fun. The weather was Yooper perfect and it seemed a shame to have to spend it trying to track down a killer. It occurred to me, though, that this weekend of murder had had one silver lining. I'd been too busy to ruminate about Jace.

Voices from the dining room reached me as I tiptoed down the backstairs. I crossed my fingers that the kitchen would be empty so that I could grab a cup of coffee and hightail it outdoors. Luck was with me. Not only did I get the coffee, the dogs waited patiently at the back door.

"Let's go," I whispered, "but no more bodies, do you hear me?" I opened the screen and we stepped out into the summer morning.

The sun glittered through the leaves creating patches of gold. Overhead the sky was that clear blue that makes you catch your breath. The waves on the lake broke gently against the shore. I know I spend a lot of time talking about the weather but when winter settles in every year like an uninvited guest who always overstays his welcome, it's hard not to rhapsodize in the summer. I headed east toward the oil house.

I had to admit that the balmy air and the scenic splendor did not make up for the fact that I was alone, that the same walk yesterday had been much more interesting just because I'd been with Max. Did that mean I really liked him? I already knew that. Did it mean I wanted more than friendship from him? Did he want more from me? I had no answers to those questions. I just knew I missed him.

Nothing seemed to have changed at the oil house. The curtains hung at the same angle they had yesterday. There was a faint layer of dust on the kitchen countertop. Even the pillows remained where we had left them. Outside, it was the same. The tufts of grass that stuck out of the foundation looked as if they hadn't grown and there were no footprints in the sand near the sauna. I glanced at the door and found the padlock hanging open. I stared it, certain that I'd seen Max lock it back up before we left. Did that mean someone had been here? Who? Captain Jack? My fingers were shaking a little as I opened the door. Whatever I'd expected to find, I was wrong. The room was empty, tidy, untouched, except for one very weird thing.

The barrel of woodchips that we'd emptied yesterday was filled to the brim, which wouldn't have been strange, except that Max had removed the box of contraband syrup. I blinked, wondering if my imagination was playing a trick on me. Nope, the chips mounded over the top of the barrel. Had someone brought Jack more chips? It seemed unlikely.

I began to excavate. This time the treasure was only about two inches under the surface. It was one of a pair of shoes, the other a few inches deeper. They were attractive shoes. Warm, caramel-colored leather boat shoes. Alex Martin's shoes.

What in the Sam hill were they doing in Captain Jack's woodbin?

I sat cross-legged on the floor and stared at the footwear. Would Sherlock Holmes consider this another clue? Probably. But I didn't know what to think. The shoes made less sense to me than the Arjeplog mitten.

What possible reason could there be for someone to have stolen the shoes of a dead man and planted them in a barrel of wood chips?

The answer, of course, was in the question. They'd been planted. Someone, the murderer, wanted the police to find the shoes and connect them with Captain Jack. They were the kind of thing Jack would take away from a scene if he was certain no one else wanted them. Had he done that? Had he been there, found the body and removed the shoes? But, if so, where had the shoes been yesterday? And why was there no sign of Jack in the oil house? I examined the shoes without touching them anymore than I already had. Would they even fit Jack who was a good six inches shorter than Alex Martin?

Larry and Lydia wandered inside to remind me that we should get back to the lighthouse. The trouble was, I couldn't decide whether to take the shoes with me or not. I mean, in the Golden Age stories, detectives would have brought them along just to make sure nobody stole them, but the modern cops on TV would have left them in the situation until a forensic team could check them out.

I figured I really should stop thinking of this situation as fictional, left the shoes in the wood chips and started the hike back down the lakefront. Meanwhile, I placed another 911 call.

This time the phone was answered on the ninth ring.

"Oh, Hatti, is that you? We've had quite a morning here.

Doc Kukka is such a nice young man but he refused to eat the Trenary toast and eggs that Vesta sent over from the diner." Trenary toast is twice-baked rusk sprinkled with cinnamon and sugar and it is sacrosanct in the UP. "Anyhow, it made the sheriff plum furious. He scolded the doctor, told him he'd insulted Vesta and Doc apologized to him and, on the phone, to Vesta, and he ate all the food. But everyone was upset and the sheriff went on down to the diner to settle his tummy with a milkshake and doughnuts. What can I do you for?"

"I'd like to speak with Ellwood, Mrs. Too."

"Well, dear, he's not here. After the diner, sheriff and Ellwood are heading out to the lighthouse."

"Oh, good. I can tell them about the shoes when they get here."

"What shoes?"

I told her about finding the deceased's boat shoes in the sauna chips.

"That's a mighty strange place to keep 'em," she said. "I can't imagine Johanna Marttinen ever told him to do that sort of thing."

"Well, I don't believe Alex put them there," I said, sorry I'd started down this unpromising track. "I think it was the murderer."

"I should have thought his mama would have taught him better, too. Those woodchips can't be good for the leather. Or are they canvas?"

"Hm," I said, noncommittally. "Do you happen to know when the autopsies will be performed?"

"Already finished, Henrikki. Doc Halonen got back from his cottage late last night. You know he's an early bird. Got in here and whipped through 'em, just like that." I could hear the snap of fingers on the other end of the line. "He said it was a nice change after spending the weekend with his grandchildren."

"Mrs. Too," I said, cutting her off. "Was Mrs. Ollanketo murdered?"

"Of course, Hatti. We've got the perp sitting right here in

the cell. That nice Doctor Kukka. I suppose he had his reasons."

I had no idea what to say to that so I said goodbye and hung up.

The dogs and I slipped in the back door and I filled their bowls with food and water. I felt as if I'd been gone for hours so it was a surprise to hear the voices in the dining room. When I walked through the door I could see that all the residents were still gathered around the table which was as strong an indication as anything that we were all upset.

"Henrikki," Aunt Ianthe said, "you went for a walk with the dogs?" I nodded, taking a chair near her.

"Let me get you some eggs and coffee cake," Riitta said, getting to her feet. She looked as neat as always but there were purple crescents under her eyes and I waved her back to her seat insisting (less than truthfully) that I wasn't hungry.

Danny, at the end of the table, looked as hollow-eyed as his mom and there was a deep scowl on his handsome, young face as he listened to Miss Irene warbling on about something. Miss Thyra was on Danny's other side which surprised me considering that she'd played the role of Judas in betraying him to me. As I watched, Miss Thyra pushed the food around her plate and kept her eyes down.

Aunt Ianthe seemed normal enough and Erik Sundback's habitual air of geniality was somewhat subdued but intact. He wore the same brightly colored shirt that he'd worn the day before but had somehow passed the night without either wrinkling or soiling it. He seemed deliberately calm as if he'd taken it upon himself to provide stability for the group.

"Good morning, Hatti," he said, when the others had finished talking. "We're having a kind of summit meeting to talk over the unusual circumstances we've experienced here, lately and what they mean to everyone.

"I know Alex Martin's return and what happened after that has been distressing to everyone, especially combined with the loss of Mrs. Ollanketo but I have what amounts to some good news and I saved it until we were all here."

"We're not all here now," Danny said. "What about Tom?"

"Danny!" His mother reprimanded him. Was it just a reflex response? Your kid is rude, you call him on it? Or did she not want Tom brought in to the discussion? If the doctor were to be released, the sheriff would almost certainly arrest Danny.

"Alex Martin's L.A. attorney has told me it is his opinion that Johanna Marttinen's gift of the Painted Rock Lighthouse and the five-million-dollar trust fund is likely to stand. As I believe I mentioned, the Marttinen property is not noted in Alex Martin's Last Will and Testament which means the typed and signed note received by Riitta Lemppi yesterday morning, is the only document that is pertinent. It will have to go through probate but Alex's attorney expects it to be accepted and I concur." He smiled at each of us for a second or two. "So it looks as if the Painted Rock Lighthouse Retirement Home is secure."

"That's wonderful," Riitta murmured. She looked at me. "Did you walk as far as the oil house? Did you see Jack?"

I heard the hysteria behind the question and wished I could give her the answer she was looking for.

"I'm afraid not."

"We're shrinking," Danny said. "First it was Alex, then Mrs. O., then Tom, now Jack. A couple more days and we'll be down to zero. *And Then There Were None.*"

"Danny!" It was his mother.

"Riitta, dear," Aunt Ianthe said, "what is he talking about?"

"An Agatha Christie novel," I said, "you remember it, Aunt Ianthe. Ten people are invited to an island by an anonymous host. Each of them has gotten away with a murder and the host has set himself to make them pay. One by one they get killed off."

"Dear me," Aunt Ianthe said. "It doesn't sound very entertaining when you tell it like that."

"An eye for an eye, a tooth for a tooth," Miss Irene said.

"It's all explained in Exodus."

Danny shot the old lady a savage look.

"You think Moses planned these murders? Or God?"

Riitta's sob was involuntary and so uncharacteristic that everyone gasped and even Erik Sundback glared at the young man.

"Let's pull ourselves together," he growled. "We have to rely on each other to get through this terrible situation."

It occurred to me that some of us (Alex and Mrs. O., for sure, and possibly Captain Jack) were not going to get through it at all.

"We must all find our *sisu*," Miss Thyra said and I thought I heard just a whiff of irony in her voice. Or, maybe it was desperation. My thoughts were interrupted by the opening and slamming of the front door which we could hear loud and clear because neither the glass-paned doors that separated the foyer from the parlor, nor the pocket doors that separated the parlor from the dining room were closed. The hundred-year-old floorboards of the lighthouse creaked and groaned as Sheriff Horace A. Clump thundered his way across them. He looked like a keg of dynamite about to blow.

"Ye gods and little fishes," he squawked. "Where in the blue blazes is everybody? You all dead?"

I'd jumped up as soon as I heard him and he swept past me, his arms flailing, his hat crooked and a snarl on his pyramid-shaped face. The buttonholes on his tan uniform shirt were stretched into almonds and the suspenders dug into his shoulders. He looked hot and cross and ready to throw us all to the wolves.

"What's up with him," I asked Ellwood.

"Bee in his bonnet. Doc Halonen says both of the autopsies were murders."

"What was the cause of death on Mrs. O?"

"Overdose."

"Of Digitalin?"

Ellwood nodded. "And Verapamil. Somehow, she got both."

"Oh, no."

"Mrs. Too called me about the shoes. What's up with that?" I told him what I'd found. He couldn't make head nor tail of it, either.

"I don't know, Hatti. This is too much like a movie. People keep dying or disappearing, like that Agatha Christie story."

"And Then There Were None?"

"That's it."

"Funny. Danny just said the same thing. Quite a coincidence."

"Not really. We were both in Mrs. Kempner's physics class. She had her baby early and they showed us movies for the last two weeks of school."

"Huh. Small world."

The sheriff arrived in front of the table of people and he took a minute or two to catch his breath after which he planted his feet about a foot apart, dug his fists into the wall of flesh that constituted his waist and spoke.

"I have had it up to here," he said, flattening his right hand and bringing it level with his massive forehead. "I don't know what's going on out here but whatever it is has gotta stop. I got two folks deader than dodo birds down at the morgue and a missing sea captain. Doc H. says Martin was pushed off the balcony and the old lady was kilt with Veramenthol."

"Verapamil," Ellwood corrected him.

"Whatever."

"I hope you know that we are very upset about these deaths, too," Aunt Ianthe said. She was, as always polite, but not cowed. It would take a lot to cow Aunt Ianthe. "We all hope very much that this is the end of it. But you are the ones who have to solve the case, is the thing. I think you should get busy."

During this little speech Clump's red cheeks had turned the color of purple plums and his small, beady eyes had narrowed over his bulbous nose.

"For your information, Madame," he said, in a tone my

mother would have described as not very nice, "I intend to get busy. A team of crime scene specialists will be brought in tomorrow or the next day."

"My goodness," Aunt Ianthe said. "That won't be very convenient for the residents."

"Exactly right," Clump said, with a note of triumph. "They are coming in, so you must go out. I want the place vacated by five p.m. today. This is now an official crime scene and you are all trespassing."

As sure as the night follows the day I expected the next words to come from Miss Irene. Trespassing is one of those words that easily lends itself to Bible references. Instead, Miss Thyra spoke.

"Some of us cannot leave," she said, with dignity. "We have no other place to go."

"Not my problem," Clump leered. "But I'll say this. If you ain't here, you can't get killed. So what's good for the goose is good for the gander."

"Sheriff," I asked, "does this mean you have decided Tom Kukka is innocent?"

"Hell, no, girl. No one's innocent til proven guilty. It's a constitutional rule. But if we're going to court, and we are, I wanna get more hard evidence, get me? Awright," he continued, "time for all of you people to vamoose."

Erik Sundback got to his feet and spoke quietly but authoritatively.

"I'd like to propose a solution to the housing problem. I don't believe that many of you know this, but I have a home in Red Jacket. I bought it last year and it's been under renovation since then. I'm happy to say it is ready for occupancy and I hereby invite any or all of you to stay there with me for the duration. There are plenty of bedrooms and bathrooms, a housemaid and a cook so it shouldn't be too unpleasant an experience."

Aunt Ianthe looked regretful and I knew she was, at that moment, wishing she did not have her own home in Red Jacket. A few days at Erik Sundback's renovated home would suit her and Miss Irene, perfectly. However, she thanked him politely and explained that she and her companion shared a home on Calumet Street.

Erik was very polite to the old lady but his object in issuing the invitation was clear from the burning look he lasered on Riitta. I saw my cousin exchange a nod with Miss Thyra and then she spoke.

"On behalf of Miss Thyra and myself, we accept your offer with gratitude," she said.

"I can bunk with a high school friend," Danny put in, quickly. The comment drew a questioning look from Ellwood but he didn't object and I thought it was just as well. In the battle shaping up between Erik Sundback and Tom Kukka, Danny was too much of a partisan to be comfortable with the attorney's hospitality.

On the whole, I thought, as we dispersed to start packing up, the exodus wasn't a bad idea and I imagined everyone would be somewhat relieved, so I was surprised to see the violet shadows under Miss Thyra's eyes and the deep crevices that bracketed her downturned mouth. She was still upset or worried or (and I thought this the most likely option) feeling guilty. I was certain she knew something important and I resolved to talk to her again.

"Where is your home, Erik," Aunt Ianthe said, conversationally, as we headed out of the dining room toward the main staircase. It was typical of my relative that she would express an interest in someone's news and I knew she was motivated as much by benevolence as by curiosity. Erik Sundback had a new house and he was proud of it, ergo, he would want to speak of it.

"It's on Cedar Crescent," he said, pleasantly. "The old Eilola place. Apparently it had been rented for a number of years and I was able to buy it for a song." He chuckled, ruefully. "Unfortunately, the renovations have been more like Wagner's Ring Cycle, long and heavily expensive."

"Oh, that's wonderful," Aunt Ianthe said, with a warm smile. "We've seen the vans and workmen over there but no one seemed to know who had bought the place. Welcome to Red Jacket, Erik. I hope this means we will see even more of you."

"And the house," Miss Irene said. "We have been so curious about the house."

"I want you to see it," Sundback said, in a kindly voice. "In fact, why don't you ladies come over tomorrow afternoon, for tea?" He glanced in Riitta's direction as if suddenly remembering he should check with her before issuing an invitation. "Is that all right," he asked, belatedly. "The cook will handle everything."

"It's lovely," Riitta assured him, warmly. "Thyra and I will be glad to see Ianthe and Irene again tomorrow." She looked at me. "Hatti, you'll come, too?" I nodded. "Oh, and do you mind keeping Lydia?"

Riitta was always gracious but it surprised me a little how easily she'd stepped into the role of Erik's hostess. Had she made her decision? Had she already (figuratively) left Tom Kukka and his devotion by the roadside?

I tried to look at Erik Sundback objectively. He was fifty years old but in great shape with blue eyes that could be warm and playful or rather cold and businesslike. He showed no likelihood of losing his white-blond hair and it complemented his ruddy cheeks. He was trim and fit and always well-groomed and he struck me as a man of controlled pride. An attractive man. I did not find it odd that Riitta was fond of him but I did wonder how their living arrangements would work out. My cousin's mission was the retirement home. Somehow, I couldn't see Erik Sundback spending the rest of his days in the fussy Victorian parlor with a gaggle of little old ladies, unlike Tom Kukka, who, though twenty years younger, fit right in.

While we were working together to get the ladies (and the rest of us) moved out, I found myself on the stairs with the attorney.

"It was generous of you to offer your house," I said.

He winked at me. "I may have had an ulterior motive." I nodded, gravely.

"Listen, I wanted to run something by you."

"Shoot," he said. In a low voice, I told him about the shoes buried in the wood chips.

"Weird," he said. "What do you make of it?"

I shook my head. "I can't figure out why they're there."

"On the face of it, it seems like Jack."

"I know. But where is he? And why would he take those shoes? They wouldn't fit him."

"Hatti," he said, patiently, "Fellows like Jack are opportunists and I don't mean that critically. He has no income except a pittance from Johanna's estate for taking care of the antique lens. A pair of calf-leather boat shoes will fetch a good price at a consignment shop."

"I suppose so. How did you know they were boat shoes?"

"Hm? Oh, I noticed them, particularly on Saturday. Caramel-colored, aren't they? I have a similar pair. Anyway, I think Jack is the most likely answer to your question."

"Does that mean you think Jack murdered Alex?"

He shook his head. "I'm not saying that. My best guess is that it was an accident. But since the autopsy says it was foul play, you can bet Clump is going to pin it on somebody. It might be Jack. It might be Tom or it might be Danny. You need to be emotionally ready to accept the outcome, whatever it is."

My heart felt heavy and he seemed to realize it because he put his arm around my shoulders and gave me a heartening squeeze.

"I'm glad you're sticking by us in this," I said. "I'm glad you're here."

CHAPTER 26

Nearly all the houses in Red Jacket were built before World War II and many of them earlier, when the population of Copper Country was three times as high as it is now. Most were typical Yooper structures with sharply slanted rooflines designed to allow gravity to aid in snow removal, enclosed mud porches and picture windows four or five feet above ground level so they wouldn't be blocked by snow. But a few of the homes were built by mine managers and other wealthy persons. Most of those great homes are located on Calumet Street, the highest point in town.

My family's Queen Anne Victorian is on the west side of the street between the Maki Funeral Home and the Leaping Deer, Elli's bed and breakfast. She inherited the shabby, rambling inn three years ago and has restored it, in meticulous detail, to a graceful, state-of-the-art inn circa 1900.

Arvo's home, in contrast, is just plain ugly. The local joke (never spoken before him) is that the architect must have had a death wish. The structure's red brick walls, darkened by time are reminiscent of dried blood and the slit-like windows make it seem as if its eyes are closed. There is a heavy, thick, low-pitched roof that curls over the gutters like a hungry python.

On the south side of the street, mid-level mine

supervisors had built smaller homes and duplexes, including the one now owned by Aunt Ianthe and Miss Irene, which, since her divorce, they have shared with Sofi and her daughter, Charlie. Frilled curtains fill the matching bay windows, each of the front doors is embellished with a surround of paned glass and each house has a stoop, three steps off the ground.

I carried in the luggage and helped the ladies unpack, refusing a cup of tea but listening to several minutes of raptures including Aunt Ianthe quoting Dorothy in the Wizard of Oz ("There's no place like home") and Miss Irene quoting Judges ("When the men of Israel saw that Abimelech was dead, each departed to his home.") After that, the dogs and I drove around the corner to the service alley that runs behind our side of Calumet Street. The alley had been built originally to provide access to the detached garages so that the expansive front lawns wouldn't have to be disrupted by driveways. I parked on the alley's narrow shoulder and let the dogs into the back garden through the white picket fence. When we'd reached the back door and the kitchen, I felt a sense of comfort and familiarity but, to my surprise and sorrow, I did not feel as if I were coming home. It was my childhood home, my past, not my present. My gut was telling me it was time to get back to adult life. I told myself I would as soon as the murders were solved. But would they get solved? How many murderers, like the ones in the Agatha Christie novel, got away with their crimes? What if we never found out what had happened to Alex Martin and Flossie Ollanketo and Captain Jack? Doc's reputation would be ruined at the very least, and maybe Danny's, too. People would think the lighthouse was haunted and no one would want to live there.

It didn't bear thinking about. It couldn't happen. We had to find out. I had to find out.

Fired with a new resolve, I decided to ignore the obvious obligation of dusting, vacuuming, running some laundry and cutting the grass in favor of making a pot of coffee to help me think.

I carried a mug into the room my mother still calls the parlor. The early afternoon sun filtered through mom's Priscilla-style curtains and dappled the chintz-covered sofa and chairs and the boards of the wooden floor, in the latter case, revealing a layer of dust that would send my mother into hysterics. The sun's rays hit the jewel-colored panes of the Tiffany-style lamp at one end of the sofa and gleamed off the old, upright piano that some misguided soul had painted white decades earlier. While the dogs stretched out on the floor, I burrowed into a corner of the sofa, held my coffee mug in both hands, closed my eyes and thought about something I'd read about detective work. Was it Conan Doyle? Anyway, the advice was to work backwards. What was the bottom line? What had actually happened? And who was affected by it? I made a mental list.

Two people were dead. Alex and Mrs. Ollanketo.

Captain Jack had disappeared.

Tom Kukka was in jail. So far, I couldn't see that anyone benefited much from these facts, in light of Alex's promise to relinquish his ownership of the lighthouse.

But there was another result here.

The lighthouse itself had been shut down. Was that to someone's benefit? If so, whose? A shadowy thought crossed my mind. Erik Sundback wanted to marry Riitta. If the lighthouse retirement home plan fizzled, she would be without a home and without a mission. And, according to Alex's letter, she did not inherit a penny, so she would be without means, too. Erik could afford to support Riitta and Danny, too. So the closing of the lighthouse was good for the lawyer if no one else. But, not only did I like Erik Sundback, I respected the stellar reputation he'd earned practicing law on the Keweenaw and I knew that reputation was important to him. He wouldn't have risked his career by committing murder, not even for the woman he wanted.

And speaking of woman, what about Chakra? I didn't want to suspect her. She was not only a friend, she'd been a mentor, an unofficial counselor during the worst months of my life. She said she'd achieved closure from her sixty minutes or so with Alex on Saturday night and I'd believed her. And then she'd turned around and lied to me about sleeping at the oil house. Why? What was she covering up?

On the other hand, unless she owned an invisible cloaking device, I didn't see how she could have been involved with Flossie Ollanketo's death. Chakra had not been in the lighthouse on Sunday afternoon. She hadn't killed Flossie and I was finding it almost impossible there was more than one murderer. Of course I was finding it equally impossible to believe that any of the rest of us had committed a murder, either. I listed the names out loud, picturing each person as I did so: Riitta, Danny, Tom, Aunt Ianthe, Miss Irene, Miss Thyra, Erik, Arvo.

All right I knew Riitta, Danny, the ladies and I had been in the lighthouse when Alex was murdered. Chakra and Sebastian had been nearby. The next logical step was to figure out who, from that group, had been in the house on Sunday afternoon, when Mrs. Ollanketo received the dose of Verapamil that canceled out her Digitalin and allowed her heart to stop.

All that thinking led me to the person who had already confessed. It led me to Tom. I needed to speak with him and there was no time like the present.

The decision of whether to take my canine assistants with me was wrenched from my hands when the two dogs bolted out the back door, down the garden path and waited, impatiently, for me to unlatch the gate and open the doors to the Jeep.

"Fine," I said, "but you can't come into the jail, okay? You have to wait in the car."

Larry regarded me with eloquent eyes and Lydia licked my fingers.

We drove the five miles to Frog Creek in companionable silence and parallel parked in front of the sheriff's office on First Street. I found Mrs. Touleheto spraying Windex onto the buttons on her rotary phone. She wore a pink tee shirt with short sleeves and an attached lace collar and a pair of white cropped summer pants on her pear-shaped body. As I came through the door, she paused in mid-squirt.

"Henrikki.You've picked up a little tan out at the lighthouse. It's good, you know? Helps your freckles blend. And I see you're growing out your hair." She peered out the window. "You shouldn't leave the dogs in the car, is the thing. Why don't you bring them inside? We can give them water and the leftover sausage from the prisoner's lunch."

I agreed to her proposal and soon Larry and Lydia were curled up on the cool floorboards of the sheriff's office.

"Have you called Waino yet," Mrs. Too asked me. "This is the time, Hatti. All he does is play video games, according to his mother."

"As tempting as that sounds," I said, apologetically, "I'm a little busy at the moment. In fact, I'm here to see the, er, prisoner."

"No can do, dear." She pointed at the plate that the dogs had just cleaned off. "He refused to finish his lunch and the sheriff simply had to punish him. The perp's in solitary."

I considered asking how a jail with only one cell could create a 'solitary' designation but decided that, as entertaining as the answer would be, it wasn't relevant. Instead, I craned my head around the corner and caught Tom's eye. He held up a hand in a kind of half-hearted wave.

"Mrs. Too, I hate to have to remind you of this, but a suspect, even an incarcerated suspect, has rights. For one thing, he's allowed to talk to his lawyer."

"Henrikki, you are not his lawyer."

"I'm nearly his lawyer. I'm in law school."

She stared at me. "I heard you quit your schooling when you got married."

"I took a break. That's pretty standard, you know. Law school is expensive. I needed to earn enough money to take the second year."

"Is that why you were working at the bait shop?"

"Yes." I'd been reared on the idea that lightning would strike a liar and, for the first time in many years, I wondered whether there was anything behind it.

"Also," I continued, thinking I had her on the ropes, "Tom is a suspect, not a perp. He is innocent until proven guilty. That's a right that's guaranteed by the Constitution."

Mrs. Toulelehto straightened her shoulders and lifted her chin. She transformed from the dithering dispatcher into the fully-in-charge Sunday school teacher.

"The Constitution is all very well and good, Henrikki, but it is not the final word on anything. It is not," she intoned, "the Bible."

I suddenly saw my opening.

"How blessed," I quoted, "are those who keep justice."

She eyed me, suspiciously. "That's not a Beatitude."

"No. It's from Psalms." If there was one thing I'd learned from Miss Irene's years of quoting the KJV (King James Version), it was that nearly everything could be found in Psalms.

"What number?"

She was testing me. I smiled.

"Three hundred."

"Hmm," she said. There was a distinct gleam in her pale blue eyes. "Go on, then. Talk to the doc. But make it fast."

"Thanks. Could I have the key to the cell?"

"It's not locked. We use the honor system. I'm running out on an errand. Could you answer the phone it if rings, then?"

I nodded and headed down to the cell.

Tom Kukka had been sitting on the thin, uncovered mattress, but when I approached the door he stood, like the gentleman he is, to open the door for me. He hadn't shaved or changed his rumpled button-down shirt and trousers from the day before and his eyelids drooped as if he'd been stricken with Bell's Palsy. He smiled at me, though, and offered me the only chair in the room before dropping back onto the mattress. He sat on the edge of it, knees apart, hands on his thighs, his head leaning back against the gray cinderblock wall.

"Nice work pulling that verse out of your back pocket, Hatti. For future reference, the Psalms only go up to one hundred and fifty."

"It seems like there are more. How do you know, anyway?" One straw-colored eyebrow lifted.

"I was in the confirmation class two years ahead of you, Hatti. You were too busy making out with Waino Aho to notice me."

I was pleased that he could make a joke, even if it was at my expense. However, it was time to get serious.

"You know this faux confession is only causing problems, Tom. You didn't kill Alex Martin or Mrs. Ollanketo but by saying you did, Clump gets to give himself permission to stop investigating. You know he's a proponent of the bird-in-the-hand school of thought."

Tom shook his head.

"I can't change my story. Clump's got a short list and the second name on it is Danny's."

"All right," I said, giving in on that. "Let's look a little further. Who else have we got swimming around the suspect pool?"

"Riitta." The name sounded stark and hollow.

"Let's stick to realistic possibilities." He shrugged again.

"It has to be someone young. Someone strong and vigorous. Someone Martin trusted enough to invite to step out onto the gallery as the storm was blowing up. That doesn't leave many folks. Me, Danny, Riitta. You, I guess, although there doesn't seem to be any motive in your case."

"Thanks. I think."

"On the other hand there are plenty of motives for the rest of us. First of all the threat of losing the lighthouse and the trust fund. In my case, the threat of losing Riitta herself. In Danny's case, fury at the father who abandoned him and his mom. In Riitta's case, the same anger, along with the belief that she'd get the lighthouse if he died."

"But he told her she'd get it anyway."

"That's what she said. You believe her and I believe her. What about Clump? What about a jury? There's no proof that he gave her the lighthouse. In fact, there's proof that he gave it to the county." He shook his head. "I have to stick to my story. I have no choice."

We sat in silence for a minute.

"Tom," I said, "we've got to figure out what happened with Mrs. Ollanketo. Is there any chance there was a mistake on the autopsy?"

"There's always a chance but that idea is unlikely to grow legs. You know how it works around here. The coroner du jour does the cutting, Jean Lasker from the Frog Creek Pharmacy runs tests on the stomach contents and a report is written. It's the no-frills version of autopsy. Something could easily be missed or misunderstood but we just don't have the set up for anything but the most rudimentary approach. Besides, this was a rather simple situation. There were two syringes and my patient, Mrs. O., got both of them."

"The question is, how?"

He thrust his fingers through his rumpled brown hair.

"I don't know. I've been over and over it. I filled one syringe with Digitalin, and the other with Verapamil. I took the latter into Miss Thyra's room and spent several minutes discussing her headache with her. I made a pretty bad mistake in filling the syringe before getting her permission– I'm guilty of that if nothing else."

"Why did you do it that way?"

"Efficiency. Or, what I thought was efficiency. I needed to get back down to the hospital to check on a patient there and so I got the syringes ready at the same time."

"So what happened when Miss Thyra turned it down?"

He eyed me. "I've told you that, already."

"Tell me again."

"Erik Sundback was out on the landing. He asked if there was anything he could do to help and I handed him the Verapamil. I asked him to wash it down the bathroom sink. I picked up the Digitalin and headed for Flossie's room. You know how small the landing is. I could see Erik go into the bathroom. I heard him turn on the water and I watched him get rid of the medicine."

"You couldn't see that, surely," I pointed out. "I mean, his back was to you."

"That's right. But after I injected Flossie, I went into the bathroom to wash out the Digitalin syringe and the other one was sitting there, drying out, on the surround of the sink. It was empty and I could see traces of the medicine around the drain. He emptied it, Hatti. I'd stake my life on it."

I nodded. "Who else was in the vicinity?"

"Besides you?" I nodded, again. "Riitta, Danny, Arvo, Ianthe and Irene. Thyra was in her room and Flossie in hers."

"What about a third syringe?"

"What're you talking about?"

"The arrest came right after that, didn't it? When you left the house, was your bag still out on the table on the landing?"

"Yes."

"Oh my gosh," I said, excitement building. How was it I hadn't thought of this before? I was brilliant! "What if, after you left, someone came back upstairs and filled a third syringe with a fresh dose of Verapamil? By that time, Mrs. O. would have been asleep. It would have been as easy as pie to inject her without anyone knowing."

"It's a good idea, Hatti," Tom said. "Shows excellent deductive skills. But it won't fly."

"Why not?"

"There wasn't any more Verapamil in the container. That dose that Erik flushed down the sink was the last of it."

I didn't want to let go of my beautiful theory.

"Unless someone brought in a new batch."

Tom smiled at me.

"You can't buy it over the counter. You can only get it if you're a doctor."

"Well, shoot."

"What else is going on out at the lighthouse?" I had the feeling he was trying to humor me.

"Actually, no one's there. Clump evacuated us this morning. He says he's bringing in a crime scene investigative team and we were sent packing. Riitta and

Miss Thyra have gone to stay at Erik's home in Red Jacket."

"I thought he lived in a condo down in Houghton on the water."

"He bought the old Eilola place last year. How he managed to keep that quiet I'll never know. It's an epic fail for the grapevine."

"I suppose he's had it renovated."

"To the teeth. He's even got a housekeeper and a cook."

A curse escaped the doctor's lips.

"He wants to marry Riitta," I said, trying to get a response from him.

"She could do worse."

"She could also do better. She could marry someone who shares her interest in creating an old folks home. She could marry someone who loves her."

"He does love her. I've heard him say so. And, he's a good man, Hatti. He can give her things that I can't."

"Like what?"

"Financial peace of mind. Stability. Age." He smiled, briefly. "That's been a big wedge. She doesn't want to marry someone my age. She's convinced I'll be unhappy without kids."

"You'd be getting a kid. Danny."

"Yeah. I've tried that argument. She's a stubborn woman, your cousin."

"She's never struck me that way," I said. "Too bad you can't convince her."

"I could convince her if she loved me." His voice was very quiet, very resigned. "Don't bug her about Sundback, Hatti. If he's what she wants, let her have him."

"Can I ask you a question?" He nodded. "If Riitta marries Erik and the county has to find someone else to run the lighthouse would you continue to provide medical services for the residents?"

"You mean assuming I'm not convicted of pushing Alex Martin off the tower and of poisoning one of my patients?"

"Yep."

His attempt at a smile did not reach his eyes but he answered me.

"Sure," he said.

I shook my head. "You're a saint. In your shoes, I'd abandon the whole bunch of them. Speaking of shoes, I found Alex Martin's shoes in the sauna woodchips at the oil house."

Tom didn't know what to make of that and I wanted to leave him on a high note, so I told him the story of the contraband syrup. It cheered him up.

At least, he said it did.

CHAPTER 27

The two-lane road between Frog Creek and Red Jacket makes for a pleasant drive on a late summer afternoon. For one thing, the entire length is paved. Visitors to the U.P. sometimes complain that they start driving on nice, normal hard-topped roads only to have them morph into cow paths and drift off into the woods. That wasn't true for Rural Route 2, aka the Red Jacket-Frog Creek to the people in Red Jacket and the Frog Creek-Red Jacket Road to the people in Frog creek.

And then there are the trees. We have plenty of pine trees on the Keweenaw but, in the heart of summer, we also have sugar maple, birch, quaking aspen, choke cherry, hemlock, cedar and black ash. The deciduous trees on either side of Rural Route 2 meet overhead and form a lacy canopy that makes the driver feel like she's inside a kaleidoscope.

On the outskirts of Red Jacket the dogs and I heard childish laughter and someone yelling, "alle, alle, in come free!" I smiled thinking of the kids playing tag but my heart was heavy. What was the future for those kids? Would they, like so many before them, have to leave home and family to find work? (I forgot, for the moment, that I had *wanted* to leave home). Our tax base was low and our population, circling the drain. Schools were consolidating or closing and so were department stores and smaller shops. Tourism was our best hope for the future. What effect would our two horrific murders have on that industry? Would it bring people here or repel them? I was pretty sure I knew the answer to that. Unsolved murders would discourage most from making the ten-hour drive from Detroit or the seven-hour trip from Chicago.

We needed to find out the truth, not just for Tom Kukka or Riitta or Danny or Captain Jack or for Alex Martin or Mrs. Ollanketo. We needed to find the murderer because if this case was left unresolved, there would be no peace for any of us. The sounds of kids playing tag on a summer afternoon would never be the same.

My brain felt scrambled as I parked in the alley and followed the dogs up the garden path. I needed a pick-me-up. Maybe a glass of wine or a piece of chocolate, neither of which I had in the house. I considered getting back in the Jeep and running to Shopko but before I could definitely decide for or against that initiative, the back door opened.

"Hey," said my sister, "where have you been? Time to wash up for supper."

"Supper? You brought me supper?" In that moment she looked like a Finnish fairy godmother.

"Well, to be fair, Elli brought it. *Suomen Makaronilaatikkocasserole.* The long, fancy word just means Finnish macaroni casserole but eggs and nutmeg give it a light, exotic taste. It is my favorite comfort food. Along with chocolate and coffee. "I brought salad and fresh *pulla,*" she said, referring to the bread. "And chocolate walnut fudge for dessert."

"You," I said, "are an angel."

As I stepped over the threshold into the kitchen, the combined scent of casserole and bread nearly bowled me over.

"Can we eat now?"

"Soon," Elli said. "Sonya's tied up with a patient and it would be polite to wait for her."

"And, as an added incentive," Sofi said, "She's bringing the wine."

As soon as Sonya arrived we took seats around my mom's round wicker table, covered with a red-and-white-checked oilcloth, and helped ourselves, family style. Afterwards we talked and laughed. It was such a relief to be with friends I could trust, friends who had no connection with the terrible events at the lighthouse. It was like slipping into a cold, clear lake after a sauna, like chugging a drink of ice-cold water. The laughter and companionship, along with the sustaining food, made me feel as if we would get through this nightmare.

We held off talking about the murders until we'd consumed everything but coffee and fudge. By then I felt refreshed enough to jump back into the fray.

"I need your help," I said, finally. "I feel like I've hit a dead end in this investigation. A cul-de-sac, of sorts. You know that Clump has arrested Tom Kukka. I can't bring myself to believe he'd have killed two people but I can't see that there's anyone else. I'd like to lay out the facts that I have and see if anything jumps out at you."

They agreed to it and I started back at the beginning, when Alex Martin showed up at the *Juhannus* Festival's faux wedding on the last day of the year following Johanna Marttinen's death and ran through events up until this morning's evacuation.

"Let's go back a bit," Sofi said. "Saturday, when Martin came back was it still within the time frame of his year? In other words, was it the 365th day of the proscribed year or the 366th?"

"Does it matter?"

"It might. If the will provided for a strict definition of a year, he might never have been in line to inherit the lighthouse at all. He might have been too late."

"I'll check on that," I said, "but it seems to me that Erik indicated the courts might be lenient within reason about a property transferring from parent to child."

"I notice," Sonya said, "there's a lot of confusion about the disposition of the property, whether it was to go to Alex Martin or to Riitta or to the county board of commissioners.

It seems to me that's a key point. That, and the letter he supposedly wrote to Riitta."

"I'd be interested in knowing more about the victim," Elli said. "What was your impression of him, Hatti? I mean he rowed out to the island with you, right? And you guys watched the Northern Lights together. Did he seem like a decent guy?"

"Decent," I said, trying to look at him objectively, "with a core of steel. On the one hand I think he had a generous impulse to let Riitta have the lighthouse but on the other, he was almost obsessive about not letting anyone take advantage of him. That seemed like his guiding principle, you know?"

"What about Chakra," Sofi asked. "She was obsessed with him, right? What if their rendezvous meant more to her than it did to him? What if she decided to sneak back into the lighthouse later to punish him?"

"It could have happened," I admitted. "The trouble with Chakra as a suspect is that she wasn't in the lighthouse on Sunday so she couldn't have poisoned Mrs. O. But, other than that, it's certainly possible that Chakra was the person Danny saw coming up the circular stairs."

"If Danny wasn't lying," Sofi said, with a sigh. "I can't believe how hard it is to sort this all out. And it's made worse by all these people lying to protect somebody else."

"The weirdest thing to me," Sonya said, "is the hiding of the body. The facts indicate Alex Martin fell on the sand just before one a.m. because of the dry surface under the body. But it wasn't there when you were out at six a.m. and it wasn't there at 8:30 a.m., either. And then, hey presto, it showed up at noon."

"So apparently it was moved," Elli said, taking up the narrative, "and if it was moved, you have to ask yourself, why?"

"Alibi purposes," Sofi suggested. "General confusion?"

"Hatti," Sonya said, suddenly, "in that timeline you gave us you said that Alex may have asked Captain Jack to deliver the letter in the envelope to Riitta's room. But there wasn't any time in there for Alex to write it."

"It's a good point but we've got to remain skeptical about all the eyewitness stuff," Sofi said. "We only know, independently, that is, through Hatti's testimony, that Danny was in the watch room from about eleven-forty-five until midnight and that Riitta showed up a few minutes later. After that we have only their words. I think we can assume Riitta stretched out her time to try to protect Danny. What we don't know is whether Danny was really up there in that alcove. His story about Captain Jack coming out of the watch room and running into someone coming up on the stairs could be a complete fabrication."

"But Captain Jack is missing," I said, accepting what I'd been fighting against. "And that argues that he saw the killer, and that the killer, knowing that the next day Jack would put two and two together, got rid of him."

"It could be Danny," Elli said, in a quiet voice. "I know you don't want it to be, but it could be. There may have been no one else up there. He could have killed Alex for whatever reason, then killed Jack to eliminate him as a witness. He could have thought Mrs. Ollanketo had lip-read something he'd said to someone and thought he had to eliminate her, too. He was on the landing, the next day, right? He could have given Mrs. O. the fatal dose of Digitalin."

"But, El," Sonya said, "what about the letter? Why would Danny deliver a letter that gave the lighthouse and the money to the county instead of to his mother?"

Unfortunately, there was a very good answer for that.

"He didn't know," I said, heavily. "He didn't know Alex had promised the lighthouse and trust fund to his mom. He could have found the letter after he killed Alex, and delivered it because it wasn't, after all, the worst scenario. Riitta would get to stay at the lighthouse and run the retirement home. All would be as it was before Alex Martin came home."

"It'll kill Riitta," Sofi said. "It just can't be Danny. Is there any chance it could just be an old-fashioned accident and that Mrs. O.'s heart wore out?"

I grinned at her. "You sound just like Erik Sundback." I paused, then spoke. "There's one other thing. I think Miss Thyra is involved."

"Good grief, Hatti," Sofi said, "she's a year younger than God."

"I know, I know. What I mean is, I think she saw something. She was up all night preparing for her seminar and she's been acting weird and guilty ever since."

"Like the way Lars acted after he'd had the one-night stand with that waitress," Sofi said, grimly. "That's what you mean, isn't it, Hatti?"

"I did think of that incident," I admitted. "In any case, there's her behavior and there's something else. The last time I spoke with Mrs. Ollanketo she asked me to give a particular mitten to Miss Thyra. At first I thought that since she had slept through the seminar, she might have thought it hadn't happened yet but what if it was intended to be a clue? After all, the murderer thought Mrs. O. knew too much. What if she did know too much? What if she was trying to pass along her knowledge with the blue mitten?"

"Pass it to Miss Thyra?"

"Well, yes, but not only Miss Thyra. Maybe she figured Thyra would understand the clue and would pass it along to someone else. The sheriff, for example. Or me."

"Have you talked with Thyra," Elli asked. "Maybe she hasn't had a chance to tell you."

"I went to her room last night. It was really late and I pretty much scared her, I think, but that's exactly what I asked her. She pointed out the pattern was roses and that roses have thorns."

"She fingered Danny?" Elli sounded appalled.

"That's how it seemed to me. But maybe it isn't that. Maybe she was just putting up a smokescreen, a kind of red herring. Maybe she's protecting the killer out of fear."

"That doesn't make much sense," Sofi said.

"It does, in a way. As she pointed out to me, she isn't mobile. It was the same for Flossie Ollanketo. They were old and poor and running away or hiding out wasn't an option. They were sitting ducks."

"So," Sonya said, softly, "was Captain Jack." She smiled, apologetically. "I'm not sure we helped you very much." Just then the doorbell rang and I glanced up at my mother's big kitchen clock.

"Who'd be here at this hour?"

"I'll check," Sonya said, disappearing through the kitchen door and down the hallway. She returned a couple of minutes later holding a package.

"Who was it," Sofi joked. "Jehovah's Witnesses?"

"Max Guthrie." Sonya's creamy complexion appeared pale and, for once, she looked every year of her age.

"What is it," I asked, frightened. "Did something happen?"

"No. He just came to give you this." She handed me the package and I opened it to find a soft, folded tee shirt printed with the word *Big Two-Hearted River*.

"Cool," I said. "It's just a joke. Why didn't he come in?"

"He said he wouldn't because you had company and besides it was late."

Sofi chanted in a singsong voice. "Hatti has a boyfriend, Hatti has a boyfriend. And she just missed a booty call."

Sonya didn't laugh. She didn't even smile. And neither did Elli. She looked at me, searchingly, and held her tongue.

Needless to say, when my visitors left a few minutes later, I was happy to close the door on them. I let the dogs out one last time then dragged up the front hall stairs to my childhood bedroom where I stripped, showered and pulled on a ragged nightshirt. Then I stretched out on my back and stared up at the glow-in-the-dark stars Pops had stuck to my ceiling twenty years earlier. The stars were yellowed and they'd lost their glow but they were still there. I was still here, too. Was this where I wanted to stay?

I didn't know the answer to that any more than I knew the answer to the question of who had killed Alex Martin.

CHAPTER 28

I had just slapped duct tape over Miss Thyra's mouth and pinched her nose shut with a clothespin when my cellphone chimed and I grabbed it. My heart was making so much noise I could barely hear the caller's voice and I was unsure whether or not I was still asleep.

"Hello? Hello? Emergency?"

There was a brief pause and then Riitta said, "Hatti? Are you all right? Did I wake you?"

I sat up and, belatedly, recognized the old wooden dresser Pops had painted pink for me the year I was ten and the plastic easy chair with the skirt that had provided a hiding place for my guinea pig during that same era. I inhaled a deep breath and calmed down. "Sorry. I was in the middle of a nightmare."

"I don't wonder with everything that's going on. I'm sorry I woke you." I noticed she sounded better, less stressed.

"What's going on? Any news about Tom?"

"Tom?"

She sounded as if she could barely remember the man.

"Oh, no. He's still in Frog Creek as far as I know." Again her voice changed. This time I thought I caught an undercurrent of pain.

"Don't worry," I said, consolingly. "Clump can't keep him forever."

"I don't know why not. I doubt if anyone else will come forward to confess."

"You're upset with him? He was just trying to keep Danny from being arrested."

"You'd think he'd get tired of always playing the hero."

The acid criticism was so unlike her I was shocked into silence while Riitta tried to justify her attitude.

"The thing is that the confession's too obvious," she explained. "There's not enough motive. Anyway, no one who knows him will believe Tom Kukka pushed someone off a tower."

"I agree."

"Yes, but don't you see? That just means everyone will know he confessed to protect someone."

"And you think the gun will turn to Danny?"

"He was up in the tower that night and he had years of pent up anger against his father. It looks like a spontaneous crime, too, doesn't it? Something a nineteen-year-old would be likely to do in a reckless moment."

"I grant you all that but then why hasn't Clump arrested Danny?"

"He doesn't have the evidence to counter a confession. Besides, you know our sheriff. He's always interested in the low-hanging fruit. But as soon as somebody proves it wasn't Tom, Danny will be in the crosshairs."

It occurred to me that Riitta's words seemed to have come straight from Erik Sundback's mouth. She sounded brainwashed.

"We've got to get this cleared up, you know? We can't get the retirement home up and running until this is over. Do you have any ideas about it?"

"The good news is, there are lots of clues. The bad news is, they don't seem to add up to anybody in particular." *Except your son.*

She sighed. "Well, I apologize again for waking you up. I really called about this afternoon's tea party."

"If you want to cancel, I completely understand. It's a tense time for everybody."

"Oh, no, no. Erik's cook is in the kitchen, as we speak, creating a banquet worthy of the Grand Hotel. You can't believe this house. Everything is state-of-the-art. Even the floors are heated in the winter! The kitchen is a perfect dream with thick, marble countertops and every appliance known to man. It's hard to believe we're in Red Jacket."

I wondered if, buried under all the years of self-sacrifice and unselfishness, Riitta coveted a home of her own. Maybe she was a little bit human, after all.

"How's Miss Thyra holding up?"

"She's still acting strange. I thought that once we were away from the lighthouse she'd get back to being herself."

"Be careful what you wish for," I said, remembering Miss Thyra's sharp tongue.

"She won't leave her room, Hatti. She won't leave her bed. I told her about all the women coming over for tea and she said she'd come out for that but she doesn't look well. I wonder if she's got another migraine."

Maybe. If migraine was a code word for guilt trip.

"My sense is that she knows something about Alex's murder."

"Then why doesn't she say something?"

"I think she will if we can just give her time."

"Time," she repeated, dully. "You know what? I'd give almost anything for this to never have happened. In the end, nothing will have changed. The lighthouse will become a retirement home whether I run it or not and that's what would have happened if Alex had never come back. Why couldn't he have stayed out of it?" And then she muttered, with apparent irrelevance, "damn Tom, anyway."

A quote popped into my head.

"Remember what Snorkmaiden said in *Comet in Moominland?* I would save your life eight times a day if only I could."

There was such a long silence and it was so absolute I

wondered if she'd hung up. When she finally spoke, she was all business.

"Erik suggested we invite the local ladies to tea, Diane Hakala, Mrs. Sorensen, Edna Moilanen, Ronja, Elli and Sofi and Sonya. He thought they might like to see the house and that they could cheer up Miss Thyra."

"The younger women are all working," I said, "but I'll check with the church ladies. I'm sure they'd love to come to tea."

"Hatti," she hesitated.

"What is it? What can I do?"

"Just ask them to bring along their knitting. You know how that is. Knitting always makes everything more relaxed."

She sounded so much like her old practical, low-key self that I suddenly couldn't hold back.

"Riitta, are you going to marry Erik?"

"I don't know. Anyway, he hasn't asked me."

"You must know whether you love him or not."

She sighed. "Life is not that straightforward. I think you've discovered that for yourself, haven't you? It's not black and white, love or not love. Wasn't it Shakespeare who talked about having one bright, particular star? Well, that's a lovely idea, like saying there is one soulmate for each of us. But it isn't true. People are generally lovable and there are always others to consider in any decision. Rest assured I'll try to make the best decision for everyone involved, okay?"

I wasn't okay with that.

"I think this one time you should just be selfish. Do what you want to do."

"You're a good friend. I'll see you this afternoon."

"Wait," I said, remembering my own agenda. "Do you have any financial papers regarding the lighthouse?"

"There's a notebook of all the stuff we've given the county over the past year, including the value of the property and plans for improvements. Erik's got a copy in his study. You're welcome to take a look at it this afternoon."

As I disconnected, I noticed the tee shirt I'd dropped on the rocking chair last night, the one from Max. I grinned, started to put it on, and realized it wouldn't do for a tea party. Since I hadn't done any laundry the previous evening, I ransacked my mom's closet and came up with a white tennis shirt embroidered with a pink cat with green rhinestone eyes and a matching pink, pleated tennis skirt. I grabbed a pair of pink Keds, too. Not a perfect outfit for high tea on the peninsula but better than cutoffs.

Larry and Lydia ate while I brewed a pot of coffee and popped some bread into the toaster. Then I took my breakfast and a couple of rawhide sticks into the parlor. The dogs settled on the floor and I sat on the piano bench as we enjoyed the morning sun.

After my first cup of coffee, I noticed the book on the music rack.

My mother, like most Finnish-American women, is a conscientious housekeeper who imposes certain rules on herself. She believes, for example, that artwork should be rearranged every few months and coffee table books rotated, in part because of the fresh environment such changes provide and in part because it is silent testimony that there is routine cleaning going on in the home.

My mom has carried out and expanded this philosophy to (some might say) an absurd degree in the swapping out of sheet music on the piano's music stand. One week, she'll post a Mozart sonata. Another week, we'll see a hymnal. Today's offering, which must have been there since before she left for Helsinki, and which revealed, all too clearly what was on her mind, was my first piano book, John Thompson's *Teaching Little Fingers to Play.* The songs inside consisted of three notes in the treble clef and they had names like *The Postman,* and *The Bee,* and *Sandman's Near.*

The message to my sister and me? *Give me more grandchildren!*

Oddly enough, the ham-fisted memo did not get my back up. Instead, it got me to thinking about Riitta. I knew she'd been concerned about the ten years or so between herself and Tom. Was this possible marriage to Erik Sundback intended to rescue Tom from a childless union? It seemed in character. It also seemed like the Snorkmaiden's words about rescuing would apply to her as much as they did to Tom.

I got up from the piano bench, called the dogs, and fetched the leashes. It was time for fresh air, a fresh perspective and a look-in on Einar. The doorbell rang just as we reached it and my heart jumped into my throat, as if the lighthouse murderer might be standing on the other side. I told myself not to be ridiculous and I practically ripped the door off its hinges, wrenching it open.

"Tennis anyone?" Max Guthrie grinned at me from the other side of the screen. "This the fashionable attire for housework?"

"Housework? What's that?" I felt a little breathless. "Thank you for the tee shirt. I love it."

"Obviously," he said.

"Oh, I couldn't wear it today. I'm going to a tea party."

"Uh-huh."

"Why didn't you come in last night? It was just a few friends, Elli, Sofi and Sonya."

"It was late. I brought someone I want you to meet."

He stepped aside and I realized he wasn't alone. There was another man with him, taller than Max and younger with rapidly thinning dark hair and an engaging smile.

"Hatti Lehtinen, meet my friend Finn."

"Finn?" I grinned at him. "As in Huck or Helsinki?"

He had a nice laugh.

"Neither. I'm from County Cork by way of the Bronx. Finn O'Leary at your service."

"Finn, in addition to being an avid would-be fisherman, is a former employee of Alex Martin. I thought you might have some questions for him."

"Geez Louise," I said. "Yeah, I do."

"And we thought," Max continued, "we could trade the answers for some coffee and prune tarts."

Very belatedly I remembered my manners and invited them in. After we'd sat down at the wicker table with fresh coffee and tarts retrieved from the freezer and thawed in the microwave, I looked at Finn.

"So you came several thousand miles just to fish?"

"I've kept in touch with Max's adventures here in God's Country and I wanted to see for myself." He gave me an appreciative wink. "I didn't expect to find a golden-haired angel."

I hooted. "Don't be impressed. You can't swing a dead cat around here without hitting a blue-eyed blond."

"Possibly," Max put in, "because you're all related to each other."

"Descendants of Finnish miners," I explained. "And, believe me, we're not angels."

"Hatti's the pick of the litter," Max said, a gleam in his coffee-colored eyes. "Not just because she's beautiful. She's smart, too."

Max thought I was beautiful *and* smart? I couldn't think of anything to say.

"Very smart," Finn said. "She can make coffee and bake."

"Full disclosure," I said, "my mom made those at Christmas time. They were frozen."

"Hey, you were smart enough to pick a mom who can bake. That's smart enough for me. Think she'll come to live with us after the kids are born?"

"Sure, as long as we buy a house across the street." I grinned at him. I'd forgotten how much fun it was to flirt. I realized I was enjoying myself but this was too good an opportunity to miss. I needed to pick the guy's brain.

"You really worked for Alex Martin?"

"I was head of his communications department for about six months. I left to go back to journalism and now I freelance for a couple of publications. Frankly, I'm writing a piece on my late boss and hoped you and I could exchange some information."

"I don't know much about Alex. I met him for the first time the night he died."

"Luckily, that's the exact night I'm interested in," he said. "It was kind of a strange situation, wasn't it? A dark and stormy night, a mysterious visitor, a bump on the head followed by a half-gainer off a tower?"

I sent Max a questioning look and he shrugged.

"Don't tell him anything you don't want him to know."

Finn shook his head. "I didn't come here to hassle you. I'll tell you what I can about Alex in L.A. You can talk or not talk. No quid pro quo."

I nodded but reminded myself I'd have to be careful. I simply could not tell the media about Riitta's long ago involvement with Alex or even about his more recent tete-a-tete with Chakra. It wouldn't be fair to the dead. And it wouldn't be fair to the living.

"What was he like to work for?"

"A roller coaster. A tilt-a-whirl. Any kind of carnival ride you can think of. The man had innovative ideas and bold moves. He was loaded with charisma. Everybody wanted to work with him, at least at first."

"And then?"

"It was something about his attitude. Hard to put into words. One day you felt like amigos, the next day there was a distance and you weren't sure how it had gotten there or why. And then if you crossed him, in any way, large or small, you got your head chopped off. It wasn't just personal relationships. It was business deals, too." Finn stopped for a sip of coffee. "I don't think I've ever met anyone who was so self-protective. He must have been royally screwed over at some point in his life because he just wouldn't tolerate anything negative. If he heard second-hand that you said something disloyal about him, you were out on your butt."

"Is that what happened to you?"

He shook his head. "I didn't get canned but the gilt had worn off our relationship and I knew it was a matter of time. I decided not to wait around with my head on the chopping block. He didn't take my defection well at all. Got me blackballed at a couple of newspapers."

"You make him sound so vindictive."

"He was vindictive, Hatti," Finn said, seriously. "You know how some people are fueled by anger? Alex got his kicks from making people pay for transgressions against him."

"He seemed pretty successful," I said.

"Oh, he was. Wildly successful. Worth something like a hundred million and climbing. Where the attitude hurt him was personally. He could and did cut off a friend or a girlfriend without a backward look. I think the shock was greater because he'd been so personable in the beginning." Finn had lost his charming smile. Lines scored his cheeks and a muscle worked in his jaw.

"The worst situation was watching what he did to his wife."

"You knew his wife?"

"We were friends, of a sort. She'd worked for him before she got her break in show business and she liked to come into the office."

"How did she react to his mercurial temperament?"

"I don't think she liked it but she tolerated it. At least until he did it to her. One day things were okay between them and the next day, it was over. I found her in the bar near the office and she cried on my shoulder. When Alex found out, that was pretty much the end for me."

"And for her?"

"Yeah. She and I spoke a few times after we were both cut off. She was a basket case and finally moved out of the area."

"She moved up here to the Keweenaw," I said. Finn blinked at me. "You knew that already, didn't you? That's the real reason you came up to see Max."

"One of the reasons," he admitted. "I liked Stella. A lot. I wanted to check on her."

"Have you seen her yet?" He shook his head. "Are you going to see her?"

"I don't know. We'll see."

"For what it's worth," I said, "I think she's found some closure." He looked startled.

"What makes you think that?"

"She told me."

"That means she met him, doesn't it? They got together?"

I shook my head at him.

"If you've got questions, you'll have to ask her. It isn't my business."

There was a long silence as Finn peered into my eyes.

"Hatti, are you certain Stella didn't kill him?"

I looked from Finn to Max then back to Finn.

"Honestly? I have no earthly idea who killed him."

After a moment, Max spoke.

"I think we could all use some fresh air, Umlaut. When we arrived you were about to walk the dogs. May we come along?"

As we carried our dishes to the sink and I corralled the canines I heard Finn speaking to Max under his breath.

"What the hell," he growled, "is an umlaut?"

Definitely not a Helsinki Finn.

On the way down Calumet Street, Finn entertained us with the story of his flight from L.A. and some other anecdotes but when we got to the corner of Third Street and Main, the point in town where you can see both the downtown area and the remnants of the mine and the railroad that served it, he stopped short, his jaw hanging.

"What," he asked, "in the name of the Father, the Son and the Holy Ghost, is Notre Dame doing here in Red Jacket?"

I laughed. "My sister calls it Quasimodo's winter home. It's a gothic cathedral, built during the height of the copper boom when the town had money to burn. These days it's St. Heikki's Finnish Lutheran Church."

"What about that," he asked, pointing at the shops on Main Street. "Who'd have thought there would be columns and cupolas and all that bric-a-brac up here in Paul Bunyan country? It looks like Victorian London without the snow."

"Oh, we have snow," I assured him. "Wait a couple of months."

"In fact," Max added, with a grin at me, "our motto is Shovel and Swat. If we're not pushing snow to one side of the road or the other, we're fighting a pestilent invasion of black flies."

"There are no flies now," Finn said.

"I know," I said. "This is midsummer, our good month."

CHAPTER 29

T he bell over the door jingled as we stepped into the bait shop. I'd never met anything but silence there so I was taken aback to hear voices. More than one, too. Was it possible that Einar was engaged in a conversation?

I quickly realized my mistake. The voices belonged to Arvo Maki and Erik Sundback who stood on either side of the gnome like pair of protective Vikings.

Arvo, gesticulating with his hands, looked over at us, registered the presence of a newcomer, broke off his conversation and started to cross the room.

"Hatti-girl," he said, with total sincerity, "just the person I want to see." He seemed re-collect himself. "Both of us want to see," he corrected, glancing at Erik. "This morning, you're the Queen of the May."

"A sight for sore eyes," Erik confirmed, walking toward us. "You have a minute to talk some lighthouse business?"

I introduced everyone and I could tell that Arvo, at least, would have liked to stay to speak longer with Finn. Finn, on the other hand, was mesmerized by the fly Einar was tying.

"Why don't the three of you go for coffee," Max said, pleasantly. "Finn can get a look at some of Einar's handiwork and I'll keep an eye on the brats." He jerked his head toward Larry, whose ears he was rubbing.

We agreed and set off across the street.

There was, as usual, no traffic at all on Main Street even though it was late on a weekday morning. We jaywalked easily toward our destination, a tiny coffee shop called Common Grounds. The hole-in-the-wall had been created by accident, during a long ago renovation project. It was too small for most enterprises and had been used, for temporary projects, like headquarters for the Copper County Homecoming Parade or take-out endeavors.

For the past year it had been vacant and Arvo had worked a deal with the business teacher at the high school to set up a coffee shop with a revolving staff of teenagers in an effort to get the young people some work experience and allow them to earn a little money during the summer. The teacher's job was to provide the kids, Arvo, always generous, provided the funding.

Today's barrista was unknown to me, which was something of a surprise since basically everybody in Red Jacket knows everybody else. The new girl looked up as we entered and I found myself staring at a heart-shaped face framed with white-blond hair pulled back into a thick single braid. Long dark eyelashes accentuated eyes of Aegean blue, or at least that's the adjective that came into my mind. Even in a place awash in blue eyes, these were stunning.

Her features were delicate and her pale, smooth complexion tinted a natural pink. Even in a yellow, company-provided tee shirt and white shorts she appeared both regal and ethereal. When she spotted Arvo, her full lips spread into a welcoming smile that revealed perfect, white teeth.

Arvo, who is always at his best in social situations, could not find a word to say. He looked pole-axed.

"Hi," I said, to cover for him. "I'm Hatti Lehtinen."

"Liisa Pelonen," she said. Even her voice was graceful.

Arvo pulled himself together and completed the introductions.

"Liisa went to the high school over at Ahmeek," he said. "Since it finally closed its doors, she's going to finish her senior year here at Copper County High, and she's done Pauline and me the honor of agreeing to stay with us." He beamed at his protégé. "Liisa has a beautiful voice, too, Hatti. She's already singing with the church choir."

Geez Louise. Sometimes I couldn't believe how slow I was on the uptake. This blond beauty wasn't just Liisa Pelonen, high school guest of the Makis. This girl was Ronja Laplander's worst nightmare. And with good reason. Liisa looked like a Norman Rockwell version of St. Lucy. She looked more like St. Lucy than St. Lucy. Astrid Laplander, with her short, squat body and the Dutch-boy cut of her straight, dark hair, did not stand a chance.

But the pang that reverberated through me as I gazed at this vision of loveliness was due to more than Ronja's disappointment. I recognized the longing in Arvo's middle-aged eyes and even though I knew it wasn't infatuation of a man for a woman, but of a childless man for a daughter, I felt an uneasy premonition and found all my sympathy was for Arvo's wife, Pauline. That look of stark enchantment had nothing at all to do with her.

Erik shepherded me to the lone, tiny table in the place while Arvo waited for Liisa to fill the order.

"It's just infatuation," he said, echoing my thought. "She's just so unbelievably beautiful. Nothing to worry about."

"Right," I murmured. Erik was a friend but he was a new friend and I didn't want to make a lot of Arvo's vulnerability. But the lawyer had figured it out.

"He and his wife are childless?" I nodded. "I imagine that's it then. This girl gives him a chance to play that role for a while." He grinned. "It'll wear off when she starts breaking curfew and refusing to help with the dishes."

"He's good with kids. He's always been a sort of honorary uncle to my sister and cousin and me. He used to dress up as *Joulupukki* at Christmas time."

"*Joulupukki,*" he repeated, "Santa Claus?"

"Literally it means Yule Goat," I explained. "But, yes, these days *Joulupukki* appears with no horns." It was time to get back to the problem of the moment. "What are we going to do about the situation at the lighthouse?"

Sundback sighed and ran his fingers through his short curls.

"The retirement home will be okay," he said. "The probate court will accept Alex's letter to Riitta as a legitimate expression of his intent."

"But what if it was a forgery?" The words were out before I could stop them. Erik blinked.

"What are you talking about, Hatti? There's no question of that, is there?" I shrugged.

"My friends and I drew up a kind of timeline last night. We can't see any reason for Alex changing his mind about the disposition of the lighthouse and the trust fund after he'd said one thing to Riitta and, more than that, we can't see that there was enough time for him to write the new letter and deliver it. There is no time unaccounted for between the end of Riitta's visit and Alex's plunge off the gallery."

"We talked about this before," he said, in a calm voice. "Alex could have given the letter to Jack to deliver."

"I can't see it. It doesn't fit. Why should he tell Riitta one thing and change his mind minutes later? I'll tell you what, Erik. I don't think Alex wrote that letter at all."

"What are you saying? If he didn't, who did?"

"The killer." I made a conscious effort to keep my voice low even though the other two people in the room were clearly not listening to us. "For some unknown reason, the killer didn't want the lighthouse to go to Riitta. He or she wanted it to go to the county."

"That's assuming a lot," Erik said. "How would the killer know what Alex had said to Riitta?"

I thought that through.

"You have a point. Maybe he or she didn't know. Maybe it has nothing to do with what he said to Riitta and everything to do with his earlier statement that he was going to keep the trust fund money and turn the lighthouse into a golf course."

"Hatti," he said, looking directly into my eyes, "think about what you're saying. Who would commit murder to make sure that a municipality wasn't cheated out of a building? Who was that desperate to save the lighthouse?"

Two names flashed before my eyes. *Tom Kukka and Riitta.*

I stared at the attorney, helplessly, at my wit's end.

"You know what? I think you might be right about the letter. Not that someone else wrote it but that it was superseded by another letter, one that deeded the lighthouse and the money to Riitta, personally."

"Why? Why do you think that?"

"Mostly based on the fact that Alex Martin was a top-notch businessman which means he was used to putting everything in writing. My guess is that, after he decided to give the property to Riitta, he wrote a letter to that effect and that the killer found that letter up in the watch room. Found it," he repeated, "and destroyed it."

"Oh."

"But don't forget, Martin had the lifetime habits of a mogul. He'd have made a copy. In this case, the situation being as irregular as it was, he'd have made a copy and hidden it."

I gasped. "You think the copy is somewhere in the watch room."

"I'd bet a cup of coffee on it."

"What-what would that letter tell us?"

"For one thing, it would tell us his real wishes. And it's possible, and even likely, I think that the letter might give us a clue as to the identity of the killer."

"You think Alex knew someone intended to kill him?"

"Maybe not that. But he was as astute as they come. How many times in your brief acquaintance did he make the point that he never let anyone take advantage of him? My guess is he was out to punish someone and that punishment was going to take the form of a public denouncement.

Hatti, we've got to get into the lighthouse and find that letter. It's the only way we'll be able to get Tom Kukka off the hook. It's the only way to keep Danny from being arrested or, worse, Riitta."

"But how? The lighthouse is off limits. Clump has locked it down. No one's allowed in."

A mischievous smile twisted the attorney's lips and his eyes twinkled. There is something appealing about a rule-follower who can, from time to time, break out of the box.

"What about the milk chute rule? Surely we can get around the sheriff's embargo."

"We?" He nodded.

"My plan is to go on out there after the tea party. I've got to run down to Houghton to the office but I'll be back late in the afternoon. I can stop by for you and Riitta and we can go on out there together. My theory, in case you're wondering, is that there's safety in numbers, if only the fact that we can't all fit into the Frog Creek jail cell." His crooked grin was very endearing.

"If we break in to steal the letter, it won't be admissible in court will it?"

"I don't think the thing will get that far," he said, the twinkle disappearing from his eyes. "Whoever did this is one of us, Hatti. I think we can count on a confession somewhere down the line." He seemed to remember Tom Kukka. "A real confession," he amended. "I think we can get this whole thing resolved in the next few hours. What do you say?"

I nodded. "What do you think really happened?"

"My gut tells me it was one of those charged conversations that got out of control. I think we can mount an effective defense based on the unusual circumstances and the family connections."

"You still think Danny did it?"

"Let me put it this way. I do not expect Danny to pay a great penalty. I expect he'd suffer a lot more if Tom Kukka wound up with a life sentence."

At long last Arvo arrived at our table balancing three

lidded cups of coffee. I didn't remember until that minute that I'd intended to drink water. I'd already had enough caffeine to send me to the moon, as Pops would say, without a rocket ship. There was a dreamy look on Arvo's face that made me very uneasy.

"Hazelnut blizzard latte for Hatti," he joked, putting down one of the cups of plain coffee, "black forest light roast for Erik and coconut raspberry lemonade cream tart espresso for me."

I thanked him but wondered, not for the first time, what it would be like to have a Starbucks franchise in Red Jacket.

"Did you know," Arvo said, "that Finns drink more coffee than any other country in the world on a per capita basis?"

"It doesn't surprise me," I replied. "I imagine we've cornered the market on Vics Vapo Rub, too."

"I love to hear stuff like this," Erik said. "I've got a lot to catch up on in terms of Finnish culture."

"What about your Swedish side," I asked, curiously. "Do you want to learn about that, too?"

"I identify with the Finns. I'm not much on those little red ponies."

"The Dala horses. I have to admit, I think they're darling. A Dala horse would be pretty on the back of a mitten. Maybe I'll speak about that with Miss Thyra." I realized I was babbling.

"Look at you," Arvo said to Erik, "you're influencing us with your Swedish culture without even trying. Well, tit for tat. I insist that you join me in a sauna sometime soon."

"I'd be honored," Erik said. "After all, it will be winter again before you know it."

"Yes." Arvo's face flushed and his eyes brightened. "Christmas. This year we will have a very special St. Lucy, one who sings like an angel."

"Uh, Arvo, don't you think we should let the high schoolers make that decision?" I eyed him, uneasily. "That's the tradition."

"Of course, of course. But there's no question of what

they will decide, is there? She is perfect for the role. Perfection." His eyes wandered over to the counter where Liisa was waiting on a new customer. "St. Lucy in the flesh. Anybody can see it."

I had a feeling Ronja Laplander wasn't going to see it.

"What did you want to talk to me about?"

"Hmm? Oh, the St. Lucy festival. This year I want to expand it. We'll draw people from Lansing and Detroit and even Chicago and Gary, Indiana. I want a new costume, one that is custom made and a wreath that can hold real, lighted candles, not just the electric ones. We can have a craft fair, too, with booths in the high school parking lot and food vendors, the way we did for *Juhannus*."

"What about the snow?"

"Hmm? Oh, we'll double the budget for snow removal. And we can have an ice sculpting contest and an old-fashioned wife-carrying contest and maybe even a dog sled race. This will be the best festival ever, Hatti! And I want you to be in charge of it." I just stared at him. "Oh, have you talked with Pauline? We decided to paint Liisa's room pink. Imagine, Hatti-girl, a pink room in our house. It has a canopy bed with a pink spread and even the carpet is pink. A paradise for a little girl."

I exchanged a dismayed look with Erik Sundback as Arvo continued to talk.

"And Pauline has chosen a sparkly pink dress for Liisa to wear to homecoming. She'll look like a princess."

The homecoming dance was held in October.

"We'll get her another dress for Christmas. Red velvet with lace? Or maybe something white with fur trim."

"Arvo," I said, unable to help myself, "Liisa is a person. A teen-ager. She isn't a doll."

He smiled at me. "I know she isn't a doll, Hatti-girl. She's the daughter we never had."

CHAPTER 30

I don't know whether I've mentioned this before but Red Jacket is a small town and pretty much everything, except the Shopko out on U.S. Route 41, is accessible on foot. Despite the heat of the day, Aunt Ianthe and Miss Irene had expressed a preference for walking the three blocks to Erik Sundback's house and I agreed to stop by to pick them up.

"Why, Henrikki," my aunt beamed at me when she opened the door. "You look so festive."

I knew she was reacting to the emerald eyes in the cat on my tennis shirt and possibly, the large plastic hoop earrings I'd added at the last minute. I thanked her.

My aunt was wearing a cotton shirtwaist with a blue-and-white polka-dot pattern and a fabric covered belt. Miss Irene's dress was a similar style but made out of seersucker with a thin red-and-white stripe. Both ladies wore strap-on canvas sandals that revealed the reinforced toes of their stockings. Both wore white beads, carried white pocketbooks and their knitting bags.

"You look lovely, too," I said. "Both of you. A breath of pure summer."

"Oh my, how poetic," Miss Irene said as we set off in the mid-day heat. "I wonder if we should have worn hats," she said, after a few minutes. "And gloves. My mother was a big believer in hats and gloves."

"The gloves would be too warm, dearie," Aunt Ianthe said, "and, as for the hats, you know what the Good Book says about lilies of the field."

It was a perfect intro for Miss Irene and she took it.

"And why take ye thought for raiment? Consider the lilies of the field, how they grow; they toil not, neither do they spin."

There seemed to be nothing to add to that.

"How have the two of you adjusted to being home again," I asked.

"Well, dearie, we can't seem to stop talking about the two murders, you know? Irene believes someone killed Alex Martin in a fit of passion."

"Really?" The fact that Miss Irene's theory coincided with Erik Sundback's idea of impulse, surprised me.

"Because he was so handsome," Miss Irene said. "Just like a movie star. Looks like that just drives a person wild."

"So you think it was a woman?"

"Not," Miss Irene said, mysteriously, "necessarily."

"I have a different take on it," Aunt Ianthe said, before I could question Miss Irene further. "Looks are all very well and good in fiction but in real life, I believe it comes down to the money. Isn't that what they always say? Follow the money. Who gets the money in the end?"

"You mean the lighthouse?"

"The lighthouse, yes, and Johanna Marttinen's fortune. But what about the rest of Alex Martin's money. Surely he was a wealthy man."

It was an excellent point and one whose answer I didn't know. Chakra had said she was owed ten million dollars but whether she got that as a settlement at the time of her marriage or it was something she'd get in the event of Alex's death, I didn't know. And, anyway, he was worth ten times that much. Who got the rest of it?

"Frankly, Hatti, human beings are self-centered and greedy."

I stared at this woman I'd known all my life. I couldn't remember hearing her speak critically before.

"Irene doesn't like to hear me say it, but, the fact is, you learn a lot about human nature in a third-grade classroom. Selfish, greedy and cruel. It takes a lot of work to turn a child into a compassionate adult, Hatti. That's why we have parents. That's why we have church. Most important of all, that's why we have community."

"But, Ianthe," Miss Irene said, "even if you are right about the reason for killing Mr. Martin, what about Flossie?"

"Flossie, my dear, knew too much. You know how she liked to listen to conversations that no one else could hear? It was her great skill and she was so proud of it. She must have discovered a secret and that secret threatened someone so she had to go. Someone was clever about the syringes. Very clever. My land! Look at the hollyhocks in Ralph Bekkala's yard. They are monstrous. We'll have to ask him whether he uses anything more than compost."

The sky was a deep blue with a few fluffy clouds along the horizon and we lapsed into conversations about the conditions of the yards and gardens we passed. It felt normal, restful, as far from murder as it was possible to get, and I was almost sorry to reach Erik Sundback's house on Cedar Crescent.

It was strange to be visiting the old Eilola house, considering my lifelong obsession with the crescent.

Small towns in Michigan, unlike those in New England, are seldom built around a quaint town square. They are more likely to be on a grid and Red Jacket is a perfect example. Our east-west streets are numbered while our north south streets have names like Oak, Maple and Chestnut.

Cedar Crescent was the exception to the rule. It started to run north and south then it unexpectedly curved as it hugged the grassed area of Quincy Park. As a child I'd been mortally envious of the kids who lived on Cedar Crescent because of their proximity to the flooded ice rink.

It was just across the street. After I trudged home from school, with my snow pants and parka soaked, I had to wait for my mom to throw them in the dryer before I was allowed to venture back outside. Then it would take me at least twenty minutes to plunge through the snow with my skates over my shoulder and by the time I reached the ice rink, I'd get about fifteen minutes of skating until the street lights came on, the universal signal that it was time to head home. Contrast that to the kids who didn't even have to take off their school clothes. All they had to do was drop their backpacks, pick up their skates and cross the street. For years I convinced myself that Sirrka and Matti Nyykonen and Edward and Peter Johansson and Maria Hulkko had surpassed me at both figure skating and hockey purely because they lived on the Crescent.

Most of the houses on Cedar Crescent were like the rest of the housing stock in Red Jacket, built with wood, steeply pitched rooflines and saunas. Many of them had been ordered pre-fabricated from the Sears catalogue and they'd arrived via cargo train from Chicago.

The Eilola house, so-called, Erik told us, because three generations of that family inhabited it in the middle of the last century, had been Sears's deluxe model and originally purchased by a mid-level mine manager. For the past several decades it had been either rented out or empty and Erik, looking around for an investment and seeing its potential had been able to snag it for a very low price.

"You'd better believe it's been a money pit, though," he told us, as he showed us around. "I had to rip out every beam, stud and strut, lay new floors and put in new drywall, plumbing and electrical. I added a couple of bathrooms and expanded the kitchen, too, but I think it has paid off."

We all agreed with him.

"It's a showplace," I said. He shook his head and smiled at Riitta who had joined us. "I know it needs a woman's touch," he said, softly, taking her hand. She smiled at him and I tried to be happy for them both.

"Quite lovely," Aunt Ianthe said, gazing around the

living room at the modern furniture and bare walls. There wasn't an antimacassar in sight.

"Very Swedish," Miss Irene added, which is her diplomatic way of calling something sleek and colorless.

"Mr. Sundback is Swedish, dear," Aunt Ianthe reminded her friend. "Not that there's anything wrong with that."

Erik laughed. "I'm not offended." He sent a bold look over to Riitta who blushed. "I'm hoping to get more Finnish influence here. Maybe a Marimekko wallhanging and some Toikka birds."

The doorbell rang and he excused himself.

"Oh, my dear," Aunt Ianthe said, gripping Riitta's forearm, "is there something going on between you and Mr. Sundback?"

Riitta looked at me and I tried to think of some way to fob off my aunt but there was no need because Mrs. Moilanen sailed into the room, her bosom extended like the prow of a ship.

"The house has good bones," she said, in her decided way, "but you really must add more color. Perhaps a few paintings on the walls?"

As the rest of the guests arrived, Riitta greeted them and Erik Sundback took me upstairs to his study, which turned out to be the first room on the right at the top of the stairs.

Stepping into the room from the dark, narrow hall, was like stepping into Charlie's chocolate factory. It was light, bright and filled with color that filtered through the stained-glass hangings on the tall windows and life, in the form of strategically placed asparagus ferns. Rows of books marched along built-in bookcases painted white and overhead, a fan, reminiscent of the café in *Casablanca* whirled, creating a refreshing breeze and a gentle monotone. A restored, antique desk and chair sat in one corner and the wooden floor was covered with a thick, brightly colored Persian rug. Photographs and paintings of sailboats and views of the sea hung from the white walls and there was a sense of peace and well-being and summer throughout the room.

"This is where I want to die," Erik said, with a wink, when I looked at him.

"It's where I'd want to live," I replied. "What a sanctuary!"

"I have to admit I spend most of my time here. It keeps me from missing the water, you know?"

I looked at him, curiously.

"Why did you move up here, anyway? What prompted you to buy this house?"

"Like I said, it started out as an investment. It just seemed like I ought to put my money into something substantial. And then, as the renovation got underway, it got more and more complicated and expensive and I started to kind of obsess over it, you know? I didn't want to admit I'd made a mistake. I had put too much into it to abandon the project but was sucking up money like a sponge. I was frustrated. And then, when I realized I'd developed feelings for Riitta, it all became clear. It was worth all the expense because I was building a home for the two of us." He grinned at me. "That may sound pretty silly coming from an old bird like me."

"Could I ask you something?" He nodded. "Why did you agree to sit on the lighthouse commission? It seems to have changed your whole life."

"You're right, Hatti." He seemed surprised to realize it. "I did it because, as Johanna's attorney, I was asked. I found I enjoyed it and I liked Arvo and Riitta."

"So you have no regrets?"

He laughed. "It's not possible to get to my age with no regrets. I have a few. I have hopes, though. I think the changes are all going to be for the better."

"What will happen with the lighthouse if Riitta marries you?"

"It shouldn't be materially affected. If necessary we can find someone else to live there. I'll admit I don't want to share her all the time. And, between you and me, I don't really want to live there."

"And Danny?"

I realized I was holding my breath. I knew Erik suspected Danny of the murders and I thought his answer would reveal just what he thought the young man's prospects were.

"Danny's set to start college at Michigan Tech this fall," he said. His smile indicated he understood the reason for my question. "He can live down in Houghton. Hell, he can live in my condo if he likes. It makes a damn fine bachelor pad."

He pulled open a drawer of the desk and withdrew a three-ring, loose-leaf notebook.

"This is everything we've given the county board about the lighthouse. Just put it back when you're finished. And, don't forget, Riitta and I will pick you up later this afternoon for the big break-in." He made it sound like another of Arvo's over-the-top festivals.

I sat in the swivel chair at the desk and leafed through the pages of boundary descriptions and dimensions and history. I noticed a paragraph that showed the small island I'd visited did indeed belong to the lighthouse property and that it was registered with the state under the name of Agate Island III because there were two other islands with the same name in Lake Superior.

There was a section on what the property was worth and proposed renovations, an application for it to become a licensed retirement home and finally, on the last pages, a reference to Mrs. Marttinen's five-million-dollar trust fund that was to go to the Copper County Board of Commissioners along with the lighthouse.

The Fund was located at Keweenaw Bank and handled by a trust officer named Rodney Q. Wheeler. There was a number attached and, on impulse, I punched that number into my phone. No one answered and I started to hang up when, at the last minute, I decided to leave a message. There was only enough time to say my name and number. And then I glanced at the last page in the notebook. I looked at it for a long minute while I listened to voices from downstairs. It was almost time for tea and I needed to get down there PDQ as Pops would say, but something had caught my eye and I picked up my phone and punched in the number of the Leaping Deer Bed and Breakfast.

During the past three years, while she's been renovating the inn, Elli has had to deal with plenty of red tape. I figured she'd know about county protocols.

Her voice sounded harassed.

"Hey, El. What's going on?"

"Noah's flood and there's not a dove in sight. This two-year-old kid has been here less than an hour and he's managed to flush various stuffed animals down various toilets. The resulting tributaries have come together on the landing where they have effectively drowned my Aubusson carpet."

"Oh, no!"

"It'll dry out or I'll know the reason why. I'm not sure the kid will survive. Anything I can do for you?"

"I was reading the prospectus the lighthouse committee presented to the county board and I was curious about something. It was approved and signed on September third of last year by board chairman William Alanen. He died on Labor Day, just a couple of days later and I thought I'd heard that he was in hospice for several months. So my question is, how could he have signed it?"

"Simple. Clara Kingsbury, the county clerk, has a machine that does what's called ghostwriting or automatic signing of a person's signature. It's done with a real pen and is used by institutions and sports figures, stuff like that. Mister Alanen was still the board chairman even though he was on medical leave so Clara used the machine to sign his name to all documents until he died. It's outdated technology, though. In more enlightened areas than the Keweenaw, people just use a computer application."

"So anybody can sign anybody else's name if they've got an app?"

"Well, you have to obtain the signature and probably get permission but, otherwise, sure.

"Elli, does that mean that Alex Martin's signature on the

letter that was delivered to Riitta _ that it might not have been signed by him?"

"You're asking if it could have been signed with an app?"

"Yep."

"I don't know. Maybe. Aren't you supposed to be at a tea party?"

"Geez Louise! I'll talk to you later."

I hung up and started to stuff the notebook back into the desk drawer when I noticed another notebook in the same drawer. I pulled it out, opened it up, and discovered it was an electronic notebook. The screensaver was a breathtaking photo of what looked like a fifty-foot sailboat tacking into the wind. The sailor at the helm grinned at the photographer and it occurred to me that while I'd seen Erik Sundback smile, I'd never seen such unmitigated joy in his face. There was no question he was in his element.

"Hatti?" At the sound of Riitta's voice at the top of the stairs I closed the notebook and slid it back into the drawer under the report.

CHAPTER 31

The oval dining room table was set with a blush-hued tablecloth of fine linen along with matching napkins. The china, fluted with little blue rosebuds, looked like Wedgewood and reminded me, oddly, of Mrs. Ollanketo's blue mitten. Luckily, it wasn't a sad reminder. The teacups were banded with the same roses and the centerpiece picked up the color with iris, white daisies and pink roses. A highly polished sterling silver tiered-dish held tiny sandwiches, raspberry scones, delicately tinted macarons, crumpets and shortbread. There were bowls of fruit cut into bite-sized pieces or, in the case of the melons, scooped into balls and at each place there was an individual fresh pink rose and a miniature trifle glass filled with something that looked like peppermint stick ice cream.

My first thought was how much all the church ladies would love it and I was right.

Diane Hakala was on one side of Riitta, with Edna Moilanen on the other. Aunt Ianthe sat next to Ronja Laplander and Mrs. Sorensen and Miss Irene was between the pastor's wife and me. The chair on my other side was empty.

"Where's Miss Thyra," I asked Riitta.

"Ssh," she said, folding her hands in front of her and

closing her eyes. "Come Lord Jesus be our guest," she said, "and let these gifts to us be blest. Amen."

No one joined in. Lutherans have a strong tradition of decorum that doesn't include touching. We don't hold hands to pray. We don't indulge in group prayers. We seldom dance and we never, ever speak in tongues or roll on the floor. The hostess is the unspoken, designated lead in praying and the rest of us fold our hands and follow along with a silent Amen.

The blessing given, Riitta stood to pour tea.

"Miss Thyra is still in bed," she said. "Erik checked on her just before he left for the office. He said she was awake but wanted to rest a little more before joining us for the knitting."

That seemed odd. "I thought this party was for her."

"You can lead a horse to water, Henrikki," Mrs. Moilanen said, overhearing us.

"She hasn't felt well for a number of days now," Riitta said, vaguely.

"Well, well, of course not," Mrs. Moilanen put in. "Good gracious, two murders at the lighthouse. It's enough to put anybody off their feed." She helped herself to a scone which she then drowned in heaping spoonfuls of lingonberry jam and clotted cream.

"Riitta, my dear, this tea party is simply spectacular," Aunt Ianthe said. "And this house. Well!"

"I know," Riitta said. "It is nice, isn't it? Do you know Erik came up with most of the ideas himself? He's understandably proud of it." She sent me a glance of appeal and I knew she wanted me to change the subject before someone launched into speculation about her relationship with Erik and I searched my mind for something to say. In the end, though, it was Edna Moilanen who rescued her.

"You know what would complement these watercress sandwiches? My vinegar cabbage."

"I thought you were going to say sauerkraut soup," Ronja Laplander said. "Or, maybe, lutefisk."

Everyone laughed.

"Of course *Joulutorttu* would go well with this meal, too," Ronja went on. "Before you know it, it will be Christmas." She was beginning to sound ominously like Arvo.

"Christmas," Ronja repeated, determined to make her point, "means St. Lucy's Day. This one will be the best one yet. I am planning to make a new crown of candles for Astrid. The old one is getting shabby. I think I'll use a grapevine wreath as a base and I'll wire in the candles and cover the whole thing with evergreens, then." She sounded almost exactly like Arvo, except she was backing a different horse.

"You intend to use real candles?" Diane Hakala sounded impressed but concerned.

"Oh, I don't know how the reverend will feel about that," Mrs. Sorensen said. "Real candles pose such a danger in the church."

"And I don't know how Arvo will feel about Astrid," Mrs. Moilanen said, pointing out that Ronja could not shape events merely by talking about them. "You know he has his heart set on that little songbird of his."

"That would be completely unfair," Ronja pointed out. Her plump cheeks flamed and her dark eyes snapped. "It is Astrid's turn."

"Liisa does look a lot like St. Lucy," Aunt Ianthe said, trying to be fair.

"No one knows what the real St. Lucy looked like," Ronja snapped. "If she was from Italy, she probably was dark, then."

"She's always blond in the pictures," Mrs. Sorensen said, doubtfully.

"So is Jesus," Ronja retorted. "But how many times have we been told that since he was from the Middle East he was most likely of a swarthy complexion?"

"Well, I don't know about that," Aunt Ianthe said. "Could all those illustrators be wrong? Why there's a picture of the Lord in our KJV where he looks just like that Finnish movie star, Viggo Mortensen."

"Viggo Mortensen is not Finnish, Ianthe," Mrs. Moilanen said. "Swedish, probably, or Danish."

"Well, the point is," Ronja said, not wanting to lose this chance of driving home her point, "this is Astrid's year to be St. Lucy."

No one took up the gauntlet, immediately but, after a moment, Mrs. Moilanen's words brought a ray of hope to Ronja's heavy bosom.

"It isn't healthy the way Arvo and Pauline are fawning over that girl."

"They are treating her like visiting royalty." The comment from Mrs. Sorensen was completely out of character. Arvo must really be making a spectacle of himself.

"It's worse than that," Diane Hakala said. "They are behaving as if she were their long, lost child. They're getting too attached to someone else's daughter."

"Mark my words," Mrs. Moilanen said, darkly, "this isn't going to end well."

"Nonsense," Riitta said. She had gotten close to Arvo as well as Erik over the past year and she clearly thought it was time to step in and defend him. "Liisa will be petted and spoiled for a year and then she'll go off to college and the Makis will return to normal. It's just an adventure for them."

No one argued because Riitta was the hostess and it wouldn't be polite. Diane Hakala changed the subject.

"I can't wait to try one of Miss Thyra's mitten patterns," she said. "The one from the work house. I want to make a pair for my cousin's husband, Hugo, who is half Swedish."

The reference reminded me that I was just sitting at a tea party when a double-murder was waiting for me to solve it. Here was a chance to see if anyone else understood the mitten.

"Do you know," I said, impulsively, "that Mrs. Ollanketo asked me to give a blue Arjeplog mitten to Miss Thyra."

"Well, dear, she used the green one in the seminar," Aunt Ianthe said. "Perhaps she wanted Thyra to have both in her collection."

"It was the last thing she said before she died."

A collective gasp rose from the women.

"Her dying words," Mrs. Moilanen said, her voice shaking, "it was a sign. Flossie was giving you a clue."

My pulse rate picked up. Could one of these ladies decipher the clue that had baffled me?

"Not necessarily," Ronja said. She was naturally oppositional. "Mrs. Ollanketo probably didn't know they were her dying words."

"Anyway," Aunt Ianthe said. "Why should she give Henrikki a clue? If knew anything about the murder, why not just tell her?" She looked at Riitta for an answer.

"Well, of course, I don't know what she was thinking," Riitta said, flustered, "but Flossie was self-conscious about her volume."

"If she had information about the murderer she couldn't have just shouted it out," Mrs. Moilanen said. "My gracious, the murderer may have overheard it."

"The thing is," I said, hoping to prime the pump, "I don't know what she was trying to say. I don't know how to interpret the mitten."

"Of course not," Mrs. Moilanen said, promptly, revealing how she'd held onto the Ladies Aid leadership for so long. "That is why she asked you to give it to Thyra. Oh, and by the way, the service for Flossie Ollanketo is scheduled for next Saturday. I spoke with Arvo this morning and the Reverend Sorensen and we agreed that would be the perfect time."

"I have a new recipe for bars," Diane Hakala said, taking the conversation in a completely new direction. "My sister-in-law, the one up in Duluth, heard about it at her Kaleva meeting. It calls for caramels and a German chocolate cake mix."

"Turtle bars," Mrs. Moilanen said, complacently. "Pecans, chocolate chips, evaporated milk. I had them at that sisterhood meeting down in Ontonagon."

"When I lived in Champagne-Urbana, we called them Illini Bars," Mrs. Sorensen said. "Scrumptious."

"If they're so delicious why haven't any of you made them for the potlucks?" Diane sounded a little resentful. There's nothing that offends members of the church kitchen ladies as much as being one-upped on food.

"I can't speak for anyone else," Mrs. Moilanen said, in a statement that was blatantly untrue, "but I have never yet returned home with any of my raspberry ribbon bars. My late husband, Arne, used to swipe half a dozen of them before we went over to the church. Folks would be sorely disappointed if I switched to turtles."

The conversation about the mitten clue was clearly over and so was the tea party. Riitta got to her feet and invited us to take a walk out into the garden and we exited out the sliding glass door that led from the dining room to the yard enclosed by a privacy fence. Because we were on the crescent, the yard belled out behind the house and it was heavily planted with white pines, pin cherries, honeysuckle, holly and bottlebrush grass at the back and several symmetrically placed beds of daisies, brown-eyed Susans, jack-in-the-pulpit, pansies and petunias in the foreground.

In the center of the yard was an ornate white bench that faced a bronze sundial.

Mrs. Moilanen asked Riitta whether the sundial, which had a kind of patina, had been there a long time.

"No. Not at all. It's brand new. See how it sits above the ground? Erik bought it to cover an old well. He said that even with the fence, the well would pose a danger to the neighborhood's children. He is always so considerate." She looked up at the sky which had morphed from cloudless to gray and changed the subject. "Looks like a storm is coming in."

"I suppose the well provided the house with water back in the day," Aunt Ianthe said. "Just like the well at the lighthouse."

"Oh, that isn't really a well," Riitta said. "It's a cistern. It was used to collect rainwater for the lightkeepers and their families."

"I've never liked wells," Mrs. Sorensen said, with a

shiver. "There was one on my grandfather's dairy farm down by Newberry. When I was about six years old, my cousin Antti told me he'd dropped the cat into it."

"Ding, dong, bell," recited Miss Irene. "Pussy's in the well."

"Did the cat die?" Ronja Laplander asked, blunt, as always.

"No. But I almost did. I climbed in to get Puss and then I realized how deep it was. I hung on, crying and whimpering until Antti got his sister Beatrice and they pulled me out."

"What happened to the cat," Mrs. Moilanen asked.

"She was in the barn the whole time. Antti just wanted to scare me. But he could have drowned the cat. And I could have drowned, too. Wells are dangerous."

"Riitta, dear, maybe you should cover the cistern at the lighthouse. The same sort of thing could happen."

"I've considered it," she said, "but it isn't really that deep. Probably about five feet. And there's no water in it these days."

I stared at my cousin.

"Hatti?" Aunt Ianthe was eyeing me with concern. "You look strange."

"Do I? Must be the barometric pressure. I think Riitta's right about the storm. We should be on our way."

"Oh, but I was hoping to see Thyra," Aunt Ianthe said.

"I'll tell you what," Riitta suggested, as we trooped back into the house to retrieve our purses and knitting bags, "come over tomorrow. Or, better yet, I'll bring her to see you. She could use an outing."

Riitta offered to drive us home then realized Erik had gone off with the only car at the house. I assured her everyone would be fine and we went off in our different directions.

"That was a lovely tea party," Miss Irene said. "Everything so pretty and tasty."

"A moment out of time," Aunt Ianthe said. "It was nice but we still have a much bigger problem. We have to find out who killed that handsome Mr. Martin and dear Flossie." I said nothing and she peered at me. "Henrikki? What are you thinking? Do you know something?"

"I don't know who killed Alex Martin and Mrs. O.," I said, with perfect truth, "but I don't think it will be too long before we find out."

"Why? What do you mean, dearie? How will we find out? When? Can you give us a clue?"

"No clue. It's just that, certain things are starting to come together in my mind, you know? Like Sherlock Holmes once said, or was it Miss Marple? 'I'm beginning to see his taillights'."

"And the light shineth in darkness; and the darkness comprehended it not," Miss Irene said. "John 1:5."

I stopped and stared at the little woman, forgetting all about the gathering thunderheads and the spatters of rain.

"Exactly."

A few more plops of rain encouraged me to hurry my elderly ladies along at a heart-attack inducing pace. Well, in all honesty, it wasn't the rain. I was wild to get out to the lighthouse. I was anxious to find out whether I could comprehend the flicker of light that I saw.

I left the ladies at their front door then sprinted across the street and entered the house from the front. The dogs were more restive than usual and I hurried to let them out in the backyard. That's when I discovered there was a figure standing on my back porch. Silent, still and ominous. I know it's a cliché but my heart seemed to jump into my mouth.

CHAPTER 32

"Geez Louise," she said. "I thought you'd never get back."

"Chakra! What are you doing here?"

"I had a visit from that flame-haired matchstick, Ellwood. He found out about my visit to the tower and he had a lot of intrusive questions. How old is that kid, anyway?"

"Nineteen. Listen, I've got somewhere to go."

"That's why I'm here. After the deputy left I did some yoga and meditation and I got into a good trance. It was during the trance that a couple of revelations came to me. It works like that sometimes. You clear your mind of all the surface trivial stuff and something important breaks through."

"What sorts of revelations?"

"Well, I think I know what happened to Captain Jack."

I thought of my own revelation earlier in the garden at Erik's house.

"I think I do, too."

We exchanged a pointed look.

"I was just heading out to the lighthouse," I said, as if the pronouncement was unrelated.

"That right? Mind if I go with you?"

I had to think fast. If Chakra was the killer it would be

incredibly foolish to go out to the deserted lighthouse with her. I decided to stall.

"Did your epiphany include the identity of Alex's murderer?"

"Not really. Nothing I'm sure about. You?"

"I'm not sure, either."

"Why do you want to go out to the lighthouse?"

"Because," she said, "like you, I believe the answers are out there. And, unlike you, I am a suspect."

"Okay. Let me just feed the mongrels and we'll go. By the way, do you remember a guy called Finn O'Leary?"

"Funny, balding, great smile?"

"That's the one. I think he's in love with you."

"Huh," she said. "I'll drive to the lighthouse."

"Why?"

"Because, my friend, in case we have to make a getaway, my car is much faster than yours. And it's air-conditioned."

We were barreling down Tamarack en route to the interstate when she spoke again.

"I checked with Alex's L.A. lawyer about his will. I get ten million but the rest of it, some ninety million plus, all goes to the same person and you're not going to believe who it is."

My heart was pounding so hard that my chest hurt. Here it was. Chakra was about to hand me the name of the murderer on a silver platter. Or maybe a gold one.

"Who?"

"He'd had the same chief beneficiary for years and years. It was Riitta Lemppi. On Saturday night he called the lawyer and substituted another name. He left nearly his entire fortune to his son, Danny."

The name sent a dagger through my heart. No jury in the world could ignore a motive of ninety million dollars. We had to find evidence that would point elsewhere. We had to. I shivered in the air-conditioning.

"Drive faster."

CHAPTER 33

Since the lighthouse had never been on anyone's milk route, it had no milk chute. Nevertheless, there was a little hook about shoulder height on the back porch that held the key. I was pretty sure that sheriff Clump would neither have known about it nor instructed Ellwood to remove it and I was right. By the time I'd retrieved the key and let Chakra and myself in the back door, we were both soaked and I was out of breath, a condition that reminded me that I needed to start jogging. The good news was that it distracted me from a heavy-duty case of anxiety. Unfortunately, the good news only lasted until we reached the door to the cellar. I sucked in a calming breath, opened the door and descended. Chakra followed me in silence.

I headed for the far wall where Riitta kept the tools and chose a crowbar, and then, with my heart slamming against my ribs, I led the way to the connecting door with the other cellar, opened it and turned that light on, too. I shot a quick look at the coal chute which was, thank goodness, empty. And then I went to the center of the room.

The cistern stood a few inches off the hard-packed dirt floor and was covered with a round iron lid. It looked heavy.

"I'm guessing we're gonna use the crowbar to get that lid off," she said. I nodded.

I worked the short end of the tool under the lid and used it as a fulcrum but even with both of us applying all our heft, we could only move the heavy iron cap a few centimeters at a time.

When we'd shifted it three or four inches I called a halt and searched for my flashlight which, as luck would have it, I'd left in the car.

"Use the light on the end of your cellphone," Chakra suggested. It was a small beam, of course, but big enough for us to see into the black interior of the cistern and strong enough to focus our attention on a worn patch on the sole of a work boot. I swallowed hard and moved the light a little. It caught the threads of stiff denim. Dungarees. I blinked back tears.

"Let me guess," Chakra said. "Captain Jack?"

There was nothing to be done. We couldn't touch the body. All we could do was call the sheriff's department and report what we'd found. Neither of us was inclined to talk. I found myself thinking about Danny Thorne. The discovery of the body seemed to corroborate his story about hearing Captain Jack on the circular stairs talking to someone coming up as he was going down. That person must have killed Alex then gone after Jack. As we climbed the cellar stairs and I led the way to the walnut staircase, I felt tears prick the backs of my eyes again.

The lighthouse was eerie, full of shadows with the wind screaming around the corners outside and the rain splatting against the windows like a hail of pennies.

"Let's hurry," I muttered to Chakra. I could feel her reluctance to climb up to the tower and I shared it but we had no choice. I thought Erik had been telling the truth about the letter hidden in the watch room and I had no confidence that it would still be there tomorrow. If there was a way to clear Tom Kukka and Danny, I had to find it tonight.

The mellow tones of my cell phone sounded like the squeal of a stuck pig and my hand shook as I checked Caller ID. It took me a minute to recognize the unfamiliar name and pick up.

"Mr. Wheeler," I said. "I had a question about the trust you set up for the late Mrs. Johanna Marttinen."

"I'm afraid I can't help you with that. We do not discuss our clients."

"She isn't your client any longer," I pointed out, "since she is dead."

"She had an heir," he started to say.

"Also dead. Murdered."

"Murdered? On the Keweenaw?"

"That's the verdict of the autopsy. We are trying to determine whether there was a financial motive for the crime."

The reference to murder must have shaken him because suddenly he was all compliance.

"Five million dollars is a lot of money," I added.

Thunder roared overhead and lightning blazed against the windows, briefly turning the gloom to dazzling light.

"Five million? Surely you mean three million. That was the value of the trust when it was dissolved. The funds were then withdrawn and deposited at Sturdy Bank down in Gogebic County. So you see, we no longer have any association with Mrs. Marttinen."

Three million?

"I have seen official documents signed by the Copper County Board of Commissioners chairman indicating the trust fund was five million," I said, in a voice calculated to neither threaten nor upset the bank officer. "Do you know what happened there?"

"Yes, of course. The bequest was originally five million but when the trust was dissolved and the funds transferred, two million was siphoned off to be used for renovations and improvements to the lighthouse. It had been the wish of Mrs. Marttinen that the Painted Rock Lighthouse be used as a nursing home for the indigent of the Keweenaw."

"A retirement home," I corrected him. "When exactly was the trust fund dissolved?"

"You mean the date?"

"Approximately."

"Sometime last fall. I had just returned from my cottage."

"Last fall? But Mrs. Marttinen died in June and I understood that the will allowed a year for her son and heir to come to Michigan to claim the property."

"Oh, yes. Now I remember. It was irregular but the Copper County Board of Commissioners contacted Mrs. Marttinen's son who waived his rights to the lighthouse and the money. The board had a list of old folks who wanted to live in the lighthouse so they decided to move early on the project."

"And that's why they withdrew two million dollars at that time?"

"That's right."

Chakra and I exchanged startled looks.

"Mr. Wheeler, who authorized the transfer and withdrawal of the money?"

"It would have been the chairman of the county board."

"Do you have the paperwork there? Could you check on that?"

"There's no need. I handled the paperwork myself as soon as I got back in the office after Labor Day. William Alanen authorized the transfer."

"You saw Mr. Alanen the day after Labor Day?"

"Oh, no. He was very ill then and died right around that time but it was his name on the papers."

"So you did the whole thing by mail?"

"Certainly not. A transaction that size must be handled in person. I dealt with a very pleasant, very competent attorney who represented the light house commission. A Mr. Sundback."

I thanked him and hung up.

"Hatti," Chakra said, and for the first time since I'd known her, I heard fear in her voice, "we need to get out of here."

"It's all right. Riitta's going to call me when they're ready to pick me up. We have a little time. Geez Louise. I can't believe the chutzpah of the man. First he lied about getting in touch with Alex then he stole two million dollars. How did he think it would never be discovered?"

"He covered his bases," Chakra said, as we mounted the walnut stairs to the second floor landing. "He handled all the paperwork between the county and the bank and the lighthouse and, just to make doubly sure he wouldn't get questioned, he proposed to Riitta. You'll notice he only did that after Alex showed up and discovered that Danny was his son."

"If Alex decided to give the lighthouse to Riitta, which he did, Erik as her husband was in the perfect position to continue to deal with all the paperwork and money," I said, continuing her thought. "It wasn't that much of a risk."

"Except that Alex must have found out," Chakra said. She sighed. "He'd have been furious."

"Erik probably tried to work something out with him," I put in. "He may have offered to replace the two million."

Chakra shook her head. "Alex wouldn't have given any quarter on something like that. He detested being crossed, especially with money."

"And so he had to die. And Flossie Ollanketo and Captain Jack along with him."

"And possibly us if we don't get out of here, Hatti."

"Soon," I said. "Erik intended to bring me out here to find the copy of the real letter Alex wrote to Riitta after which I'm sure he planned to destroy it. We're not going to let that happen."

CHAPTER 34

W e'd reached the tiny landing in the tower. The doors were closed and the place looked and smelled like a school shut up for the summer. We'd only been gone a day but there was already a faintly musty odor. I went past my old bedroom and opened the door to the watch room and crossed over to the desk where I turned on the banker's lamp. I caught Chakra staring at the carpeted floor where she and Alex had shared their last moments together.

"Memories?"

"I was so sure he was the one. I thought we could have everything, you know?"

"I know. Why don't you look in the secretary over there and I'll take the desk. We'll get through this as fast as we can and get the heck out of Dodge."

She opened the glass doors in the hutch and started removing the books and the other objects like the clear deck prism, a diamond shaped glass object that had once been inserted in the deck of a sailing vessel, a hand-hammered copper pitcher and an antique mariner's storm glass.

I sat in the old-fashioned swivel chair with the faded leather pads and examined the row of cubbyholes along the top of the mahogany desk. They were mostly empty except for three brass-barrel keys which, I assumed, would unlock the drawers of the desk. After a few abortive tries to get the right key into the right lock I accidentally jiggled the drawer at the top and it edged an inch. None of the drawers was locked which made sense since Alex no doubt had been using the desk right up until he died.

The top drawer contained pens and pencils, an eraser and some pre-stamped, one-cent postcards. The second drawer, a telephone directory and a Finnish language Bible. The third drawer held a stack of papers some five inches thick. Leafing through them I recognized thirty-year-old tax returns, receipts, insurance bills, doctor's reports, a deed to a house in Rhode Island and so forth. Alex had said his mother never threw away anything and apparently he'd been right. Near the bottom of the stack I found a homemade card with a very inexpert picture of a reindeer and a crayon message written in a childish hand: *You are my deer. Happy Valentime Day, Mommy.*

"Finding anything," Chakra asked.

I murmured something, afraid to trust my voice.

I put the papers back then ran my fingers over the top surface of the desk after which I got down on the floor in the kneehole and did the same on the underside. The wood was unfinished and a little rough but there were no seams, no indication of a secret drawer, no place to hide a copy of a letter.

I dropped onto all fours to examine the wooden floorboards under the desk when an exclamation from Chakra brought me bolt upright.

"What's wrong," I asked, as I cracked my head on the desk and slid off my knees, balancing my weight with the heel of one hand. The board under my hand popped up as if released by a spring.

"Nothing. I just found a photo of Alex as a small boy."

"Handsome?"

"Unbelievably. We could have made beautiful babies."

She sounded wistful and I wanted to comfort her but not only was my head throbbing, I was excited about what I'd discovered. I pried up the board and found a cache that was two inches by about eighteen inches and probably six inches deep. I grabbed my phone and turned on the flashlight. The largest item in the hole and the one that made my heart beat faster, was an envelope with Riitta's name on it. The flap was not gummed down and, with trembling fingers, I unfolded and read the typed letter.

Dear Riitta,

I have apologized for the past and will not bore you with a repetition of that. By the time you see this, I will have told you of my intentions. This note is to provide you with something in writing but know that, at one word from you, everything will be taken care of through my L.A. lawyer, J. Hampton West.

You now own the light station and the trust fund amounting to approximately five million dollars. You can continue to run the old folks home or sell the place. You can use the money to support the lighthouse and/or to support yourself and Danny, or a combination of both. More than that, I am making Danny the chief beneficiary to my estate which, at present, is worth some one hundred million dollars, give or take. Don't get too excited. I don't intend to die anytime soon!

There is something else I want you to know. Erik Sundback, using authority he took upon himself, dissolved my mother's trust fund ten months ago, transferred the funds to another bank and, in the process, managed to keep a couple of million dollars for himself. It is not necessary for you to address this issue as I have my own plans to deal with it. I just want you to know. He obviously has designs on you.

I will get back the wandering two million for you.

All the best,

Alex Martin

I should have grabbed the letter and Chakra and taken off as fast as possible but I couldn't resist looking into the cache in the floor. It was so obviously a boy's hiding place.

It was full of arrowheads and Petoskey stones, granite, copper and agates. There was a calcified bird's egg, a slingshot, rubber bands, pennies and string. There were old erasers and pencils, a plastic protractor, an ivory coated slide rule and a tin compass with a stub of pencil still in it. Had he been a pirate burying his treasure? A spy? A prisoner of war trying to leave a record for future generations?

My heart ached for the boy Alex had been and the man who'd lost his life in his prime. I gripped the compass and wished, for a furious second, that I could stab the point into Erik Sundback's black heart.

My phone chimed, echoing in the enclosed space and causing me to jump high enough to hit my head again. This time I didn't check caller I.D.

"This is Hatti."

"Hatti! *Voi kahuia!*" Riitta sounded hysterical. "It's Miss Thyra. She's gone! Kidnapped!"

Maybe it was caused by the bump on the head but I caught a quick vision of Miss Thyra wearing her long black dress, her wrists bound behind her and a black scarf tied around her eyes. She was walking a plank.

"Kidnapped? Did you get a ransom note?"

"No note. She just disappeared."

"Maybe she went out for a walk."

"Hatti, it's raining cats and dogs. She didn't leave of her own accord. She was abducted."

"How can you know that?"

"Because. Listen to me, Henrikki. *She left without making her bed.*"

No other phrase could have conveyed the situation more clearly. Finnish American ladies, especially those in Miss Thyra's generation, never left the house with their dishes undone or their beds unmade.

"When was the last time you saw her?"

"Erik spoke to her before he left for the office, just as we sat down for the tea party. She told him she'd join us later and, after he gave me the message, he left. I thought she was asleep. I went to check on her a few minutes ago."

So there was only Erik Sundback's word for Miss Thyra's whereabouts.

"Erik's on his way back from Houghton. He told me to sit tight and he'd pick me up, then we'd come get you and go over to Frog Creek."

"I don't think you should wait for him," I said, trying not to communicate my anxiety. Now that I suspected that Erik had proposed to Riitta to hedge his bets, I didn't think she was safe with him. "You go ahead on over to the sheriff's office and talk to Ellwood about this."

"I can't go anywhere. Danny's got my car."

I muffled a curse. "Okay, then. Just call 911 and tell Ellwood. He'll understand about the unmade bed."

"Hatti? Why don't you want me to wait for Erik?"

I hated to tell her but she was going to have to know sometime.

"I've got some bad news on the Erik Sundback front."

"He's the killer?"

"You knew?"

"No. Not for sure. I was hoping I was wrong. He's seemed, I don't know, different, since we've moved in here. Not as kind, you know? More lord-of-the-manner. And I know Miss Thyra's afraid of him."

"Are you very disappointed?"

"Yes. He's been good to all of us. But don't feel sorry for me. I was never going to marry him."

"You'd already decided that?"

"It didn't feel right. Marriage just isn't in the cards for me."

I wanted to argue with her, to point out how well she and Tom Kukka suited one another but it wasn't the time or the place.

"Where are you, anyway?"

"At the lighthouse with Chakra. We've just found some evidence that exonerates Tom and we're on our way home."

"Good," she said. "I'll never be able to thank him enough for what he did for Danny."

"Maybe Danny can find a way to thank him. Alex made him chief beneficiary in his will. The boy's worth a pile of money."

"That's nice," she said. I knew she meant it in just that way, too. She was pleased for Danny but not overwhelmed. Riitta never had and never would be motivated by worldly considerations. "Have you found Jack?"

I made a face. "In the cistern."

"Oh!" She started crying.

"Call Ellwood," I reminded her. "I'll see you soon."

"A false promise, Hatti."

The attorney's deep voice was like a knife to the gut. He was here. The killer. I took a tiny bit of comfort from the fact that I was on the floor behind the desk and he couldn't see me but I knew it wouldn't make any difference in the end. He'd come to kill me. And now he'd kill Chakra, too. I closed my eyes.

"You shouldn't have meddled," Erik Sundback said. "But since you did, you'll have to pay the price. In the meantime, I assume you found the hidden copy of the letter. I'll take it, if you please. Now. And don't expect any assistance from your friend here. She's a bit tied up."

Tied up? I grasped the letter in my left hand and the tightened my fingers around the compass in my right and I lifted my head above the desk. Chakra was standing near the sliding glass door to the gallery and when she saw me she moved enough so that I caught a flash of metal. Sundback had handcuffed her to the door handle.

Geez almighty Louise.

"Don't bother to stall," he drawled. "I called the sheriff's department on my way out here and told them Captain Jack's body was found in the reeds near Dollar Lake. The clown brigade is heading down there as we speak."

That was a blow. Without really thinking about it, I'd assumed Riitta would be able to get Ellwood, at least, out to the lighthouse within half an hour. Stalling had seemed like our best bet. Our only bet, really. Unless I could find a way to overpower a hundred-and-eighty-pound man who had already killed three people.

I stood up behind the desk, although my legs felt like the Sunshine salad my *mummi* used to make with yellow Jell-O, crushed pineapple and grated carrots.

"First I want you to answer some questions," I said.

"Offhand, I'd say you're not in a position for negotiation," Sundback said. He waved something in his right hand and it felt as if I'd put a wet finger into an electric outlet. The way the pistol gleamed reminded me of his smile. It seemed like pure evil. "But I don't mind giving you some details. What, exactly, do you want to know?" He made a little movement with his head and drew my eyes to the person standing next to him. Or, more accurately, drooping next to him.

"Miss Thyra!"

"The wages of sin is death, Henrikki. But I'm sorry you have to be involved."

For an instant I thought she was going to confess to the murders but only for an instant.

"Miss Thyra, what are you talking about," I asked. "Riitta thinks you've been kidnapped!"

CHAPTER 35

"She came willingly," Sundback said. He'd lost all of his courteous friendliness and sounded just like a schoolyard bully. "Guilt has taken hold of her. She plans to throw herself off the tower in a fit of remorse. If it makes you feel any better, you are going to try — unsuccessfully — to stop her. You will die a hero."

I tried to ignore him.

"Miss Thyra?"

"It was my fault about Alex Martin. And Flossie. I was to blame." I was so astonished I didn't know what to say. I'd suspected she had some kind of guilty knowledge but surely it was the attorney, not Miss Thyra who had killed Alex and Mrs. O.

"I don't understand."

"It was I who hid the body. Mr. Sundback saw me. It was Sunday morning before dawn. I saw something from the dining room window and came out to investigate. When I realized Mr. Martin had fallen from the tower, I panicked. I went down to the cellar, opened the window then fetched the wheelbarrow from the backporch and hefted the body into it. After that I trundled him to the window and deposited him on the coal chute. I haven't felt one moment of peace since my fall from grace. I haven't been able to say my prayers."

"Miss Thyra," I said, still confused, "why did you panic? Why didn't you just call the police?"

"Don't you understand? It was because of my vanity. I knew that if a body was reported at the lighthouse the seminar would be canceled. It was so important to me that the history of mittens be allowed to go on. Too important. I sold my soul for it."

"Then why did you send me down to the cellar?"

"It was a ruse." She sounded exhausted. "I was already sick with guilt. I wanted you to find the body. I was very upset when you came back with nothing more than a clothespin, one I must have dropped when I was depositing the corpse."

I switched my attention to the attorney. "How do you come into all of this?"

"I saw her move the body. I'd gone down to Houghton but had come back to check on my, uh, handiwork, when, to my surprise, I found Miss Thyra struggling with the wheelbarrow. When she was finished and safely back upstairs, I removed Martin's body from the coal chute and hid it in one of the empty steamer trunks, which was no small task. I needed it to be discovered under the tower so there was a chance of a verdict of accident or suicide but, by then, it was light and the house was stirring. I couldn't move the body again until everyone was occupied with the mittens."

"Miss Thyra, did you know who had killed Alex Martin?"

"Not then. Not until you gave me Flossie's mitten. The Arjeplog mitten, blue for a man, the pattern made up by Finnish girls at the workhouse in Swedish Lapland."

"Half Finnish, half Swedish. So when you talked about the thorns on the roses that was just a diversionary tactic. You never thought Danny had killed his father."

"Another sin to add to my account. I was afraid of Sundback. I knew he'd killed Mr. Martin. I suspected he'd killed Flossie." She didn't look at him. "I suppose he killed Captain Jack, too."

"All right," Sundback said, "that's enough chit-chat. Bring me the letter, Hatti."

"Hang on," I said, "I'd still like to know why you killed three people." He didn't respond immediately and I held my breath. He could shoot me or Miss Thyra or even Chakra with a quick twist of his body. Chakra was totally neutralized and he could take Miss Thyra out to the gallery and pitch her into the storm. Except that if he did that, he couldn't control me and I'd be able to lock him out on the gallery. Maybe. I tried to think. There must be a way to save all three of us.

"The old lady had to go. She lip read a conversation between Martin and me outside the sauna. He'd found out I borrowed some of the trust fund money."

"Two million dollars."

"Ah. I see you found out, too. Well, I had every intention of paying that back and I told him so but he wasn't having any. Martin might have looked like a sun god but he was a vindictive so-and-so. He refused to let me pay it back. He said he'd ruin me, a man who had spent a lifetime building up a reputation beyond reproach."

"Why did you steal the money?"

"A ridiculous question, Hatti. It was there. It was available. It wasn't needed for anything immediate. The lighthouse commission couldn't touch it until the year was up. Why shouldn't I make use of it? That's just good economics. But Martin found out. He accused me of abusing his mother's trust. He accused me of theft. I went up to the watch room and told him I apologized and I was ready for whatever punishment he had in mind. We stepped out on the gallery to watch the storm and I managed to hit him with a rock then push him over."

I swallowed the bile that had risen in my mouth.

"And Captain Jack?"

"Wrong place at the wrong time. He was coming down the circular staircase as I was going up. He didn't suspect me. Why should he? I found him in the kitchen, asked him to help me with something in the cellar and took care of him there."

"With the rock?"

"And the knife in his belt."

Jack's *puukko* knife. My stomach turned over.

"And then you dumped him in the cistern."

"That's why I couldn't use it the next day to hide Martin's body. The whole thing got too complicated."

"It doesn't seem to me you used much finesse," I pointed out, not sure why I was taking a chance on goading him. "I mean, a caveman could have bashed two people over the head and pushed one off a tower. I suppose you smothered Mrs. Ollanketo with a pillow."

"You suppose nothing of the sort," he said. His voice was a little strained as if he were reining in his temper. "That was a piece of sleight of hand. Kukka asked me to empty the syringe and I did so, right into the bathroom glass. I cleaned out the syringe and later came back and refilled it. It was, as you might imagine, child's play to inject the old lady while she was asleep."

"You think you were so clever," I said, with some bitterness. "You'd never have been able to trick Tom if he hadn't trusted you."

"His mistake. Bring me the letter."

I was out of time. I'd tried stalling but no one had come to rescue us. I tightened my fingers around the compass. It wasn't much, especially against a loaded pistol, but it was something. I had some idea of thrusting the letter at his left hand, the one not holding the pistol, and then swinging my arm up to gouge his eye out. Hopefully, the shock and pain would make him drop the gun and I'd be able to kick it out of the way.

"What about Riitta," I said, as inspiration struck. "Don't you think she'll be a little upset when she finds out you killed all three of her retirement home residents, to say nothing of her cousin?"

"Not my problem," he said. "We are finished."

Of course he'd figured that out.

"Did you ever want her?"

"I wanted to marry her. As soon as I found out Martin planned to leave her the lighthouse and the trust fund. I'd have been home free. If the lighthouse went to the county, I'd have been the one in charge of finances and I could pay back the loan at my leisure. If it went to Riitta, and we were married, she'd have given me full responsibility for the project with the same result."

"But you switched the letters from Alex Martin on Saturday night. You couldn't have known by then that she wasn't going to marry you."

"I knew. She was pretending to think about it but she was fooling herself. She'd never have married me."

He had, I thought, a lot of insight for a murderer.

"Did you care for her?" I had a sudden thought. "Did you steal the money to renovate the house for Riitta?"

"I *borrowed* the money to buy a new boat," he said. "Life is not a fairytale. Now, if you haven't brought me that letter by the count of three, I'll blow all three of you to kingdom come, starting with the old lady. One... two..."

Was he serious? I had no idea but, considering that he'd already killed three people in cold blood, I couldn't take the chance. I lurched around the desk and toward him, deliberately stumbling so that when I slammed the letter at his left hand, it would look like an accident.

The plan went perfectly. Well, up to a point. I thrust the letter at him, he grabbed at it and then I raised my arm to stab him in the face.

Turns out taking an eye for an eye is harder than you might think. I couldn't do it. As a result, he had enough time to recover his own balance and to swing the pistol around so that I was facing the barrel.

Time seemed to stand still. I was aware of Miss Thyra drooping like a sack of potatoes next to Sundback and of Chakra over by the door. My body felt frozen but my mind was anguished with my missed chance. We were all going to die. And then Chakra Starshine, yoga instructor and widow of Alex Martin, saved the day. She barked a command at me.

"Hatti! Defensive cross!"

CHAPTER 36

Reflexively I tensed my arms, slammed my elbows together, jerked them upwards and scissor-ed them hard. I distinctly heard the snap of a bone breaking followed by an outraged cry and the sound of the pistol hitting the wooden floor. I'd done it! I'd disarmed him. Miss Thyra sprang to life and kicked the gun out of the way and, at the same time, Chakra once again came to my aid.

"The door, Hatti."

She'd managed to open the slider and the screen and rainwater sheeted into the room. I raced toward the door and out onto the slippery concrete of the gallery.

Once again my mind slowed down but this time I wasn't paralyzed with fear and indecision. I could save us all if I took this one step at a time. The next move was to find the stationary ladder, a series of some six iron rungs permanently attached to the side of the lantern room. I could see virtually nothing and the gallery itself felt like a skating rink but I knew the rungs were located about ten feet away, on the side of the tower that faced the lake. I held my left hand on the wall and counted my steps, moving as quickly as seemed safe.

My hope was that he'd follow me, thereby allowing Chakra and Miss Thyra to hole themselves up in the watch room. Once I'd climbed to the little door into the lantern room, I'd be okay. I could bar the door against Erik. I could call Jace. He'd come. I knew he would.

I felt the first rung with my left hand and my spirits rose even more. In fact, I had to fight a sense of pure invincibility. I'd faced a loaded gun and I'd prevailed. I'd employed a self-defense maneuver and broken an adult man's arm. Ulna or tibia? Did it matter? I raised my right hand to the second rung and swung myself up just as a gust of wind knocked me to the side and lightning flashed. All of a sudden I remembered that I was on a fifty-foot tower trying to balance on an iron rung in an electrical storm. Had I vanquished Erik Sundback only to turn into a Benjamin Franklin science experiment? Geez Louise! I told myself to focus. I hoisted myself upwards, grabbing another rung, climbing from one rung to another with my feet.

I needed to stay calm. I thought about the mighty lake beneath me. I tried to remember the statistics, the numbers of men who had died in the angry waves. Tens of thousands of them. And what of the Painted Rock Lighthouse? It had stood here for a century. It had been active only a part of that time and yet it had stood between sailors and death. It stood between me and death now. I found myself thinking of words from *Moominpappa at Sea.*

"She found it slow going but somehow she managed. She had time. She had nothing else but time."

An instant later, as I lifted my left foot to join my right on the third rung of the ladder, time ran out. Hard, angry fingers curled around my ankle and jerked my leg. An image of myself battered and broken on the wet sand at the foot of the lighthouse flashed before my mind's eye. I thought of those I'd leave behind: Mom and Pops, Sofi, Charlie, Elli would be sad. Jace would be sad, too. At least at first. In the long run he might be relieved not to have to go through a divorce.

The jerk came again and, along with it, a muttered curse. Rain spanked my face and body. It got into my nose and mouth and made it hard to breathe. I focused the way Chakra had taught us to do, as if the entire world is a tiny camera aperture. All I had to do was shake off the manacle. I kicked back hard but the gripping fingers just tightened. Maybe I hadn't broken his arm. Or, maybe, he had more *sisu* than I. That thought made me angrier than anything else. Was I going to let him flick me off the tower like an annoying insect? I was not. I had one arrow left in my quiver. One very small arrow. I was still clutching the schoolboy compass. I steadied myself from the most recent jerk, then swung my arm down, hoping to bury the tin point into Erik Sundback's muscular shoulder.

It would be risky. Once I let go with my right hand, I'd be even more vulnerable. I had to hit the target. I had to inflict enough damage to make him let go of me. I sucked in a breath and went for the Hail Mary moment.

I missed.

Well, not entirely. I'd contacted with his shoulder but he'd brushed off the attack as if I were a spider. I was now holding my entire weight up with my left hand and I needed a miracle. I got as far as "please, dear Lord," when it happened. The dark and stormy night exploded into a fireball of light and the last trumpet, in the voice of an old-fashioned foghorn, blasted the news that the end had come.

And it had come for Erik Sundback. Already off balance from my pitiful attack, he reeled backwards letting go of my ankle to wind-mill his arms in a desperate attempt to catch himself. I glimpsed a look of pure rage on his wide, handsome face.

And then he was gone.

CHAPTER 37

It was over.

Well, mostly, over. All but the part where I had to scrape myself off the stationary ladder and limp back along the gallery. Now that I could let go, safely, it was hard to do it. The hold that had felt so precarious only seconds earlier, felt secure. I felt an odd mixture of relief (that I was not splatted on the ground like a fried egg) and inertia. My limbs felt rooted in place. My fingers felt numb. Even my eyelids were heavy. I didn't want to climb down. I just wanted to go to sleep.

This would, I thought, be an excellent time for a caped superhero to appear. Superman or Batman or even Aquaman, considering how wet everything was. No one showed up, though, and I supposed I should be grateful for the one miracle and not expect another. I pried my fingers loose from the rung and slowly made my way back down the ladder then I hugged the wall with my right hand. The gallery floor seemed more treacherous than it had with someone chasing me. It seemed to take forever to get back to the sliding door and the shelter of the light keeper's study.

Chakra was still attached to the door and Miss Thyra was standing where I'd left her, her hand on the switches on the wall. She asked a question which I had to lip-read to hear.

"Is it over, then?" I nodded. "Is he dead?" I nodded, again. She flipped the switches off. The sudden silence was deafening. She disappeared onto the landing and came back with the comforter from my old bed. She placed it around me then moved to Chakra. I watched her pull a hairpin out of her tight bun and work the mechanism on the handcuffs.

"You saved my life," I said, finally. "The light and the foghorn caused him to lose his balance and fall. What made you think of it?"

"You use what is at hand," Miss Thyra said, her attention on the lock she was picking. "The difficult part was deciding when to use it. Too early and it might have been useless. Too late, and," she shrugged and left the thought unfinished but I knew. Too late and I'd have already been plucked off the tower like the unlucky Itsy-Bitsy spider.

"I tried to stab him with the pointed end of a compass." I thought it might be better if I told them everything. Just in case Miss Thyra felt guilty for another death. "I didn't make contact but I think he was a little thrown off. It really was a joint effort."

"A joint effort of more than just the three of us," Miss Thyra said. "God helps those who help themselves." She smiled, and, for the first time in days, she looked happy. "It says so in the *Moomins*." She looked at me. "Henrikki, I think we should use your little wireless telephone to call the police."

The cellphone in my pocket was as drenched as I, so I used Chakra's phone. Mrs. Touleheto responded after only eight rings.

"Good evening," she said, cheerily. "What can I do you for?"

"Hi, Mrs. Too. It's Hatti."

"Oh my land. Well, bless my stars."

"Why are you blessing your stars?"

"Catastrophe! Are you sitting down?"

My heart started to race. "Yes. What is it? My parents? Sofi?"

"Waino," she said. "I ran into Hilda Aho this morning down at Jokinen's Bakery in Hancock. She said Waino is smitten with the goalie on the Nimrods hockey team."

"A boy?"

"No, no, the girl's hockey team. He's been helping coach them this summer. The trouble is she's only a freshman so she'll be around for a while."

"She's fourteen? Waino is interested in a girl who's fourteen?"

"She may have been held back a year. He was, you know."

"It's all right, Mrs. Too. Waino and I are just friends. I'm married, you know."

"That hardly counts, Henrikki. You can't have a baby with a husband who is living somewhere else."

"How true. Well, I called for Ellwood and the sheriff. We've got another body out at the lighthouse."

"That is certainly very careless of you, Hatti," she said. "There's simply no more room at the morgue. In any case, I got a call from Riitta Lemppi some time ago. They're all on their way out there. Even Doc Kukka. But you had better call Arvo Maki. There's no way they can get a body into the Corvette."

The first pair of booted footsteps sounded on the circular stairs right after I hung up. Suddenly the little watch room was full of people, one of whom scooped me up, blankets and all.

"Hatti," Max said, his face an odd color. "Are you all right?"

I couldn't help grinning. My superhero had finally turned up. I sighed, reached up and wrapped my arms around his neck and he brushed his lips against my cheek.

"I'm taking you downstairs," he said, roughly.

Downstairs? To the bedrooms? My heart gave a little jump.

"I need to talk to her," Ellwood said.

"Not," Max said, "until she's had some coffee."

The words might not be out of Prince Charming's playbook but they worked for me. I grinned at him.

"You know me so well."

Sometime later, coffee cups in hand, Miss Thyra, Chakra and I got through our entire story. We had to tell it several times as Sheriff Clump did not immediately grasp some of the details. He couldn't, for example, understand why Miss Thyra had moved Alex Martin's body on Sunday morning or why Erik Sundback had moved it back.

Riitta and Tom sat next to each other on a bench, chosen, I suspected, because it allowed them to touch from shoulder to hip. It looked as if they were friends. I hoped it was more.

"Erik seemed like such a good guy," Arvo said. "A great guy. He devoted hundreds of hours to the lighthouse project. I don't know what we would have done without him, in fact. He handled all the paperwork. All the finances."

"A prince among men," Max murmured in a voice that only I could hear.

"I think the temptation was just too much," I said to Arvo. "He as much as told us that. He had his eye on a big new fifty-foot yacht and there was all that money just sitting there with no one paying any attention to it. I suppose he was justified in thinking Alex Martin wasn't interested since he'd never shown any interest in his mother or her fortune during the past twenty years."

"You said the trust officer was informed that Martin was told about the will and its provisions last fall," Ellwood said. "Do you think that was true?"

"I think Erik told them it was true. I think he produced paperwork to that effect. I don't think he actually contacted Alex. If he had done so, Alex would have shown up on the Keweenaw a lot sooner."

"Five million dollars plus a lighthouse is a lot of property," Tom Kukka said, "but not worth a man's life. It's too bad he ever came back at all."

"Except," Riitta pointed out, "that he found out about Danny. And Danny found out about him."

"So that's it, then," Clump said. "The lawyer's the one

that did the deed. He kilt the old lady, too. The deaf one."

"And Captain Jack," Chakra reminded him. "Hatti and I found his body down in the cistern in the cellar."

"Criminently," Clump said. He looked at Arvo. "That's two bodies down at the morgue and two more here. Good thing you brought the meat wagon and whatnot."

CHAPTER 38

Ten days later, on another Saturday night, we gathered again at the lighthouse. This time it was essentially a family party, an attempt to banish ghosts, to launch a reset for the Painted Rock Retirement Home, to welcome back my globetrotting parents and, most importantly of all, to celebrate an engagement.

"You'd never know this was the same place," I said to Chakra as we strolled along the shoreline, admiring the slowly setting sun, the mild ripples on the lake, the slight, fresh breeze and the fact that we were no longer in the clutches of a murderer.

We both gazed out at the island.

"It looks so forlorn," she said.

"It isn't. Not really. Agate Island is just waiting for the next child who wants to explore its hills and caves, to collect rocks and shells and to lie on the grass and daydream." I swallowed hard then added, "I'm sorry about Alex."

Her eyes were red but she nodded.

"I'm sorry, too. In any case, it's time to move on. I've decided to go back to California, but not to Hollywood. I like teaching yoga and meditation and self-defense. I may even keep my name."

"May I make a suggestion? Look up Finn once you get there."

She grinned. "Maybe I'll do that. As I recall, he had a great sense of humor. What about you, Hatti? Are you going to stay here?"

"I think so. Everybody's excited about the yarn shop, especially Aunt Ianthe, Miss Irene and Miss Thyra."

"Watch out. Pretty soon they'll start calling you Miss Hatti. What about your husband? Has he gotten in touch? He must have read about this in the paper or online."

I stared out at the lake. Tonight the waves were gentle. They reminded me of lacy-edged doilies.

"I called him," I said, unsure of why I was telling Chakra. I hadn't told anyone else. "His office manager told me he's in South America working with a small tribe on a land-and-water issue. No Wifi. No internet. No television, apparently." I hesitated. "The thing is, he didn't go alone. He's hired somebody new since I was in D.C. A recent law school grad. A Native American." I took in a deep breath. "The woman I spoke with had been my friend. She said this new employee has a big crush on Jace. I guess that's not surprising."

Chakra looked at me.

"What was the problem between you, two, anyway?"

"I told you, I don't know."

"You must have some idea. Was it ethnicity? Is that why you feel threatened by this new lawyer?"

I made a face. "I don't even know if the problem had anything to do with me. Jace had a tough childhood, unemployed, alcoholic, single mother, a much younger troublesome half-brother, life on a Canadian rez where they were never really accepted. Did I tell you he never even met my family? We met and eloped and moved to D.C. Probably not the best way to start a stable married life."

"You can't just drift, you know, Hatti. I don't say stalk him the way I did with Alex, but you have to resolve this one way or the other if you want to be free of it. If you want to move on."

She looked over at the dock where two people were silhouetted against the sunset. One of them was Max Guthrie, who was leaning against the railing with his arms crossed over his chest. Next to him, and half-hidden, was a woman facing the other way, looking out at the lake. She had her arms crossed, too. They appeared both intimate and hostile and I squinted into the lowering sun.

"That's Sonya," I said, with a start. "Normally she and Max give each other a wide berth."

"Hatti," Chakra said, with concern in her voice, "how interested are you in Max?"

"I like him. Why?"

She shrugged. "That doesn't exactly look like a neutral scene. Do those two have any history?"

"I doubt it. They're both newcomers and, from everything I've seen in the last few months, Sonya's the only woman on the Keweenaw who doesn't start drooling when he saunters into a room."

"Just watch your step, okay? I'd hate for you to get hurt again. I've got to get home. I want to make an early start in the morning. Walk me to my car?"

We hugged good-bye and I watched her drive off through the pines in the slanting rays of the sun and then I trudged around the house and back to the lawn. Riitta, standing by a makeshift lemonade stand, waved to me and I made my way toward her, pausing briefly to speak with my parents, the pastor and his wife, the Hakalas and Laplanders, Arvo and Pauline Maki and Mrs. Moilanen who were seated in a circle of webbed lawn chairs. Sofi, her daughter, Charlie, Elli and Danny Thorne, along with Barb Hakala and Astrid Laplander were lighting sparklers for the younger Laplander girls and the Sorensens's grandchildren and Aunt Ianthe, Miss Irene and Miss Thyra were on the porch playing a game of canasta, with Tom Kukka as their fourth.

Riitta handed me a glass of cold lemonade and we sat in a couple of lawn chairs on the side of the yard.

"This is loaded with sugar but it's to die for. Have I thanked you enough for what you did for me?"

I took a long swallow and licked my lips.

"More than enough. The lemonade hits the spot."

"C'mon, Hatti. If you hadn't taken charge of the investigation, Tom would still be in jail. Sheriff Clump would have accepted his fake confession and that would be that. Thanks to you, I'm happier than I have any right to be." She looked over at the front porch and, as if he felt her eyes on him, Tom looked up and grinned at her.

"That's a guy in love," I said, feeling a pang of self-pity.

"We both are. I'd have married him, anyway, but, oh, Hatti, I'm just so thrilled I'll be able to give him a family."

"Have you told anyone else yet?" She shook her head.

"I asked him not to mention it to the ladies. They wouldn't approve of us, you know, anticipating the wedding vows."

"Tell me the truth," I said. "You never planned to marry Erik Sundback did you?"

"I considered it," she said, honestly. "He was so helpful with the lighthouse and he's older. It wouldn't matter to him if we didn't have children. But I'd abandoned the idea before I found out about the baby and, luckily, before I found out he was the murderer. There was some quality in him that I didn't trust. Something similar to that streak in Alex. I have no problem with masculine strength but this was something different, a selfishness that bordered on cruelty. You know, Alex could have forgiven Erik. He could have accepted Erik's offer to pay back the money and four people who are dead would still be alive."

"How's Danny taking the fact of being a multi-millionaire?"

"Surprisingly well. He's investing it until he finishes college and then he wants to do something useful with it like starting a foundation to promote economic growth and education in the UP. He'll use Alex's money responsibly, and that's all I can ask."

"He had a good role model growing up," I said.

"The best," Riitta agreed. "There is no one more unselfish than Tom Kukka."

"I meant you," I said. "Tom's a dear but you're a saint."

"He is a dear, isn't he," she said, ignoring the compliment to herself. "He's just about perfect."

"Henrikki!" My Aunt Ianthe was yelling at me from her seat at the canasta table on the front porch. "When are you going to open the yarn store then? Irene and Thyra and I want to buy yarn to make a layette for Riitta and Tom!"

Riitta made a face at me.

"I'd trust him with my life," she said, "just not with my secrets."

"And Henrikki," my aunt continued, in a voice that reached everyone in the lighthouse yard, "we will need yarn for lots of layette sets. Your biological clock is ticking, too. Now that Jack is gone, maybe you could get back with your other husband."

"Forgiveness is mine, saith the Lord," Miss Irene said. "And there is a time for every purpose under heaven."

Riitta laughed at me.

"What's a little humiliation if you're happy?" And then her smile dimmed. "Are you happy, Hatti?"

I put aside the twinge of doubt about whether or not to stay on the Keweenaw and the regret about my short-lived marriage. We only had today. I'd learned that when I was up on the tower hanging on by my fingernails. We only had today and today I was with the people I loved most in the place I loved most.

"Yes," I said, honestly, "I am happy. And I'm home."

Turn the page for an
excerpt from

A
DOUBLE-POINTED
MURDER

The Bait & Stitch Cozy Mystery Series
Book Two

Ann Yost

The girl with the hole in her chest was no Jane Doe. She was not only known to me, she was a relation.

If you count adultery as one of the ties that bind.

Cricket Koski, a barmaid from the Black Fly Roadhouse down in Chassell, had been the catalyst in my sister's divorce three years earlier, a breach that was only now beginning to heal. I shook my head. I was pretty sure, like ninety-nine-point-nine percent sure, that the reconciliation between my sister Sofi and her ex, Lars, would not survive the discovery of the 'Insect' in Lars's bed. The fact that Cricket was dead would not make that much difference to my sister.

I should probably point out that I'm not a cop or even a private detective but I've had a year of law school and, even more importantly, I'm available. Up here on the remote witch's finger of land called the Keweenaw Peninsula, that's a big deal. So when Lars called me from his jail cell, of course I came.

The barmaid was about my age (twenty-eight) and, as far as I knew, had lived as innocuous a life as my own. (Although, in my own defense, my professional life had experienced a slight uptick recently when I took over the operation of pops's bait shop and added knitting supplies. My personal life was, of course, a more dismal story.) But the point was, that I could think of no reason for anyone to want to turn Cricket Koski into a shish kebab. Anyone other than my sister.

"Weird wound."

I jumped. I'd completely forgotten that my presence at the

Frog Creek morgue at zero-dark-hundred was thanks to Waino Aho, the sheriff's deputy with whom I'd experienced my first kiss fifteen years earlier during Vacation Bible School at St. Heikki's. I gazed up at the handsome, if vacant, Nordic features then back at the perfect shape of the aperture underneath the victim's perky left breast. The surrounding skin was smooth and the wound was bloodless.

"A wormhole," Waino said.

I knew he wasn't referring to the hypothetical, topological feature that would be (if it exists) a shortcut through time and space. When Waino said "wormhole" he was referring to the orifice in a piece of fruit created by a burrowing maggot.

"A nail-gun coulda did it."

"Maybe. Or a skewer."

His eyes widened. "A what?"

"One of those long, metal things that people roast marshmallows on."

"I use a birch stick."

I nodded. Birch sticks come in very handy up here in Northern Michigan, especially as vihta in the sauna.

"Something long and thin," I said, following my own train of thought. The truth slammed into me with the force of a felled tree. Triumph at my extraordinary deductive powers caused my voice to shake. "A tool with a long shaft, tapered at the end, and made out of the same carbon fiber composite that is used in stealth fighter jets and formula one racing cars."

Waino stared at me, uncomprehendingly, as I paused for dramatic effect.

"A knitting needle," I said. "A size-five, double-pointed knitting needle like the ones we use on mittens and socks."

His blue eyes met mine and my childhood buddy's sudden mental leap made my heart plummet.

"If she was kilt with a knittin' needle, Hatti," he said, "your sister musta did it, then."

A DOUBLE-POINTED MURDER
available in print and ebook

Hatti's Favorite
Oven-Baked Pancake
(Pannukakku)

Ingredients:

4 eggs

$\frac{3}{4}$ tsp. salt

$2\frac{1}{2}$ c milk

1 c. flour

$\frac{1}{4}$ c. sugar

1 tsp. vanilla

4 T. butter

Preparation:

1. Preheat oven to 400 degrees. Put butter in 9x13 pan (glass works best).
2. Put into oven until melted and slightly bubbly.
3. Whisk together eggs until combined.
4. Add flour, milk, salt and sugar and blend until batter is thin.
5. Carefully pour batter onto melted butter in pan.
6. Cook for 30 minutes or until golden brown around the edges and bubbly over the sides.

Serve immediately with fresh berries or whipped cream or, ideally, Lingonberry syrup (available at IKEA).

Scrumptious. Just ask Sheriff Clump!

THE
BAIT & STITCH COZY MYSTERY
SERIES

A Pattern For Murder
A Double-Pointed Murder
A Fair Isle Murder

Ann Yost comes from Ann Arbor, Michigan and a writing family whose single greatest accomplishment is excellent spelling.

After six years at the University of Michigan she completed her degree in English literature and spent ten years working as a reporter, copy editor and humor columnist for three daily newspapers. Her most notable story at the Ypsilanti Press involved the tarring and feathering of a high school principal.

When she moved with her Associated Press reporter husband to the Washington D.C. area, she did freelance work for the Washington Post, including first-person humor stories on substitute teaching and little league umpiring.

She did feature writing for the Charles Stewart Mott Foundation on building community in low-income neighborhoods and after-school programs throughout the country.

While her three children were in high school, Ann began to write romantic suspense novels. Later, she turned to the Finnish-American community in Michigan's remote Upper Peninsula for her Hatti Lehtinen mystery series.

She lives in Northern Virginia with her husband and her enterprising mini-goldendoodle, Toby.

Lightning Source UK Ltd.
Milton Keynes UK
UKHW011516070121
376605UK00001B/430